BRIDGEND LIBRARY AND INFORMATION SERVICE

3 8030 02240

CW01523083

To Al Mancheski, whose pers...... ....u
.... by.

 **Llyfrgelloedd**
awen Libraries

MGA

Please return/renew this item by the last date below
Dychwelwch/adnewyddwch erbyn y dyddiad olaf y nodir yma

- 2 AUG 2019

2 1 MAR 2020

WEDI'I GYMRYD ODDI AR Y CYFLENWAD
WITHDRAWN FROM STOCK

awen-libraries.com

Also by Janson Mancheski:

The Chemist

Trail of Evil

Mask of Bone

Shoot For the Stars

The Scrub

The Greatest Hits—Best of The Chemist Series

TRAIL OF EVIL

Janson Mancheski

CONTENTS

PROLOGUE 1

PART ONE
HEAD SHOTS; HEAD GAMES

CHAPTER 1 5
CHAPTER 2 11
CHAPTER 3 18
CHAPTER 4 22
CHAPTER 5 27
CHAPTER 6 33
CHAPTER 7 38
CHAPTER 8 44
CHAPTER 9 52
CHAPTER 10 61
CHAPTER 11 67
CHAPTER 12 74
CHAPTER 13 84
CHAPTER 14 94
CHAPTER 15 101
CHAPTER 16 112
CHAPTER 17 120
CHAPTER 18 126
CHAPTER 19 134
CHAPTER 20 140
CHAPTER 21 147
CHAPTER 22 153
CHAPTER 23 162
CHAPTER 24 166
CHAPTER 25 173
CHAPTER 26 179

CHAPTER 27 186
CHAPTER 28 193

**PART TWO
SEASON OF THE WITCH**

CHAPTER 29 202
CHAPTER 30 211
CHAPTER 31 218
CHAPTER 32 228
CHAPTER 33 244
CHAPTER 34 242
CHAPTER 35 248
CHAPTER 36 252
CHAPTER 37 258
CHAPTER 38 264
CHAPTER 39 272
CHAPTER 40 276
CHAPTER 41 282
CHAPTER 42 288
CHAPTER 43 296
CHAPTER 44 303
CHAPTER 45 310
EPILOGUE 316
ACKNOWLEDGMENTS 318

Copyright © 2013 **Janson Mancheski with Fearless Publishing House**
All rights reserved.
The characters and events in this book are the creation of the author, and any resemblance to actual persons or events are purely coincidental.

No part of this book may be copied, shared, or used without the author's permission.

All rights reserved. No part of this book may be reproduced in any manner, except for brief quotations in critical articles or reviews, without permission.

Website: JansonMancheski.com

PROLOGUE

Inside a mountain cavern on a rainy African night, the drumbeat slows. The crowd of worshippers shuffles in place, swaying, a devoted maelstrom gathered in the wide central chamber.

Near the granite altar a witch doctor—a *botono*—raises a fiery torch. Garbed in a dark robe, he touches the brand to the fire pit and sparks roar up in a sizzling display. The drums increase their intensity. The participants—first ten, then twenty—dance to the sound of the shakers, whirling in place, shimmying, enraptured by the guttural throb of the drums.

Another burst of flame erupts from the pit. Across the room, a *mambo* eases her way to a fern-woven basket. She opens the lid and withdraws a fat, green serpent. The snake coils itself around her arms, its shimmery tongue flicking in the firelight. Near the center pole, the mambo begins to sway as if entranced. The celebrants form a circle around her, stepping in and out, clapping to the drumbeat.

At the altar, the witch doctor raises his left hand in the air. He is summoning a *petro loa*, a dark god he hopes will grace the ceremony with its presence. The throb of the drums continues to echo off the craggy rocks.

The village chief steps forward, leading a goat by a tether. A pair of shirtless men assists, and they maneuver the animal so its neck drapes over a wooden basin. The goat offers a frightened bleat, black eyes wide with fear. The botono steps toward the creature.

After the flash of a long, gleaming knife…warm blood gushes…the animal's twitching legs…as a fountain of crimson spurts and splashes into the basin.

When drained, the men hoist the carcass above their shoulders and are swallowed by the frenzied crowd. The drumbeat lowers to a dull throb.

From an antechamber off the main room comes a silent parade of young girls. Each is clad in a white tunic. Twelve in number, they march forward, lining themselves near the shadowy black wall of the cavern. They stand barefoot, still, expressionless; and each has a "sponsor" who stands behind her.

At the altar, the botono turns to the crowd. He holds a carved wooden bowl filled with bits of "seasoned" bread. The chief and villagers watch, eyes rapt.

At the basin, the snake adorns her, and the mambo fills a chalice with the steaming blood of the goat. She joins the witch doctor, and together they face the line of virgins. The botono dips a piece of bread into the mambo's chalice. He feeds it to the first girl, who opens her mouth to receive. He makes no holy utterance, for wherever Christ might be, He is nowhere near this mountain cavern on such a bleary, rain-sodden night.

The witch doctor progresses down the honor line, administering his "offering." Before he reaches the fifth young virgin, the first one sways and collapses into the arms of her sponsor. She is carried off to a shadowed chamber, out of sight. By the time the unholy pair reaches the end of the line, the first half-dozen girls have collapsed.

When the final virgin is eased from the cavern, the *tanbu* drums resume their more intense pounding, with the shakers rattling, all accompanied by the frenetic, jerky, wanton dancing of the near-naked celebrants. A possessed teenage girl suddenly lurches about, zombie-like. An invisible spirit has taken hold and is riding her.

Guzzling from a rum bottle, the contents seeping down her smeary cheeks, the mambo cackles. A frenzied pack of worshippers rush to the dead goat—tearing the animal's limbs apart, waving steamy entrails in the air.

By this time, the witch doctor has vanished. The drums and twirling revelry of the voodoo celebration will continue long into the night, until dawn arrives to scrub the mountainside with clean purple light.

PART ONE

HEAD SHOTS; HEAD GAMES

CHAPTER 1

Nothing but toys. Life-sized baubles. Each no more than a robot encased in warm human flesh. To Colonel Tazeki "Taz" Mabutu, every young African maiden was but a trinket who existed for his own amusement, or a commodity to be sold or traded on the open market.

These were his thoughts as he emerged from an invisible back exit in the mountain, a dark slice of crevice between the rocks. Thirty yards away, a large military truck sat with its cargo loaded: twelve fresh young females, ready to be transported to the port city of Monrovia. There, the Liberian freighter *Kwensana* floated in the harbor, awaiting her final deliveries before departure. Destination: The United Kingdom.

Colonel Mabutu strode to the driver-side door of the vehicle. He was now wearing military garb. The truck's engine was running, and to the driver he said, "You have the papers, Shoppa? In case the U.N. dogs are out tonight?"

The man in combat fatigues nodded. "Yes, Colonel. All is in order."

"My signature at the bottom?"

"As you ordered, Botono."

The soldiers in the truck's front seat carried TEC-9 assault pistols—spitting jackhammers of death—in their laps, eyes gleaming white in the rain-cast night. Around them the whispering tree branches and broad jungle ferns dripped, swaying in the humid breeze. The mountain peaks stretched to the heavens in the background, providing a looming backdrop against the sky's velvet curtain.

"Text my mobile when the ship is loaded," ordered Tazeki. The men saluted, and the colonel watched the truck as it rumbled away down the mountainside.

Puffy, soot colored clouds swept across the night sky, serving to blot out *Lshne* and her handmaiden stars. Tazeki thanked the loa for the letup in the rains. It would allow for a smoother helicopter ride back to his compound, where a long night awaited him.

To a nearby aide, he ordered, "Start the helicopter. And put the girl on board."

The man saluted and scurried away down the narrow path in the darkness.

***

The young girl awoke in the opulent bed, tangled in satin sheets. The colonel's bedroom, she remembered. Having come from a small inland village, these were by far the most elegant surroundings she had ever experienced. Like a dream, when compared to the tarpaper shack where she lived with her parents and nine siblings. She considered rising, visiting the commode, but was fearful of disturbing such an important man as the colonel. She'd seen him cross last evening, ordering his men about, and was fearful of his wrath. Those eyes—warm and coffee colored when he smiled—were bloody daggers when angry. She did not wish to test those blades.

"You're awake. Good," said the colonel's voice, hollow in the high-walled bedroom. "I've got a lot of work to do."

The fern ceiling fan spun lazily above the room, providing comfort against the humid, mist gray morning. The young girl arose, swinging her bare legs free of the sheets.

"No. Remain where you are." His voice was stern, used to giving commands. "I'm the one who needs to get moving." And he was up, while she scooted back beneath the covers, pulling the sheets to her chin.

She watched as he padded across the floor of polished teakwood, short of stature but sinewy strong. He moved to the wet bar, where he donned his loose robe and poured himself a glass of fresh mango juice. Sitting on the bar stool—his silk robe of colorful African shapes and forms parted halfway up one dusky thigh—he emptied a vial of white powder onto a glass serving tray. Lowering his head, he took an extended snort, rubbing his nostrils while ignoring her presence.

"I'd offer you some," he called to the girl, "but you are still a child."

"I'm fifteen. Old enough."

The colonel smiled. "Perhaps. But where you're going, you won't be needing it."

***

Twenty minutes later, Tazeki Mabutu had showered and was sitting behind the work desk in his private study. The walls were covered with African artifacts: crossed spears, thatched battle shields, colorful masks depicting gods and demons. On the mantle above the fireplace, amid the pottery and knickknacks, sat a female shrunken head. Strands of what had once been wheat-colored hair hovered over her blank, remorseless expression.

His young guest, now garbed in the same white shapeless dress she'd worn on her arrival, sat in an armless wooden chair a few feet in front of the desk. He noted her uneasy countenance. She looked like someone who had been summoned for interrogation.

Tazeki was holding his pewter statue of Pazuzu, shifting the object in his hands as if weighing it, like it might hold some clue to the fate of the adolescent sitting before him.

"Is everything"—she spoke, hesitant—"was it all right, sir? Me, I mean?"

"Your performance last night," Tazeki said, his eyes sincere, "the zombie dance. It was enchanting."

"I don't remember much."

"No. Of course you don't."

He set the statue atop his desk, next to the screen of his computer. He pondered a moment while steepling his fingertips in front of his chest. "You are quite beautiful." Tazeki spoke with calmness, staring into her warm brown eyes. "A work of art. Exceptional."

"Thank you, sir." She looked down at her lap.

"Allow me to speak freely." His lips gave no hint of a smile, and his eyes bore into hers with intent. "Would you do me the great honor of becoming my wife?"

The girl could not have appeared more stunned. She was incapable of a reply. His words jolted her. Tazeki pictured the thoughts tumbling around in her youthful brain: *the colonel's wife*? Living in this palace of splendor. The servants, the chauffeured cars, attending opulent balls and state-sponsored political events. Arm-in-arm with Tazeki Mabutu, head of the Liberian National Police. It would be too much for her mind to grasp, too sudden a shift in fortune for a girl straight from a shanty village steeped in poverty and squalor.

"You speak for real, sir?" She hesitated. "You not make a joke? To tease me?"

Tazeki heard her voice catch. Her eyes were cautious, wary against his playing a cruelty at her expense.

"This is short notice," he said with sincerity. "I will allow you all the time you need to ponder such an important decision. By the way, what was your name again?"

"Safron," she said, her voice soft.

"Safron. Very well."

Before the young woman could utter any further sound, the colonel reached beneath the surface of his desk. He flipped a metal switch and watched as, a moment later, she dropped through the polished wooden floor—chair and rug and all—too surprised and shocked to even scream. He pictured her body crashing against dark stone walls, thrown into tarry blackness as the trapdoor above her snapped closed. In seconds, she would hit the deep pool of brackish water. He imagined her scrambling for her bearings, inhaling before she went under, far beneath the house. She would struggle to find the surface, clawing about, trying to cling to whatever final breaths she might manage.

Before her fingers would gain purchase on the slippery rocks, however, the eels in the pool would swarm. She would scream—a sound Tazeki could not hear, of course—and within a matter of minutes the flesh would be torn from her meager bones in raw, bloody strips. She would bleed profusely, and by the time she realized the true extent of her horror, she would be devoured.

***

The room was quiet. Like a pond after a fish had jumped. Tazeki rang the bell for his servant. When Kasim appeared, wearing his customary red Nehru jacket, Tazeki ordered the young man to procure a new woven rug from the supply they kept on hand. To place it in front of his large mahogany desk, where it covered the seams of the trapdoor. The servant performed this task without comment, before disappearing from the room, silent as an insect.

Tazeki stared into the hooded eyes of Pazuzu and a devilish smile formed across his lips. "Precious, wasn't it, my friend?" he murmured aloud. "Did you see the look on her face?"

Pazuzu conversed only with his thoughts. His sly expression remained enigmatic.

"No—not when she dropped through the floor." Tazeki crowed effusively. "I mean, when I asked her to *marry* me!"

CHAPTER 2

Whenever Detective Cale Van Waring was in the same room with the man who had kidnapped and almost murdered his fiancée, he wished he'd handled the man's arrest in a more primal fashion. Instead of wounding him in the thigh, if he had aimed his Glock four inches higher, he could have blown the bastard's balls clean off.

This correction—in Cale's opinion—would have rendered a more befitting form of justice. But then he'd be working parking meter duty somewhere, if he still even had a job on the force.

It was Monday morning now. As lead investigator in the case, he'd been requested by the DA's office to appear at the Brown County jail. As Cale parked his vehicle and strode toward the glass front doors, however, he thought he could detect the first faint whisper of foreboding as it surfed on the playful May breeze.

In a private interview room, Cale took a seat beside John Zachary, the assistant district attorney. The parties were seated around a long, ash-hued table, where Zachary had arranged for jail officials to set up audio and video recording apparatus. He wanted a clear record of the accused's physical demeanor, along with every verbal utterance Tobias Crenshaw might make.

A pair of the suspect's attorneys sat to one side of their client. Guards had rolled the shackled man into the room in his wheelchair. Crenshaw—a.k.a. "The Chemist"—had occupied the chariot since recovering from the ordeal of his arrest. The leg wound was bandaged, Cale imagined. His shoulder, where he had received a stab wound, courtesy of Maggie Jeffers, Cale's fiancée, would be likewise wrapped. His left arm was encased in a sling, worn over his jailhouse jumpsuit. A fitting fashion accessory, as far as Cale was concerned. Crenshaw deserved every ounce of pain he'd been dealt.

The attorneys present were hired guns from a notable Milwaukee law firm called Murray, Murray, and Wine. They appeared smooth and efficient, possessing a quiet confidence, which rendered in Cale a feeling of unease each time he'd had the displeasure of being in their presence.

After everyone was seated and the suspect indicated that he was ready, Zachary clicked on the recorder and video camera. He spoke in a steady voice and stated they were conducting the third interview with Mr. Tobias Powell Crenshaw. He mentioned all those present in the room.

Turning his attention to the accused, Zachary said, "You wish to make a statement today, regarding the charges you're facing, Mr. Crenshaw?"

The charges. Cale was aware the DA's office had decided to add a first-degree murder charge to the initial six counts of felony abduction. Even though they didn't have absolute proof. The hope was they might pressure their suspect—who had a healthy fear of prolonged incarceration—into a confession. Or at least force him to provide them with more evidence, such as revealing what he'd done with the bodies of a pair of still-missing victims.

It was all a game of legal cat-and-mouse.

Despite the wheelchair, Tobias Crenshaw looked to Cale not much different than he'd been on the night he was arrested. His shaggy dark hair could use a trim, and the tortoiseshell eyeglasses served to narrow his face. The ankle and wrist shackles, the prison jumpsuit, none of these hid the fact the man was a dangerous sociopath. On the outside he appeared calm and confident, the demeanor of a successful businessman. Looking into his eyes, however, Cale could discern the predatory nature of the monster lurking beneath the surface. Crenshaw's twilight gray eyes possessed a chilling quality. He stared out at the world with a narcissistic, self-centered contempt, looking as if he'd rather employ a filet knife to your inner organs than converse with you.

In his wooden chair, two feet from where Zachary was positioned, despite the bolus of hatred rising in his throat, Cale couldn't help but shudder at the sinister portrait Tobias Crenshaw projected. His was an aura of death, shrouded in its most treacherous form: benign normalcy.

"I'm here because of the plea deal you discussed with my attorneys," said the prisoner, his voice a prickly monotone.

Zachary's eyes registered no surprise.

Cale felt his own breath catch. A plea deal? What plea deal? The revelation came as a shock to him. He wondered what sort of compromise the DA's office had concocted behind the scenes. Was he the only one present who did not know the true nature of what was going on here? And to this point, was he even sure he *wanted* to know?

"You mean concerning the reduction of the charge of murder in the first degree?" said Zachary. "Is that the plea bargain you're referring to?" Crenshaw stared straight ahead, nodding imperceptibly.

"I need a verbal response, Mr. Crenshaw."

"Yes." Crenshaw turned toward the camera. "It's about dropping the murder charge."

"Not 'dropping'. *Reducing*," said Zachary. "For the record."

"All right, then. Reducing."

Cale noted how John Zachary, his blond hair coiffed, shared a meaningful look with the defense attorneys. He spoke in the direction of the microphone positioned at midtable: "Let it be noted that the accused, Tobias Powell Crenshaw, the abductor known as 'The Chemist,' has indicated his intent to explore the possibility of reducing his current charge of first-degree murder—"

"Alleged," interjected one of Crenshaw's attorneys, a bald man with a wreath of dark hair. "The *alleged* abductor." When Zachary shot him a look, the man added, "We're not pleading guilty to anything, here. This is a discovery discussion. Intent on exploring a reduction in presently filed charges."

"Point taken, counselor," Zachary allowed. To the camera, he said, "The *alleged* abductor known as the Chemist...discussion on reducing the new first-degree murder charge down to aggravated manslaughter." Zachary jotted a note on his legal pad.

"And for the record," Cale said, interjecting his opinion to the quiet room, "this is *alleged* bullshit!" When he had their attention, he added, "The guy chopped the head off one of his victims. With a machete. How does that add up to anything short of premeditated murder?"

Zachary turned his eyes back to the camera. "Let it be noted that Lieutenant Cale Van Waring, of the Green Bay Police Department, has registered his protest regarding any reduction in charges against Mr. Crenshaw. Detective Van Waring, it should be disclosed, possesses no degree in jurisprudence."

"Maybe not," Cale said, scowling. "But I possess a degree in common-*fucking*-sense!"

Cale wondered if he was the one person here who gave two shits about the victims. Close to snapping his pen between his fingers, he shot a steely gaze in Crenshaw's direction. The man returned it with a smirk, while Zachary indicated it was time to explain the *true* reason the group was gathered in the room today.

"To our second point." The ADA cleared his throat. "Mr. Crenshaw, in exchange for the possible charge reduction, you have indicated through your attorneys that you have information pertinent to the death of Ms. Kimberly Vanderkellen?"

"That's right."

"Would you mind stating the nature of your claim?"

Crenshaw eyed the camera like a stage performer. "It concerns the identity of the man who murdered the Vanderkellen girl." He glanced around the room at them all. "His name is Kinsella—and he's from Liberia. Africa."

"What?" Cale heard his voice skip off the room's painted walls. He turned to Zachary, saying, "This is just more game-playing BS!"

Zachary, sober, scrutinized the prisoner. "And you received this information how, Mr. Crenshaw?"

"I didn't receive it—I *know* it!"

Zachary was holding his breath. "This person you are naming...you know this for a fact? That he murdered Kimberly Vanderkellen?"

"You wanted the name of the man who killed the dead girl. His name is Kinsella. Chopped her head off, execution style."

Cale began to protest again, but Crenshaw spoke over him, saying, "He used a ceremonial sword. Not a machete. Dumped the body in Lake Michigan."

Silence choked the room. "Fact is," Crenshaw added, "he's the one who kidnapped them all!"

"This is total nonsense!" Cale roped them all with his eyes, shaking his head in dismay. "He's giving you a hand job,"—directing his gaze at Zachary—"and you're liking it!"

The attorneys remained silent, expressionless.

Zachary set his pen aside. He stared across the table at Crenshaw. "Kinsella. It's his surname? His first name? What?"

"First or last." Crenshaw shrugged. "Who the Christ knows?" His scornful look challenged them. Believe him or not; he didn't care either way.

"And he resides in Liberia? In Africa?" Zachary asked skeptically. "That's what you expect us to believe?"

"I don't give a damn what you believe. It's where he's from. Repeat: *Liberia*. Repeat: *Kinsella*. That's what you asked for—that's what I'm telling you."

"Can you give us a reason—a motive, if you will—as to why this man would kidnap and murder any of these women?"

Crenshaw smirked, before cutting his eyes back to the ADA. "The simplest reason of all: Because he's a trafficker—that's why. A *human trafficker*."

Rising from his chair, Cale's look of frustration ping-ponged from the prisoner, back to Zachary, then to the pair of poker-faced defense attorneys.

He strode to the door and rapped. When the guard outside opened it, allowing fresh air into the now claustrophobic room, Cale stomped out into the corridor. He'd seen enough dog-and-pony shows in his years as a detective. Enough to last a lifetime.

He was not going to be part of another one.

CHAPTER 3

"The old ball and chain!"

Detective James "Slink" Dooley hooted this in the fashion of a yokel tasting his first morning moonshine. It caused a few of the investigators in the Robbery-Homicide duty room of the Green Bay Police Department's downtown office to glance over. "You're thirty-seven. It's about time you got tied down like the rest of us mopes."

"I knew you'd be pleased," said Cale. He continued to work the computer keyboard, back at his desk after returning from the meeting at the county jail. His jaw was still tight from grinding his teeth at the idea of Tobias Crenshaw's attempt at a plea reduction. He reached up and loosened his necktie, releasing some of the pressure.

Slink asked, "So when's the blessed event?"

Cale and his fiancée, Maggie Jeffers, had made the decision over the past weekend. He dreaded revealing the news to Slink, but figured his longtime friend, partner, and no doubt best man, would have to know sooner or later.

"Not sure yet. Maybe sometime in August. Soon as Maggie can make the arrangements. Get a hall and stuff. I guess it's tricky on short notice."

Slink had spun around in his chair two desks away and was smirking like a rascal. "Two months from now. Almost like a shotgun wedding. I like that—seems old fashioned, in sweet kind of way."

"I'm glad you approve."

"You know what this means, don't you?"

Cale lifted his eyes, issuing his best blank stare. He was reluctant to provide Slink with the slightest ammunition. He knew better, considering the topic.

Slink answered for him. "One word: *bachelorparty*!"

Cale frowned. With fifteen years on the force, he'd been to more bachelor parties than he could count. They paraded through his mind in a blur of drunken revelry...the kegs of beer, the shots of Jägermeister, the inevitable sloppy visits to the local strip clubs, followed by poker games till sunrise. At least these days they had the good sense to hire a limo or have a driver's service cart them around, often in an oversized van from Impound. Not good for the department's image: a bunch of inebriated cops cavorting around the city, acting more like fraternity dickheads than upstanding law enforcement officials. But then again, boys will be boys.

Around them, Cale could hear the buzz of quiet conversations, detectives and uniforms moving about, phones ringing, computer keyboards clacking. Another day of solving crime in Titletown, U.S.A.

"That's two words," Cale said after a while, his eyes never leaving his computer screen. "'Bachelor party.' Two words."

Slink rose from his desk. "Not where I come from. One word. '*Bachelorparty*.'"

Cale studied his partner. Slink appeared to be back to his former agile self. There appeared no indication of the man's recent brush with a 9mm slug. Left shoulder, a through-and-through tag. "So, you come from the Land of Illiteracy? I'm not sure I'd be bragging about that."

"What I'm bragging about, is I get to be best man for the downfall of this department's most eligible bachelor." He enjoyed the grimace on Cale's face. "At least this'll shoot down all those rumors about you being a fruit."

Before Cale could respond, a booming voice echoed behind them. "Who's a fruit?" Anton Staszak was lumbering toward his desk, carrying a stack of manila folders. More case files. He headed the department's Missing Persons Unit. Staszak gave them both a weary look as he plopped his significant bulk behind his desk. "My brother-in-law's gay. A great guy. Huge Packers fan."

"Cale's marrying Maggie," Slink reported, turning the screw, "to squelch the gay rumors. Once and for all."

"Takes one to know one," Cale shot back, guessing he sounded like a sixth-grader on the playground. Not caring. Slink Dooley, they all understood, had an innate talent for getting under a person's skin.

Staszak gave them a shake of his oversized head. He'd received significant cranial injuries during the recent Chemist case and had had the bandages removed just three days ago. His shaved melon glistened in the morning light, curved and lumpy with scars and stitches, looking like a misshapen honeydew.

"Good a reason as any, I suppose," Staszak said. "Now can you both get back to work? Before the Captain comes around bitching?"

They were silent for two good minutes, returning to their paperwork. The thing they never told you when you chose a career in law enforcement, Cale ruminated for the millionth time, was the never-ending paperwork. He finished logging off his case and printed out the forms, which required his written signature. A cough came from Staszak's nearby desk, and Cale turned his head toward the oversized detective.

Staszak was near the size of a mature grizzly, and Cale noticed the man was eyeing him with a cagey gaze. With a large paw cupping his mouth, Staszak stage-whispered (for Slink Dooley's benefit), "Hey, Cale, do you think this tie goes with this shirt?"

"Screw off!" Cale groaned, watching as his two friends cackled with laughter. He rose from his desk and strode across the room, heading for Captain McBride's office door.

"Oh no!" cried Slink, his eyes still moist. "He's reporting us to the principal!"

Cale's response was an upraised finger over his shoulder. He knocked twice and disappeared inside the sanctity of the captain's office.

CHAPTER 4

Captain Leo Hortense McBride—the Investigations Unit commander—was dark-skinned, overfed, and seldom in the mood for idle chit-chat. As Cale entered the man's office that Monday morning, he understood any number of things could be in the works for him to be called in for a private conference with his boss. First, he'd been confined to desk duty since the arrest of Tobias Crenshaw three weeks earlier. Something about his involvement in a weapon fire incident. Something about the Internal Affairs review board determining if his shooting of the suspect during the arrest had been warranted.

Cale believed his wounding of Tobias Crenshaw had been justified. The man had been brandishing a weapon: How could a bottle filled with liquid sedatives *not* be construed as a weapon? It might have been hydrochloric acid, for all anyone knew at the time. Despite this fact, he had aimed his weapon low. Wounded the suspect in the thigh. He had not employed deadly force. A fact that had to work in his favor, shouldn't it?

It was the reason McBride wanted to meet with him this morning—Cale guessed—to let him know IA had exonerated him. His desk confinement had been lifted. Cases were backlogged. He was needed back out on the streets.

The captain was seated behind his desk. He motioned his detective to a chair inside the room, where Cale performed a quick study of the office walls covered in amateur artwork—if one could call it that.

Collecting garage sale art was their boss's captivating weekend hobby.

"IA's decided that you had a 'clean shoot' with Crenshaw," Captain McBride said, the relief visible in his eyes.

Cale had been certain he'd be cleared, since his captain, a witness to the event, had testified on his behalf. But when it came to the politics of the Department, he also understood Internal Affairs could hang him out to dry if they chose to do so.

"I hear you walked out of the ADA's meeting with Crenshaw earlier," the captain said, shifting the topic.

"They're offering him a charge reduction. In exchange for some BS information about another perpetrator being behind the Vanderkellen girl's murder." Cale matched McBride's stare. "What puzzles me is how no one happened to mention any of this beforehand."

The captain rolled a silver/black gel pen between his fingers. "Fact is, I just found out last night. If it makes you feel any better." Leo pressed his lips together. "I was going to give you a heads-up but figured you should hear it for yourself. Get a feel for whether he's telling us the truth."

Cale cast his gaze out the window, the swaying tree branches, before turning his attention back. "Oldest play in the book. What perp accused of murder *doesn't* try to put the tag on someone else?"

The captain rotated one round, arthritic shoulder. "Regardless. Our investigation still has to check it out."

When Cale nodded his head, his boss let the second shoe drop, informing him that while IA had exonerated him in the Crenshaw shooting, they were suspending him fourteen days for the unauthorized break-in of a private citizen's home in the case. A break-in he, Cale, had directed. Captain McBride arched his bushy eyebrows. "Remember? The one where your partner almost got his arm blown off?"

Staring across the room at a chalky Degas rendition, Cale's expression stayed grim. He did not need reminding of Slink Dooley's significant injury. Slink was his partner, and Cale had been beating himself up ever since the incident had occurred. This despite the fact Slink had taken to wearing the slug on a chain around his neck for—supposed—good luck.

Even though Detective Dooley had volunteered for the "assignment," that still didn't make it kosher. Cale was the Officer in Command. And although the action helped break the Chemist case open, it fell short of acceptable department procedure. Cale sat and listened as McBride's voice droned a tired litany he knew by heart: "Rogue cops could not be tolerated...he was aware of the rules...an unauthorized home invasion of a private citizen...terrible precedent...the officer review board's recommending a two-week suspension...a lesson to other cops considering lone-wolf activity...a true suspension; not just restrictive duty."

Leaning with his elbows on his knees, when the captain finished, Cale said, "Slink? Staszak? They're in the clear on this, right?"

"They were deemed subservient in the affair. Grunts following orders." After a pause, McBride added: "Their records are clear of any wrongdoing. Pensions intact."

Nodding, Cale kept silent.

"One other thing. If you want to call it a silver lining," the captain continued, "your own pay's intact. Review board figures they'll dodge flak from the union that way."

Cale rolled of his eyes.

"And I wouldn't bother with an appeal, Cale. Take the lumps. Live to fight another day." The captain was doodling on a notepad atop his desk. "You'll still receive your commendation for capturing Crenshaw—that part's etched in stone."

Whatever, Cale thought. He'd never been one for awards. Or medals; or accolades. Leave the trinkets for guys with a need to prove their self-worth. "This suspension? Am I on house arrest? Or can I do whatever I want for two weeks?"

A flicker of compassion in the captain's eye. "Let's start the damn thing tomorrow. Okay? Turn in your sidearm and badge before you leave tonight. And for the record, no, I can't stop you from doing whatever the hell you want while you're gone."

"Good. I've got a call into the FBI already," Cale informed him. "Agent Redtail's tracking down the bullshit info Crenshaw's shoveling us. Seeing if this Liberian human trafficker—*the real killer*—actually exists."

Captain McBride made a note in his desktop file.

Cale's mobile phone buzzed, and he glanced at the readout. He rose from his chair. "That's him now, Cap. I'll let you know if I've got something."

Exiting the captain's office, Cale knuckled his boss a half-hearted salute.

***

Away from the ringing phones and bustle of the duty room, Cale slipped into one of the vacant interview rooms. He closed the door and hit the redial on his phone. After departing the jailhouse earlier and returning to the downtown Adams Street Station, he had launched a computer search. Ten minutes after doing so, Cale had phoned the FBI's Milwaukee Bureau and left a message with his friend, Special Agent Eddie Redtail. He'd wanted to offer the man a heads-up in the latest turn of the Green Bay kidnapping case.

The agent was now returning Cale's call. "Kinsella? That's it?" Agent Redtail exhaled, his frustration evident. "First name? Last name? You got anything more for me?"

"Last name, I'm thinking. Like I said in the message."

"You said he's a Liberian? As in Liberia, Africa?" the FBI man said. "*Kinsella* doesn't sound too African to me. But I'll check the NCIC database, see if we get any kind of hit. I'll also check offshore." He exhaled. "No offense, Cale, but you guys did a Google search, I'm presuming?"

"We're kind of slow up here in Aww-Shucks, Wisconsin, Eddie, but we have heard of computers." Cale kept his tone light. "It's a popular name of Irish ancestry: a clan name. At least a thousand Kinsella's live in the U.S. I also found a large investment banking group. Not to mention a half-dozen authors by that name."

"Give me a couple of hours," Agent Redtail said with a sigh. "I'll get back to you."

CHAPTER 5

Cale's thirty-eighth birthday was coming in August, and he was getting married—circumstances permitting—right afterwards, over the Labor Day weekend. It wouldn't surprise him in the least if Maggie tried to coordinate the two events: turn his ritual yearly day of mourning into one of joy. It would be just like her. She was clever that way.

Maggie's cleverness was but one of the reasons he loved her.

Despite happy days coming over the horizon, however, on this day a cloud of uncertainty darkened the atmosphere around him. When you worked homicide cases, certain tasks, no matter how uncomfortable, went with the territory. Talking to the family members of victims was one of them.

Yet today, in spite of the news of his forthcoming ten-day paid suspension, things weren't as bleak as they might have been. With the midday sun a blister in the blue enameled sky, Cale was at least the bearer of hopeful news for a change.

The home of Gene and Laureen Dowd was a sturdy little A-frame set in a quiet, treelined neighborhood adjacent to a city park. One with mature trees and bushes and a kids' jungle gym. A tall swing set, swings removed—no doubt due to city liability concerns—stood forlornly in the center of it all. But the merry-go-round looked functional, and the park gave off an aura of children's happy laughter and more pleasant times.

Automobiles were already parked in the driveway and at the street curb. They belonged to members of the Mothers of Missing Daughters group: family members who'd been victims of Tobias Crenshaw's kidnapping rampage.

Cale rapped on the brass door knocker. The door was opened by Cynthia Hulbreth, one of the Chemist's previous victims. One of the lucky ones. One who'd been rescued. She gave Cale a warm smile and a hug as she welcomed him inside.

"How's Maggie holding up?" A serious expression shadowed the young woman's smooth features. Maggie had escaped Tobias Crenshaw's clutches, as well.

"She's good." He shot for sincere, hoped he hit the mark. "She tell you we're getting married? End of August, if we can find a hall on short notice."

"Oh, Cale! That's great. Congratulations." Cynthia gave him a second hug. Heartfelt for the detective credited with saving her life. "Tell her to call me next week. We'll do lunch."

"I'll do that."

The young woman escorted Cale into the Dowds' spacious living room, where coffee, date bars, and a fruit tray had been assembled. After shaking hands with a handful of guests—he was already acquainted with them all—he took a seat near Gene Dowd. At the front of the group, left of the big bay window, right of the tall entertainment center. He couldn't help but notice the pictures of Leslie Dowd—one of the victims still missing—which graced the shelves and the room's walls. Always smiling back at him.

Will I ever find her? he wondered. *Is she even alive?*

The present lineup included Samantha and Shirley Koon, Cynthia Hulbreth and her mother, Agnes, the Dowds, and Frank and Inez Moore. These familiar faces made up the core of the group. Their plight had been documented over the past twelve months in the local newspapers and on television and radio reports. They weren't a group looking for publicity, but just a measure of justice and as much closure as was possible.

They were staring at him with anxious, expectant eyes, uncertain if Cale's words would slam them in the gut or cause their collective hope to soar. Thankfully, he'd had the foresight to render both the Dowd and Moore families a heads-up on the phone, prior to his arrival. Cale had informed them he hadn't any word, one way or the other, on the fates of their missing daughters. Leslie Dowd and Mary Jane Moore remained absent. No word of their whereabouts.

Then why was he even here? They were no doubt confused by the reason for his visit.

"I've got something to tell you all," he said, after the room had quieted. "I wanted you to hear it from me first." He spent the next ten minutes replaying the morning's jailhouse meeting with Tobias Crenshaw. When he finished, a long minute of silence crept through the room like an invisible burglar.

"Reckless manslaughter?" Gene Dowd's voice sounded incredulous. "This in exchange for Crenshaw's telling us who the actual killer is?"

"It's something to go—"

"Oh, come on, Detective Van Waring," groaned Inez Moore. "The 'real killer'? Sounds like O.J. Simpson, if you want to know the truth."

They were all in agreement, grousing, frowning as they considered the frustrating reality of what they were hearing.

"Look," Cale said, holding up his palms, "every one of us wants Crenshaw to pay for his crimes. And believe me, he will. It's just that the DA doesn't want to hang his hat solely on the first-degree murder charge. The charge reduction—to reckless manslaughter—is a way of hedging our bets. Making sure we convict him of as many serious crimes as possible."

"He's not denying the kidnapping charges, then?"

Cale shook his head.

Cynthia Hulbreth spoke: "So, we're still going to nail him, aren't we? I mean, you've got enough evidence to send him away for forever. Right?"

Cale's look at her was tight. The young woman had been through hell and back at the hands of that monster. "We've got enough forensics from his house to convict him on at least seven felony kidnapping counts. So, the answer is *Yes*. But the main thing is this: he's given us a second suspect. One who may be connected to your missing daughters' whereabouts." He roped them all with his eyes.

There were nods this time, blended with lingering murmurs of uncertainty. Cale brought home his argument. "The man's wife has left him. He's losing his kids, his fancy cars, homes, business. Everything."

When Gene Dowd spoke, his eyes locked on Cale. "One question: How can you be certain Crenshaw's not just toying with you guys? From day one, his whole crime spree has been one big game of cat-and-mouse, hasn't it?"

"You're right. We can't be certain. But I'd ask you this—what is the alternative?"

No one spoke, and Cale continued. "The main problem is the guy Crenshaw's fingered might be a Liberian national. Someone involved in the human trafficking business. We're not sure yet. I've already contacted my connection at the FBI. They're searching their database to try and confirm his identity, as we speak."

"Human trafficking?" The words were repeated by Laureen Dowd. "But don't they kidnap young girls, for the most part? Ten? Eleven? Twelve-year-olds?"

"Not all the time," Cale said, but it was not his area of expertise.

Gene Dowd was a burly man and frustration colored his face. "If this guy's from another country? I guess what I'm asking...is there any chance we'll ever see our Leslie again?"

"That's the State Department's job—to find out all they can." Cale rose, the uncertainty in the room creating a stifling atmosphere. "They've got a multitude of international resources at their disposal. Interpol will know if this guy has a record. As soon as they can locate him, they'll question him. They'll extradite him back here, if need be."

Shirley Koon's brown eyes appeared even larger than Cale remembered. She said, "It just makes me feel so...so *helpless*. Our having to trust Tobias Crenshaw—of all people—that he's telling us the truth."

Cale's nod was one of quiet camaraderie. They were all in this together. He departed from home, out into the sunny day, heading to his vehicle. Headed back to the station and the dreariness of desk duty. At least for one more day.

Yet the feeling troubling him most, at the moment, was that he wasn't sure he'd accomplished a single damned thing with his visit.

CHAPTER 6

Milwaukee, Wisconsin

As an FBI criminal profiler, Agent Eddie Redtail was no slouch. He'd overseen the Wisconsin Bureau, located in downtown Milwaukee, for the past eight years. During his tenure, law enforcement investigators across the state had requested his assistance on a variety of cases. In fact, the Green Bay Police Department—his friend, Detective Cale Van Waring, specifically—had asked him just four weeks earlier for profiling help in a serial kidnapping case. Though not one to pat himself on the back, Agent Redtail knew he'd scored a direct hit at predicting the subjective emotional makeup of this unknown subject: the criminal who'd come to be known as "The Chemist." He had built the profile, and now the perpetrator was in police custody, ready to be tried for first-degree homicide and multiple abduction counts.

The case, however, remained active. As well as anyone, Agent Redtail understood there remained a pair of victims listed as "unaccounted for." And one thing he knew about Detective Van Waring: when it came to closing a case, Cale was as dogged as any investigator he'd ever met.

Although they had captured the suspected purveyor of the crime and put an end to his kidnapping spree, Van Waring would not give up on finding the missing victims. Even if Tobias Crenshaw was tried and convicted, sentenced to prison for the rest of his natural days, the file would not be closed. Not with certainty; and not until every last avenue was exhausted.

To this point, it came as no surprise when Agent Redtail received a voice mail message Monday morning from the detective, himself. The investigators had received the name of one of the Chemist's possible accomplices. That someone, somehow and somewhere, knew something, did not strike Agent Redtail as odd. His suspicion all along was that Crenshaw was being aided in making his victims—along with their automobiles—vanish without a trace. It was unlikely that he was acting alone.

Redtail had guessed that sooner or later a name would surface in connection with the baffling case. After hearing Cale's message, he began a criminal data search for the name "Kinsella." Agent Redtail understood that because they were dealing with, perhaps, a foreign national, that the government channel to best go through would be Homeland Security.

In a concise conversation, Redtail had explained the circumstances to an Agent Rowdy there. And two hours later, he'd received a response.

Through Interpol, Homeland learned that a Liberian national—"Kinsella," single name—had been arrested in Great Britain on a human trafficking charge in 2010. The man had been printed, photographed, and processed. He'd spent one night in custody before his lawyer had arranged for his bond release. The charges were dropped thereafter, due to lack of sufficient evidence. Though a free man, it had been suggested that Mr. Kinsella vacate the United Kingdom, and he'd been listed with both New Scotland Yard and Interpol as an "undesirable."

They had no further record of him after that.

Agent Rowdy had forwarded the suspect's photo and processing information, e-faxed it to Milwaukee's FBI field office. Upon receiving the photo, Agent Redtail couldn't help but study the features of the large Liberian individual: the deep set, beady eyes, and their sinister dullness. The shaved skull. The man's barrel chest and muscular neck reminded him of an adult anaconda. Something about the picture cried out, *Danger*. And Agent Redtail didn't doubt it for a second.

It had been three hours now, since he'd received Cale's initial phone message, and Agent Redtail was contacting the Green Bay detective with what he had discovered.

"Homeland's been in contact," Agent Redtail informed Cale, "with Liberian law enforcement. The ICPO—International Crime Police—office there claims they've got no criminal history on anyone named 'Kinsella.'"

"Figures," Cale said grumpily. "Friggin' third-world countries."

"I wouldn't give up hope just yet." Agent Redtail's tone was upbeat. "Agent Rowdy indicated DHS is very interested in any international angle involving human sex slavery. That's in their wheelhouse."

"'He's a human trafficker.'" Cale repeated out loud the words Crenshaw had told them. Yet in his mind, major pieces of the puzzle remained unanswered:

If it was a slave trading ring they were dealing with, why the Green Bay area? The locale seemed obscure on an international scale of things. And why had there been six victims total? And why all in their early twenties? These victims were older than standard trafficking targets—and not druggies, and not runaways. And how was Tobias Crenshaw involved with these people?

They were questions Cale had no answers for.

Agent Redtail said, "These days, whenever female victims go missing, trafficking red flags go up."

"I always thought it was most often preteens? Or adolescents? You know? Young girls from impoverished countries?"

Agent Eddie Redtail couldn't disagree. "It's anyone. Anywhere. There's a never-ending market out there for either sex—male or female. And it's getting worse." He exhaled. "It's a worthy avenue of pursuit, Cale. That is if you can procure a warrant on your slime ball."

"I'll get a warrant. Our ADA's got Crenshaw implicating this guy—on the record."

"Fax it to me. ASAP. I'll forward you the suspect's photo that Interpol sent us."

Agent Redtail was silent for a minute. He imagined what type of action Cale might be pondering. "You're considering chasing him down yourself, aren't you?"

"I didn't say—"

"You don't have to." Agent Redtail's tone was blunt. "But let's see if our people can locate him, first. Go through the proper channels."

"'Proper channels,'" Cale repeated, dismissive. "No offense, Eddie. But in my world, that's code for moving at a snail's pace."

"All I'm saying is, there's no sense running off half-cocked. Not to a foreign country." Redtail's pause held weight. "Besides, we don't even know if your suspect's anywhere near Liberia."

"If he's there, I'll find him."

At his desk, Agent Redtail removed his glasses. He pinched the bridge of his nose. "American justice doesn't mean shit to these people, Cale. And extracting one of their citizens? Forget about it." He loosened his tie and exhaled. "Look, Homeland's got a crap house of intel on trafficking. It's a nasty bag of snakes."

"Snakes are my specialty."

"If you say so," Redtail countered.

After ending their discussion, Agent Redtail decided to make another important, backup phone call. One thing he had learned about Cale Van Waring over the years: the man was prone to acting on impulse, rather than with any calculated plan. It's what made him a good investigator, if also somewhat of a loose cannon. If Cale was serious about flying halfway around the world in search of a suspected trafficker—a potential sadistic killer, no less—well, Eddie Redtail decided he had better make certain the guy had every available resource at his disposal.

"Liberia." Redtail muttered the location in a low voice, searching his personal notebook for a private number. "Talk about the armpit of the world."

Having located the number, he placed the call.

CHAPTER 7

Green Bay, Wisconsin

Gazing around the vacant evidence room, Cale's eyes swung around to the single box, which sat on the long table in front of him. The double-height, curtain-less windows became a blank canvas for the late-afternoon sun, and the breeze tickled the leaves of the high trees outside. The cardboard container was marked "The Chemist—Serial Kidnapping Case." As a personal note, Cale decided he could have added: *Solved but not over*.

He removed a pair of photographs from the manila envelope on top: the pair of still-missing victims. He studied the smiling faces—Leslie Dowd, Mary Jane Moore—knowing they would be etched in his brain forever. Branded there the way a red-hot iron sears cowhide.

The other victims had either been murdered or had barely escaped with their lives—Maggie included. If Agent Redtail was correct, and the motive behind the abductions was, indeed, human trafficking, then it rendered them at least a fragment of hope: Any victim missing was worth more alive, than dead.

In an otherwise random affair, this fact, at least, made some degree of sense.

Cale's thoughts were interrupted by a cough from the doorway behind him. "Sad, isn't it? When a case ends?" Slink Dooley pocketed his phone. "It's like when a house of cards falls down."

"There's always a new house of cards. Nature of our business."

Slink issued him a rueful look. "Card houses? Cops and robbers? Why's it seem like we're still stuck playing kids' games, kemosabe?"

Cale's attention was drawn to his partner's left shoulder, the shoulder where he'd taken the slug. Though the sling had been removed, Slink still moved his arm in the way of a boxer who still remembered a particularly jarring punch. "I'm sure the round that split your shoulder didn't feel like any cap pistol."

"I catch a bullet from some street scum...you get reamed out by Internal Affairs." Slink shrugged. "Sometimes I wonder which is worse." Silence for a beat. "Hey, remember what that old cop told us? Back when we were rookies? 'If you ain't getting shot at once in a while, you ain't doin' your job.'"

"You mean Harvard? That old *dead* cop?"

"Yeah. Him."

Cale placed the pair of photos back in the evidence box. He gave his partner a questioning look. "You're turning into quite the armchair philosopher these days."

"I'll send you my bill."

"Philosophers charge by the hour?"

"We charge by the drink."

"Sounds like a better deal." Cale closed the box's flaps. His pager sounded, and he checked the number, clicked it off. "You been getting that shoulder looked at? Sure it's healing okay?"

"Only hurts when I play the violin."

"That would hurt a lot of people."

Stepping toward Slink, Cale handed his partner a photograph of the man Scotland Yard had arrested.

Crenshaw's supposed accomplice. The man known as "Kinsella."

Slink studied the picture. "Not your new cellmate, I hope."

"I should be so lucky."

Accepting the photo back from his partner, Cale inserted it into a manila case folder. He was nearing the end of his shift—the reality of his suspension beginning to sink in. The pager had told him Captain McBride was summoning him to his office. Slink told him he'd return the box back to Evidence and moved toward the room's exit.

Cale trailed behind him. "I might be taking a little trip. Figured I'd let you know."

Slink smirked. "Where? Vegas?"

"More like Africa. Maybe."

"Nothing like a good safari to get the juices flowing. *Bada bing!*"

The partners exited out into the hallway. "It's not a sure thing."

"Got it. You're being cryptic."

Cale began walking down the corridor. Up ahead, uniforms were moving about, a shift change in progress. Phones bonged and cheeped.

Slink called out behind him: "My invite better be in the mail."

***

Captain Leo McBride's brusque demeanor caused a lump of unease to swell in Cale's gut. Though the captain's stoic expression betrayed little, the hitch in his voice gave Cale a sense of foreboding. The way a pilot senses his radar has fritzed out before glancing at the gauge.

The clues Tobias Crenshaw had given them earlier that day infused Cale with a glimmer of hope. That is, if they turned out to be genuine. In a case peppered with more dead ends than a hedge maze, this might be the break he'd been praying for. The DA's office had already indicated they'd have a "Wanted for Questioning" warrant on the mystery man Crenshaw had fingered. First thing tomorrow morning.

After dropping into his usual chair, Cale explained how he'd contacted the FBI. How Agent Redtail had employed his connections with DHS to track down their new suspect; or almost track him down, as things stood. The man's exact whereabouts remained unclear. But an international search was in progress nonetheless. He watched his boss take it all in with a few nods and grunts. Not much change in his expression.

"I'm aware of your contact with Special Agent Redtail. I spoke to him myself," McBride said, matter-of-fact.

"That's good, Cap. Great."

It meant the communication lines were open. And for this Cale was grateful. He did not want to appear the lone wolf on this, working with either the FBI or Homeland outside the boundaries of the department. He would have guessed the captain might display more enthusiasm, however, and the fact he wasn't was speaking volumes. It set off Cale's internal alarm, telling him there might be a secondary reason he'd been summoned for the meeting.

Cale glanced at the wall clock. A little after five p.m. He fished inside his jacket and rose from the small chair.

He set his holstered Glock 9mm and golden detective shield on the captain's desk. "Making it official," he said, his tone subdued.

McBride stared at the objects with reluctance, as if having little desire to reach for them. "Like I said earlier, Cale, you're free to do whatever you please. It's coming up on June. Why not go fishing? Or catch a Brewers game? Hell, take Maggie to Hawaii and call it an early honeymoon."

"She could use a getaway." A few ticks of silence followed, before Cale added, "I was thinking of heading east."

"Florida's hotter than a rat's ass this time of year."

"Further east." Cale kept his expression tight. "You wouldn't happen to know what the weather's like in, say, Western Africa these days? Around Liberia, for instance?"

Captain McBride set down the pen he'd been rolling in his fingers. "It's the rainy season. So Agent Redtail tells me. I'd suggest you take along a decent umbrella."

"Good to know."

Cale held the captain's stare before glancing away. If his boss had already conversed with Agent Redtail, then it stood to reason he'd been briefed on the latest intelligence—the human sex-trafficking angle involving their case.

McBride closed the open folder on his desk. "You'll keep me updated on your whereabouts, right?"

"Shouldn't be a problem," Cale agreed.

"Like an old bookie friend told me once"—McBride gave him a smile at the memory—"I'm only a phone call away."

CHAPTER 8

Uncertainty. It was one of the things Cale Van Waring feared most in life: the fear of *not knowing*. The time spent pondering this or that. Time wasted. That was the beauty of death, he decided: when you died, at least you knew where you stood. Being suspended from your job was kind of the same way. It was cut-and-dried. Either you were suspended, or you weren't.

Comfort could always be found in certainty.

Departing from the office, Cale waved a few unsentimental good-byes. The duty room was sparse on a dinner hour, and a pair of detectives issued him nods. A couple of uniforms did the same, all quick to return to their paperwork. Watch it! Leper on the loose! Nothing sentimental about a guy going on suspension.

Cale drove his silver Bronco, taking Riverside Drive home, moving along the curling brown Fox River. With the steady breeze, the river flowed northward, headed toward the mouth of the emerald bay. It was after six and the post-work traffic congestion was beginning to thin. The local sports talk show was touting the Brewers' chances as a playoff team, while allowing it would be a long summer if the starting pitching failed to stiffen.

Keeping pace with the traffic, he pressed Maggie's mobile number. She suggested they go out for a quiet dinner instead of cooking. Just the two of them. Cale chose not to let on about his suspension. Wait until after a beer or two. Or three. Considering he didn't have to be at the office first thing in the morning, nor worry about a midnight phone call. He wondered, briefly, what the hell he would do all day. Mow the lawn? Some inanity like yard work, where he didn't have to waste time thinking about a world gone mad?

Then a call to his travel agent. But he wanted to sleep on it first, before seeing how the logistics might play out.

An hour later, with the summer sun dodging behind a bank of flat clouds in the west, they settled on a modest downtown café serving Greek cuisine. The crowd was meager on a warm Monday evening. At a small table toward the back, they ordered drinks while perusing menus. Before Cale could drop the news of his suspension, Maggie beat him to the punch: "Guess what? Chloe thinks she found us a house."

The beers arrived—Red Stripes—and Cale took a healthy swallow. "Last time I checked, we had a house." He meant his parents' old house, where he had grown up. He'd moved back to the place after they'd relocated to Arizona ten years ago. Maggie had lived there with him for over a year now.

"Not for us. I mean for the new detective agency."

The new detective agency. Cale's blank stare revealed he'd already dismissed the idea as whimsy on her part, thinking she had abandoned the pie-in-the-sky plan.

Since her ordeal as a captive of the Chemist—where she had been in Tobias Crenshaw's clutches for over four hours, and due to fentanyl exposure, had come close to losing her life—Maggie had gone on extended medical leave from her job as a state public defender. Her contract would be up in the fall, and she informed Cale she might not return.

"Call it burnout, or whatever." Maggie had decided she could not defend society's helpless anymore. Tobias Crenshaw had stolen something from her, some deep part close to her soul. She felt as if her heart had shrunk.

Two weeks after the incident, Maggie had informed Cale that she and her sister Chloe were considering starting a new business venture together. "We're calling it Jeffers Private Investigators." Maggie would handle the legal end of the business, along with computer traces and background checks. Anything to do with electronic investigations. Cale was forced to admit that eighty percent of private investigations were handled via computer these days: Everything from identity theft to tax fraud to skip traces.

As a lawyer, Maggie would be well equipped to handle this end of the PI business.

For her part, Chloe would work the investigative side of things. Her gift of gab, they decided, made her a natural. Chloe's tasks would include taking photos of suspected marital infidelity, insurance fraud cases, tailing suspicious spouses, and locating missing persons or teenage runaways when the police suspected no foul play. Chloe would also handle the more esoteric side of their cases: the psychic angle—her specialty—if and when a situation called for those means.

Thanks to her involvement in the Chemist case, Maggie's sister had become a minor celebrity in the weeks following the arrest of Crenshaw. As lead investigator, Cale had chosen to reveal to the news outlets Chloe (Jeffers) Ravelle had indeed provided the detectives with valuable information in the rescue of the kidnapped victims. Consequently, Chloe had been interviewed by newspapers and electronic media from as far south as St. Louis. She'd done a half-dozen late-night radio specials on paranormal crime detection, in addition to several blog interviews. She had become an overnight celebrity, though in Cale's opinion, of temporary repute.

Nonetheless, he had legitimized her.

Cale was comfortable with Chloe's newfound attention. *Why not let her have her day in the sun?* he reasoned. Her fifteen minutes of fame. What was the harm in that? Besides, having her mojo back did wonders for Chloe's self-esteem. And it sure as hell made Maggie happier. It meant the positive karma, Cale calculated, would be coming back around to him in spades. Nothing like making the new wife-to-be happy.

Was he a believer in Chloe's "talents" himself? A former Doubting Thomas now turned convert? Cale didn't think so. Still, he could not deny the fact Chloe's "visions" had proved invaluable in helping track down Tobias Crenshaw, and in saving Maggie and the other victims from hell on earth. So, he allowed that there had to be something to it. But from skeptic to wholehearted believer in the paranormal? Cale was doubtful it would happen anytime soon.

In support of the sisters' new venture, he had agreed to assist the fledgling business by utilizing whatever connections he had inside the Green Bay Police Department. It was even considered—with amusement by all—how after he retired from the force, Cale might even join the agency as a full-fledged investigator.

They'd been sitting around the dining room table a few days after the sisters had first hatched the idea. Chloe, fresh from her job as a hair stylist, had been adorned in her usual array of beads and bangles, her hair fashioned in a sideways sweep. She was wearing one of her colorful printed pantsuits. Cale had thought of suggesting she dress more subdued, in order to be taken more seriously as a psychic, but caught the oxymoron.

He decided, instead, that he was not qualified to comment. When you're a skeptic, he reasoned, it's often best to keep your opinions to yourself.

Maggie had been wearing jeans and a T-shirt that evening, and they were sipping chardonnay, chuckling over the concept of Cale working for the new agency. "When the time comes, I'll consider it," he had joked. "If you're still in business by then."

Maggie shot back, "If you're still an asset by that time, Barnaby Jones."

He ignored the *Barnaby Jones* jab. "Oh, I'll be an 'asset' all right." His smirk was playful. "I'm the only one here who can hit the side of a barn with a nine-millimeter."

"Guns and PI's—what a concept!" Maggie's expression was colored by playful sarcasm. "Didn't that stuff go out with Sam Spade and Mike Hammer?"

He decided against reminding her how three weeks earlier his trusty Glock had saved her life. No. She was smart enough. She needed no reminding.

Chloe had added to the discourse: "These days most things are done with computers, anyway. Aren't they?" Maggie's plump tabby Hank was perched on Chloe's lap, purring as she scratched his furry neck. "Along with—" She'd tapped her temple with a crimson lacquered fingernail.

She meant *intuition*, and had a point, Cale was forced to admit. He'd played more than a few hunches himself in cornering Tobias Crenshaw. Intuition and "gut instinct" were factors in good investigative work. It was seldom all facts and evidence alone. Solving a case seldom played out as written in any manual.

Now Maggie's voice was reeling him in from across the restaurant table. They had ordered a gyros plate for two, and Cale could smell the lamb and olives and variety of tangy spices. Perhaps they'd finish with ouzos afterward, celebrate his suspension, when he got around to revealing it.

"You're not planning on getting shit-faced, are you?" she asked, cautioning.

"Why not? You're a fun person to get 'shit-faced' with."

She issued him an odd look, taking a sip of her beer. "What? Crime take a summer holiday? No devious masterminds in need of urgent pursuing?"

"They suspended me." He blurted it out. "Fourteen days. With pay," he was quick to amend, as if it somehow lessened the offense in her eyes.

"Desk duty?"

"Uh-uh. The real deal. I had to turn in my service weapon and shield." He took a long swallow of beer. "Screw-up probation. For breaking into Lester Paprika's house."

"They can't be serious."

"As a nun with hemorrhoids."

Cale explained how Internal Affairs had reviewed his "creative methodology" (his term) in the Chemist case. How Captain McBride had given him the word earlier that day. He also shared with her the synopsis of the morning's interview with Tobias Crenshaw. How the kidnapper was casting an incriminating finger at a new player in the case: a man who went by the single name of "Kinsella". A resident, purportedly, of Liberia. A man with a history—presumed, anyway—of being involved in the sordid arena of international human sex slavery.

"The BS never ends with that guy, does it?" The topic of Tobias Crenshaw caused a noticeable chill in Maggie's demeanor. She finished off her beer, flagged down their waitress, ordered another round for them both.

"His wife left him, I hear," she continued. "Moved out east somewhere. Took the kids."

"Shouldn't be much of a custody battle. Not when he gets convicted of first-degree murder."

"Incarceration for life does tend to throw cold water on a marriage. Not that I'm unhappy for him."

Cale set down his bottle. "That's part of what's in play here, with the DA's office. Crenshaw's giving us this Kinsella character in exchange for a plea down to aggravated manslaughter."

Maggie's expression darkened. "No way! They're not that stupid, are they? The guy's a...a pathological liar! And that's low on his particular list of psychoses."

He informed her the prosecutors were considering the option. Especially if Crenshaw pleaded out. They could dodge a messy trial and save the taxpayers a huge bill at the same time. The DA, mayor, and police chief would all end up looking like winners.

"And meanwhile, the lead detective gets suspended?"

"*C'est la vie*." Cale raised his beer bottle in a mock toast.

"It all seems so damned *convenient*." Maggie shook away a strand of dark hair looping over her left eye. "For Crenshaw, I mean. This mysterious tip of his. I say if it smells like a turd, it's most often a turd."

"Agreed, counselor. And I commend your colorful use of legalese." Cale smirked. "But it's Zackary's job to verify the tip's accuracy. The lead's got to be a hundred percent on the money, or the deal's off the table."

Maggie sighed. She stared off into one dark corner of the restaurant, her mind seemingly miles away.

"Here's to never-ending BS!" Cale toasted, his tone bitter. She drank with him, before he added: "You know, there is a chance Crenshaw might be telling us the truth." He paused a beat, then said, "Eddie Redtail's helping us. FBI's pulling all the intel they can find on this Kinsella guy, as we speak."

Maggie's deep exhalation spoke volumes. She was tired of the topic.

They spent the rest of the meal making small talk, each trapped in their own private thoughts. The topic of Tobias Crenshaw served to rob them of much appetite. Three beers later, and a shot of ouzo each for good measure, they strolled outside into the glow of the pleasant summer evening.

The sky was tar-black by then, clouds sliding across a yellow teardrop of moon. Moths and fireflies buzzed around the streetlights, which were lit up and down the downtown business district. Cale could smell the musty river, spirited with the reflections of blue lights on each bank. The muted strain of music eased through the wall of a nearby tavern. Monday night. The only souls about were college kids, whose weekend hangovers had melted away. Whatever small crowd existed, he guessed, would be an early one.

And for this every cop on patrol would be thankful.

CHAPTER 9

The city's first serial criminal had been captured and arrested and was at present incarcerated in the Brown County jail. It had been three weeks since the arrest. The shock was wearing off, and publicity was at last beginning to subside. Green Bay's jut-jawed inhabitants were ready to accept how big city crime had swept through their midst like the most ill-tempered of winter ice storms.

As Cale stood at the downtown intersection of Washington and Walnut Streets, the sweep of traffic headed west over the bridge, he could feel the alcohol beginning to infuse him with resolve. Holding Maggie's hand, with the summer evening sighing around them, he decided that if he did little else with his life, at least he'd be satisfied he had accomplished one goal: Tobias Crenshaw would never do harm to another innocent person.

When the stoplight turned, and they crossed the street, Cale felt as if a giant burden had been lifted from his shoulders. Screw the suspension. Screw the frustrations of battling crime in this asinine world of bureaucracy and political correctness. He would continue to do things his own way. The right way.

He would fight the good fight.

They meandered along the lighted avenue, window shopping, laughing arm-in-arm like a pair of lovers strolling the Champs-Élysées. Cale noticed a dingy brass bassoon in an antique shop and threatened to purchase it, practice at home in the evenings. To counter his sadistic threat, Maggie dragged him through the doors of a quaint Irish bar with Killian's signs in each window. They would order a Guinness each. Then they would hightail it back to the sanctity of the modest castle they called home.

Parked outside the tavern, Cale noted a trio of Harley Davidsons. Bikers inside. A club? Or they were mere riding enthusiasts. His antenna was up, his natural cop's wariness.

They seated themselves on barstools inside the sparsely inhabited place. "I bought you a gift," Cale said. "Slink's bringing it over tomorrow morning."

"Hmm." She sipped the dark liquid in the tall pint glass. "If it takes two of you to lift it, that's my clue, right? I've got to start thinking like a detective." She feigned deep thought. "I'm getting a Chloe vibe here. It's a new washing machine?"

"I'm not blowing the surprise." He watched her frown.

Cale's quick scan of the tavern had revealed a quartet of college guys and one gal taking turns at the dartboard. Monday night baseball muted on the big screen. Three biker dudes in leather vests shooting pool, behaving themselves. No one was acting suspicious or looking, so it appeared, for trouble. Cale turned to Maggie: "I'm thinking of going after him."

"Going after who?"

"Our guy. In Africa. If Crenshaw's story turns out to be true."

Maggie offered no reply. Bono was singing on the jukebox, expressing concern for the poor Northern Ireland working class sods. Cheery stuff. She dabbed beer foam from her upper lip with a paper bar napkin.

"A piece of advice: I wouldn't get my hopes up too high. Remember, Crenshaw's on a first-name basis with his pal Satan."

"I said *if* his story turns out to be true. Big *if*." Cale sipped his Guinness. "Agent Redtail will let me know. Tomorrow, I'm guessing." Bono's band mate was playing a guitar riff. "How much do you know about human trafficking?" It felt as if, regardless of the amount of liquor he poured down his gullet tonight, Cale couldn't shake free of the disturbing topic.

"You mean young girls being stolen? Kidnapped? From poor, impoverished countries?" Maggie frowned, revealing her revulsion. "Forced into the sex slave racket? That kind of trafficking?"

Cale's mind moved down the dark path it had visited many nights during the past few weeks. The question he kept asking himself, regarding the Crenshaw case, was always *why?* Why would a successful businessman, a family man to boot, out-of-the-blue begin a kidnapping spree? Crenshaw was living the American dream: a mansion on the river, a bright and attractive wife, two well-adjusted young kids. Why risk it all by snatch-and-grabbing adult females? In broad daylight? Despite his near fool-proof MO.

It made no sense to Cale. It hadn't since they'd first tabbed Tobias Crenshaw as a possible suspect in the case.

Of course, Cale hadn't yet perused the psych-eval report the judge had ordered at Crenshaw's arraignment hearing. There was little doubt the Chemist had a serious psychopathology. The report would indicate as much. Cale hoped it would shed some light on the lingering mystery of the motive.

He set the quandary aside like a tricky math problem. To Maggie, he answered, "You're right. That's the *usual* sex slavery scenario." He gave her his full attention. "But what if there's something deeper involved? What if the traffickers wanted to narrow their victims down to a definite *type*? Instead of the usual impoverished or homeless adolescents?" Cale took a drink of his beer.

"By 'type,' you mean like Mary Jane Moore? Like Leslie Dowd? Cindy Hulbreth?" Her look at him was tight. "You guys profiled Crenshaw's victimology. He targeted females in their twenties. Right?"

"That's correct, counselor."

They sat in silence, allowing the bar sounds to buzz around them. "It will all come out in the trial, won't it?" Maggie said in a lawyerly tone. "If the psych report says Crenshaw's a nutjob, then whatever his sick motive was hardly matters."

Cale shrugged. "Assuming it ever comes to trial."

Maggie rose and gave his shoulder a squeeze. She moved down the tavern's main aisle, walking a worn path leading to where the restrooms were located. Cale sipped his beer and watched her departure. Her raven hair shone in the dim light, starlight off black onyx. Damn, she was a knockout, he caught himself thinking. His eyes drifted beyond the bar to the pair of harsh yellow lamps above the pool tables: the trio of palookas holding wooden cues. One of them was lining up a shot while his pals had their eyes glued to Maggie's ass, strolling past. Cale's gaze fell upon the large guy with a goatee, sleeves ripped off his denim shirt. Leather vest, biceps more flab than cut. Although he no longer had his badge with him—thanks to the Internal Affairs geniuses—he was in no mood for a confrontation with the trio of bikers.

When the alpha palooka shot a whiskey glance in his direction, Cale met him head on with an iron stare, followed by a slow shake of his head. A clear warning to the guy to not even go there with Maggie.

Something about the way he looked now, Cale guessed, something in his eyes, the intensity there, conveyed an unmistakable message. Even through the boozy haze of the Irish tavern, his look carried a warning: Don't mess with me right now. Maybe some other time. Not tonight. Don't do it. It's a no-win for you and your buddies.

The biker turned his eyes away from Cale: the dark-haired guy alone at the bar, quietly sipping his Guinness. The alpha was up in the pool game. He looked content to refocus on the table and didn't look their way the rest of the evening.

Maggie returned to her barstool the way a tart slides into the cushioned booth of out-of-town salesmen.

Cale's mind, however, was far from hookers or cracking pool cues over heads, or even kiss-ass review boards playing politics. The discussion concerning Tobias Crenshaw and his madness—real or imagined—had served to focus his thoughts on the topic of human slavery. Suppose this guy, Kinsella, turned out to be on the money. Suppose they discovered he was in the thick of some international trafficking ring. It still didn't explain why Tobias Crenshaw had developed a taste for crime, all of a sudden, in the first place. Cale couldn't shake the fact some integral piece of the puzzle was still out there, waiting to be found. Until he discovered what the missing part was, the whole *why* of the Chemist case would remain an enigma.

The grim topic of the evening's conversation had turned Maggie equally somber. "Do I have any say in this hypothetical little excursion of yours? The convoluted logic involved in traveling to Africa, of all places?"

"It's not convoluted. Not if the guy turns out to be relevant to the case." Cale sipped his drink. "Crenshaw's fingering Kinsella as the actual killer, remember?"

Maggie set her glass on the bar coaster. "No offense. But since when does a Green Bay police detective—a suspended one at that—go chasing five thousand miles after a sketchy criminal?"

"There are certain promises I made. Promises to some good people." Cale sipped his beer. "Folks who are counting on me to bring them closure."

"Even if it involves chasing after some ghost? Halfway around the world?"

"That's the general idea. Yeah."

Maggie stayed silent for a minute. "What about the promises you made to me? To us? Where might those fall on the Van Waring Master Promise Scale?"

Cale stared beyond her at the bank of dark windows, which offered up a view of the shadowy street outside. Their reflections, backlit, cast an angelic halo around Maggie's head. The irony wasn't lost on him and he reached for her hand, studied her palm as if reading it. "I plan on keeping my promises, Mags. To each person I promised. But especially to you."

She forced a weak smile.

Whatever was to happen, Cale acknowledged, he had little desire to fly off to Africa. But if that's what it took, then so be it. It was the price you paid for making promises you meant to keep. It was harsh logic, no doubt. But as far as Cale was concerned, it held up nonetheless.

Fighting the good fight.

***

In the upstairs bedroom, after getting undressed, Maggie held him tight. She decided there was no point in arguing about his possible trip. It was something inside Cale, his sense of honor or duty. Some part of him she understood, but still didn't know the fabric of. Would she ever? In the future someday, she guessed, when they'd known one another longer than two years.

They made love with a relaxed gentleness, yet it felt as if each might be holding something back. Maggie decided it was a fear of abandonment—at least in her case. But soon the passion increased, and they became trapped in a blaze, bright and leaping, hot enough to burn yourself in the tangle of their limbs. Together they staved off the darkness, chasing the room's bleak shadows to the edge of the walls, where they clustered like shy schoolboys, alone and filled with hope.

"You ought to get suspended more often," she said afterward, her voice breathy in the dimness. "I think we just discovered a new brand of energy."

"How about we blame the Guinness?"

"Then all of Ireland would be purified, wouldn't it?"

"And Scotland. And Wales." Cale said this while lying on his back as if crucified, arms spread in pleasurable exhaustion. "You're not quoting Bono, I hope."

She turned to him in the absent light, wrapped in the sheet, weight on one elbow. "I could be mad at you, you know. But I'm choosing not to be."

"I appreciate it."

Silence for a few long beats. "If you don't come back from Africa, then what? I'm trapped in this bed each night? Alone? How fair does it sound?"

Cale chuckled. "I'm certain you'll manage. And anyway, that's not going to happen."

"You sure take the fun out of being a drama queen."

"Besides, you've got the new business with Chloe to keep you energized." He rolled to the mattress's edge and sat upright, feet on the floor. "You'll likely have your first case solved by the time I get back... I'm grabbing some aspirin. You want a couple?"

"Four. I don't want to feel as hungover as you tomorrow."

"Trying to outrun the bear, are we?" He said this with a snicker. "All you've got to do is run faster than me? Is that it?"

"Something like that." She pulled the blankets close to her chin.

He rose and made his way off into the shadows, where his dark form disappeared around the doorway.

For her entire life, as long as she could remember, Maggie had possessed what she referred to as a "sleep switch." It was a talent many people—Cale included—would die for. She decided not to worry about things she could not control. What would happen, would happen, she reasoned. Maggie fluffed her pillows, positioning them into the usual private nest. *To hell with the aspirin.* She turned onto one bare shoulder and was asleep within seconds.

CHAPTER 10

Tuesday morning broke clear and clean, like the glorious summer mornings of his youth. Days of baseball and bike riding and fifty-cent candy bars. Though Cale's head felt the size of a medicine ball, he rose and plowed through his morning workout routine. Hank sat on a nearby loveseat grooming himself, watching as Cale put himself through thirty minutes of torture aboard the rowing machine. Hank bore the calm expression of someone comfortable in the presence of lunacy.

Afterward, in the kitchen, Cale poured himself a glass of orange juice and watched as Maggie came into the room. She was wearing gray shorts and a wifebeater, and carried her tea mug in one hand, a stack of bills in the other. She appeared to be a little pale, her eyes clouded.

"You feeling all right?" Cale asked. "Couldn't be a bit of hangover, could it?"

"I'm fine," she said, not looking him in the eye. "Just a bug I'm fighting." Hank sauntered into the room, brushing her ankle, signaling it was time for his breakfast.

Setting the stack of bills atop the counter, Maggie added, "Last night I was thinking. When we were in bed—"

"Meaning you weren't consumed by the burning passion of our lovemaking?"

She frowned. "It's called multitasking."

"Shatters my illusions a bit. But all right, I'm listening."

"You mentioned the bastard Crenshaw? Giving you a tip on a suspect—the African gentleman?"

"I'm sure he's many things, but I doubt 'gentleman' is one of them."

"All right, killer then. Or murdering psychopath. Or sadistic human trafficker. Take your pick." She paused. "Assuming this man can't be legally extradited back here, then you're considering going off to try and—what—locate him on your own? Is that about right?"

Cale had a towel draped over his shoulders, gripping both ends. "If it comes to that. Yes. That's the gist of it. But we'll have to see how things play out."

Maggie took a sip of tea. "I was thinking. How about if I come with you? You know, to Liberia or wherever? I could help out."

He issued her the same stare Hank had given him earlier. "This isn't some vacation we're talking about, Mags. If we're dealing with a human trafficking ring, trust me, these are not pleasant people."

"I understand that—but you're forgetting one thing: I'm a lawyer. Remember? I can help out on a lot of different levels."

"The answer is, one: *not*. And two: *happening*!" He let out a breath. "I have no idea what I'm even dealing with or what kind of danger I might be wading into. I can't risk having to worry about you while I'm doing it."

She crossed her arms, defiant, mindful of her tea mug. "I can handle myself, you know." She set the mug on the counter and glared at him.

He didn't want to bring up the incident with Tobias Crenshaw, wherein she'd been kidnapped from their home, raped, almost killed. He knew it wasn't fair. "The point is, I'll be able to do my job a lot better if I know you're right here. Home. Safe."

The silence built between them, each locking eyes without looking away. This was not a fight—not a real one—and neither wanted to turn it into one. Cale heard a car outside as it churned up the driveway. Through the gauzy curtains of the dining room, he watched the pewter-colored Taurus ease to a halt on the driveway apron.

"Cavalry's here," Cale said lightly. The presence of his partner, he hoped, might serve to defuse the tension inside the kitchen. He watched Slink exit the vehicle. He was carrying a shoebox in one hand, and in his white short-sleeved shirt and narrow tie, Cale decided his partner could be mistaken for a Jehovah's Witness carrying his bible.

"You don't have to be a hero, Cale." Maggie's caustic tone reeled him back, caused him to turn his head her way.

"Right now, the FBI is running the case. Not me."

"And you sure as hell can't save the world. Not even with Agent Redtail's help." She took a slow sip from her mug. "Besides, it's not a very healthy job choice."

***

Slink Dooley rapped on the back door and turned the knob, allowing himself into the Van Waring home. It was a little past 8:00 a.m. Spotting them standing and stink-eyeing one another like prefight boxers, Slink decided it didn't take a genius to know he was wandering into the middle of something. Just what, he wasn't sure. He'd been married himself for six years now, and he understood one truism. Ask any street cop: they'd rather wrangle an alligator than venture into the eye of a domestic dispute.

With Hank pausing from his breakfast bowl long enough to stare up at the visitor's entrance, Slink said, "Hey, Dr. Phil here. Your lucky day. You guys have just won a free therapy session at my basement clinic. First six-pack's on me."

Maggie groaned, giving him a shake of her head. "Please don't mention beer. You want some ginger tea?" Then, glancing at the box in his hand: "Not an early wedding present, I hope."

Slink, clever detective that he was, picked up on the clue. The wedding, at least, did not seem to be in jeopardy. He shook his head to the tea, waving the box in the air. "Might be the waffle iron you always dreamed of, little lady?" To Cale, he said, "And you, Kemosabe. Thought you'd be heading out to Lake Winnebago, by now. I hear a little worm drowning helps take a guy's mind off things."

"Wouldn't be the same without you there."

Slink chortled. "That, my friends, is what women are always telling me."

"In your dreams," they both said at once, before Cale shifted his eyes to the box his partner held. "Is it what I think it is?"

Slink played the room: "Day one of suspension and his detecting skills haven't slipped a bit." He moved around the counter past Cale, set the cardboard container on the dining room table, and pulled off the lid. Unpacking the crumpled newspaper filler, he withdrew a soft leather holster with a small handgun tucked inside.

Cale had followed Slink into the room. Maggie, more restrained, trailed behind. Removing the handgun from the holster, Slink held it up for Cale's inspection. "Kahr PM9," he reported. "A slick little invention from even slicker minds."

Maggie stepped closer to the men, eyeing the diminutive weapon in its holster. "A toy gun?" She scowled at Slink. "You better not be buying one for Little Jimmy. Janet will have a fit."

Slink issued her a scowl. "Little Jimbo's a Colt .45 man. At least he's going to be, when he gets to third grade."

"Do I have to pry it out of you?" Maggie arched an eyebrow at them both. "Or are you going to tell me what crazy scheme you're up to now?"

"I was going to get the mouse killer. Like we said," Slink reported, handing the holstered weapon to his partner. "But this one's got way more *savoir faire*. And it comes with a healthier kick."

Cale began his professional examination. He checked the dot-the-i-sight, stared down the barrel, flipped it around.

"We call these 'tossers'," Slink informed Maggie. "Small enough to fit in an ankle holster. Or a handbag. Lethal enough to send Mr. Bad Guy six feet under with one well-placed bye-bye."

"She's a beauty, all right," Cale said, ejecting the empty clip. "We'll need to register it. And apply for a concealed carry permit."

"Up to you guys. But it's brand new. Cleaner than an Amish bride on her wedding night." From the shoebox Slink withdrew a box of nine-millimeter ammunition and a spare clip. "Six in the true mag. Seven in the backup." To Maggie he said, "You can't hit *Señor Hombre* with six shots, darlin', time to turn your pretty tail and vamoose."

Maggie frowned. Her eyes shifted from the small weapon. back to their faces. "What do you mean if *I* can't hit someone? Why are you both looking at me like that?"

Slink's grin was playful. "Far as wedding gifts go, this sure as hell beats a punch bowl."

CHAPTER 11

Cale stood at the end of the dining table, both hands planted on the polished surface. He watched with amused interest as his partner explained the workings of the Kahr PM9 to Maggie. How to load the clip, how to aim with both hands, the proper stance, trigger pressure, how to reject a spent clip, where the safety was. Slink had already procured a time for them to visit the department shooting range later that afternoon. The sooner the better, as far as Cale was concerned. Maggie had been lucky to survive an assault with a gangbanger in the county juvenile detention jail. Then she'd been kidnapped by the sociopath Tobias Crenshaw. Though she'd managed to escape both encounters in one piece, Cale concluded that if she'd had access to a firearm, her chances of being victimized would have been greatly diminished.

"Forewarned is forearmed"—so the saying goes. There was no way he was going to allow his fiancé to place herself in such a position of vulnerability again. Not if he had any say in the matter. Besides, as soon as she had her official PI license, Maggie would be granted a legal permit-to-carry. It was a matter of personal protection.

Cale watched her eyes now, keen with intelligence, taking in all the nuances Slink was explaining about the small but deadly weapon. What he admired most about Maggie was that, despite her recent encounters with evil, she refused to play the victim. She was leaving the frustrations of practicing law behind her, on her own terms. She was beginning a new business venture. And now, here she was, learning to use a firearm, learning to defend herself. Learning like a duckling taking to rain.

Cale's phone chirped. He answered, walking away from Slink's lesson, moving into the airy living room. The vertical blinds allowed in golden spears of sunshine. The call was from Agent Redtail, and while he listened, Cale noticed his reflection in the tall leaning mirror, which Maggie had angled near the room's entrance. The man gazing back looked like him, but the morning light cast his reflection as a smeared version of himself. He watched how the glass surface distorted his face as Eddie Redtail's words reached him. Cale observed his reflection's reaction: the grim slice of his mouth, his narrowing eyes. He watched himself nod, respond, then end the phone call.

He was aware Slink had ceased his lesson. Both he and Maggie were staring at him, concern coloring their expressions.

"Eddie Redtail," Cale said, minus any emotion. "Crenshaw's story checks out. They located a Liberian national by the single name of 'Kinsella.' The Liberian government, no surprise, is refusing extradition. For political reasons, they say."

"And this means what? In reality?" Maggie asked.

"It means Redtail's got me booked on a flight to Atlanta. Then to Rome. He was unclear on the rest. Says he'll brief me when I land."

Maggie set the small handgun on the dining room table, on one of the place mats, checking to make sure the safety was on. She moved across the room to face Cale. "So, this is honestly going to happen? For real?"

"I'm scheduled to leave here"—he glanced at his watch—"in a little over two hours."

"There goes your cozy fishing trip," Slink said, ever the jokester.

"I'm still going fishing." Cale's voice was sober. But the fish I'm after just got a little bigger, that's all."

"A fish who won't take too kindly to a big fat hook in his mouth," noted Slink.

Cale smirked. "Name me one that does."

***

Slink volunteered to drive Cale to Austin Straubel International Airport, on the city's far West Side. The noon flight to Atlanta. It made more sense than his taking the Bronco or popping for a twenty-dollar cab fare not counting tip. Maggie remained unenthused with his decision, smoldering quietly at the reasons he'd listed for her remaining at home. Regardless, she was not one for melancholic goodbyes. She insisted she had important things to get done anyway. But after fifteen minutes of pouting, her mood relaxed. Like an attorney realizing she had no true defense, she resigned herself to the inevitable.

After Cale had showered, packed, and returned downstairs, they exchanged a tender hug. Maggie whispered, "You promise to come back to me? In one piece?"

"Two good legs and upright." Bravado colored Cale's words. His comment suggested the image of a Civil War son who hugged his mother before venturing off to Antietam.

With Slink navigating the Taurus over the bridge spanning the broad Fox River, they made small talk during the drive. Slink asked if Maggie was taking an extended medical leave, or if she was serious about resigning as a public defender. Cale answered vaguely, revealing she had discussed several new projects. He figured Maggie would let the world know her plans when she was good and ready. She was an independent thinker. An unstoppable force when she set her mind to something.

"Keep an eye on her, right? While I'm gone?"

"Damn straight." Slink rolled his neck. "Who else is going to teach her how to use the cannon you gave her?"

They drove in silence for the next five minutes, and Cale's mind was already five thousand miles away, imagining his plane setting down in Rome's Fiumicino Airport. The starting point in the search for the mysterious man Tobias Crenshaw had fingered. Cale's ruminations were traversing along shadowy paths, when Slink asked, "Who you like tonight? Brewers over Phillies? Or Orioles at home against the White Sox?"

Cale glanced at the radio, thinking he had missed something.

Slink added, "Just because you're flying halfway around the world, kemosabe, doesn't mean you forget the national pastime." He turned the Taurus into the airport entranceway. A minute later, easing the vehicle curbside, throwing it into park and turning to Cale, Slink asked:

"How long have we been partners?"

"This still about baseball?" Cale narrowed his eyes.

"Twelve years. Two in Narcotics; another ten now in Investigations." Outside the terminal people were moving in and out, a parade of taxis and shuttle vans at the ready. Slink continued: "I'm going to tell you something, hombre. Only because I'd want to know myself, if it was me."

Cale felt a tightness in his chest. "Do I want to hear this?"

"I'm sure you *do not* want to hear this. But I'm going to tell you anyway."

Searching his partner's face, Cale watched as Slink cast his gaze out the window at the sliding front entrance doors of the terminal. The familiar looking strangers.

"Maggie might be...pregnant. Geez. No other way to put it," Slink said, turning toward Cale and allowing his words to hit home. "Or something's up. I overheard her and Janet on the phone yesterday. Before work. Girl talk, you know?"

Cale turned his head away to stare at some invisible point far across the fence bordering the runways. Without turning back, he said, "This couldn't have waited? Till I got back?"

"Key thing here: I said *might be!*" Slink let out a breath. "Like I said, if it was me, I'd rather know than not." He matched Cale's stare out the windshield. "One to ten? How pissed off at me are you at me?"

Cale swung his head back, eyes narrow. "Ten, if you're the father."

Silence for a beat, before Slink gave a sheepish smirk.

"Your comedic timing's still intact. I'll give you that much." He exhaled, then: "I'm not saying it was intentional. But...something happened to her with Crenshaw. When he had her for those hours." His eyes were intent, staring at Cale. "That's my theory."

Cale was silent for a minute. A large plane gunned its engines, started taxiing down a distant runway. "Why hasn't she told me?"

Slink shook his head. "I don't think she knew. At least not for sure. So, there's…I suppose she's got things to think about."

Silence filled the interior of the Taurus, expanding, until Cale opened the passenger door and stepped outside.

"Guess you've got your own thinking to do," Slink said, joining him, popping the trunk. "Long plane flight. If it's good for anything, must be for thinking."

"Good as any, I suppose." He pondered the situation for a minute. "Think I should ask her? Say anything?"

"Hell, no. It may not even be true." Slink popped the trunk and opened it wide. "She'll tell you when she's ready."

Cale supposed Slink was right. Besides, his friend was far superior when it came to understanding the feminine psyche than he had ever been.

Slink put a steady hand on Cale's shoulder. "Catch the bad guy, Cale. Bring him home." He advised this in a somber voice. " You can deal with all the other BS when you get back."

After pulling his two pieces of luggage from the car's trunk, Cale slammed the hatch closed. They nodded farewell, and he watched the Taurus slide away into the lane of moving traffic.

Turning, Cale made his way through the entrance doors. Near the check-in area, he was quick to spot an old face—Luke Charles, a former street cop. Never made it past sergeant grade but retired with his twenty. He now worked airport security. Cale chatted Charles up and while talking he cast his gaze out the glassy front windows of the main terminal. Although it was over two hundred yards away, he spotted the Taurus as it drove through the distant intersection. Slink failed to take the right turn that would take him back downtown. Instead, the pewter-colored vehicle cruised through the stoplights and entered the main drive of the Oneida Casino.

Charles was babbling on about his son having graduated college at Marquette, but Cale wasn't listening. His mind was replaying the conversation he'd had minutes earlier: *Baseball games, Maggie pregnant. The sick bastard Tobias Crenshaw. Maybe pregnant; maybe not.* His expression soured. Why was Slink visiting the casino, instead of heading back to work? Especially with his, Cale's, suspension in effect? They'd be short-handed on the rotation.

"Anything the matter, Lieutenant?" The former cop's voice was at his shoulder, following his stare through the broad bank of windows.

With a shrug, Cale said, "Nothing at all, Sergeant." He withdrew his phone and checked for messages. "At least nothing that can't wait."

Giving Luke Charles's shoulder a pat, Cale headed off toward the check-in line.

CHAPTER 12

Château du Carthairs, Belgium

The snap of the riding crop. It stung the taught right buttock of the filly as she pranced, pulling the riding cart with her trio of pony mates. Around the grounds they moved, knees high. Their thick-booted heels pounded the turf. With their arms harnessed behind them, heads upright and backs straight, they cantered in unison, performing with trained precision.

Beneath the stand of shade trees adjacent to the riding stables, Prince Mir Al-Sadar stood and viewed the proceedings with keen interest. To his trainer beside him, he said, "Most excellent, Mr. Anselm. You have groomed this team well. You will be rewarded with a generous bonus."

Mr. Anselm was a diminutive Belgian with a craggy, cratered face beneath his customary brown fedora. "Thank you, Your Excellency. It has been most fulfilling work."

The prince, his sharp black eyes on his ponies as they rounded the far turn, nodded. "And an added gift as well, of course, if they win the upcoming competition."

Mr. Anselm bowed graciously before lifting his head. He watched His Highness take his leave, heading back to the sanctity of his splendorous chateau.

***

Late afternoon, the summer sun still arched and bathing the country landscape with coppery light. The bells of a distant church tolled out the hour, answered by the far-off whistle of a high-speed train. The air, warmed by the sun's caress, carried the sweet scent of lilacs. The tall spires of the château cast lengths of shadow across the adjacent courtyards. In the surrounding hills, over the next few hours, the sky would turn from bronze to burnt orange to scarlet, before at last giving way to twilight's purple surge.

Situated in the heart of a three-hundred-acre forest, sixty miles southwest of Brussels, the château was constructed in 1798 for a wealthy Turkish nobleman. The original purpose was for holding diplomatic meetings with the French ambassadors, away from their home soil, where it was hoped they might express their opinions in a more open fashion.

From the third-floor windows, one could gaze out over the treetops, the manicured lawns, study the sunlight reflected off the calm waters of the natural spring-fed lake. Swans floated leisurely, moving as if by an invisible motor. Foxes foraged in the woods, chasing wild hares and chipmunks. Deer moved in silence, dining on leaves and berries, ever vigilant of the stalking hunter's arrow.

Inside the château, in the great hall—one of six buildings comprising the estate—spectacular French details complemented the evidence of splendor. Huge tapestries dripped from the walls. By day the tall windows allowed in splashes of glistening sunshine. Masterpieces by Rubens and Renoir and Gauguin rendered proof that wealth trumped any semblance of modesty within these walls. The grand reception rooms stretched upward, greeting twenty-meter-tall ceilings, complete with murals of high-country living, soft and feathery, appearing as if brushed by The Master himself.

The château was owned by Prince Mir Al-Sadar, a member of the Emer Saud royal family. For all its nobility and grace—for as with many things, they mask what they truly are—the dark underbelly of the place was one many people might find troubling. Repulsive, even.

Surrounding the entire inner compound was an eight-foot tall, wrought-iron fence, reputed to be electrified. It was designed to keep curious intruders out, but even more important, to contain the château's most precious commodity: the prince's harem of twenty succulent females. The ladies came from around the globe, purchased by His Majesty for his private amusement. They also provided a budding source of income from those fortunate—or wealthy—enough to be favored by the prince. A few nights a week he leased out a handful of his harem to those willing to pay the exorbitant fees. Thus, the ladies were "earning their keep."

By turning his hobby into a profitable business venture, Prince Mir was indeed pleased by the fruits of his noble endeavor. His ladies were under constant guard by his henchmen, not to mention their being hooked on heroin, and therefore stripped of their own free will. But business was business, after all. And consequently, no one either protested or seemed much to care.

Behind the main house, beyond the stretching slope of grassy lawns and century old oak, elm, and willows, stood the stables. Thoroughbred stallions and mares were housed there, fed and groomed and trained to be champions. They were raced all over Europe. Even shipped to the United States to display their talents. Set apart from the horses, in a private stable of their own, a different kind of pony was trained alongside the equine variety.

Pony girls.

These were owned by the prince, molded at the hands of Mr. Ernst Anselm, one of Belgium's most respected equine tutors. For some of the harem members, it was a source of great pride to be selected as a "pony." Akin to being named a prima ballerina. They considered it a step above the degrading work as one of the prince's fancy prostitutes. For others, the task was no less off-putting: being trained to "perform" by prancing around the grounds in tight latex and equine gear, little more than an animal, themselves.

"To each their own," thought Leslie Ann Dowd. She was back in the stable, having been granted permission to remove her halter and bit. She would be bathed, lathered, rinsed by the assistant trainers. Then Leslie, along with her pony mates, would be shuttled back up to their rooms inside the château. Dinner and comfortable accommodations awaited them. Along with an injection of the magic juice that would send each of them on her private journey to the moon every evening. A welcome escape from the rigors of training.

This day, however, was different for Leslie. Her plan had been in place for weeks now. Like most things in life, its successful execution depended upon timing. As magicians always said, it was *everything*.

Over a year ago, Leslie had been purchased by the prince from the large Liberian man they called "Kinsella." In his too-snug sports jacket, which covered his large muscular torso, the man had been an intimidating sight. He was responsible for her clandestine transportation by ship, from America to Africa. Then further into Europe. Leslie and another American girl—named Mary Jane Moore—had talked at length during their eight-day voyage. Mary Jane had likewise been purchased by Prince Mir and brought to the opulent country château.

Except that during the journey, Mary Jane had proved recalcitrant to the program, and had been punished for her insolence.

Inside the château now, within the comfort of her private bedroom on the third floor, Leslie thought of Mary Jane. Of what had become of her friend. Was she imprisoned somewhere? Being tortured? Subjected to the lash or whip like the other girls? Or was she dead—as many in the château were known to whisper—having been roasted over a fire pit? Consumed by the prince (a repulsive rumor that Leslie chose not to believe!), and his cannibalistic henchman, Kinsella?

Sitting at her bureau, Leslie cast aside these troubling thoughts. She had more pressing matters on her mind: namely her escape. Her dark-blond hair was still damp from the rinsing she'd received, so she fluffed it with a towel, combed it through, pulled it back and fashioned it into a ponytail. Thankfully it wasn't too long, wasn't going to be a nuisance. She'd be running through forests and fields, hiding in barns or farmhouse basements. Who knew where? The last thing she needed to worry about was her hair.

Rising, she glanced at the clock: 4:20 p.m. The prince took his afternoon siesta from four till six. The staff nurse who came to administer the shots arrived sometime around five. It meant Leslie had little more than thirty minutes to slip free of the château, get past the stables, and into the expanse of thick woods. All before anyone realized she was missing.

She slipped into her navy-blue tracksuit. It matched those of the other girls. They were provided for workout purposes. Staying in peak shape was essential, after all, for each member of the prince's harem. She donned her cross-trainers and grabbed her fanny pack from the deep corner of her closet. The pack contained a bottle of water and four dinner rolls she had managed to pilfer from the kitchen. These were all she had for sustenance, and Leslie imagined she could subsist for at least three days on the meager provisions. Also, inside her pack was a jackknife she'd stolen from the stable. Her only weapon. She hoped she would not have to employ the knife. She would not hesitate to use it, however, if it came to that.

***

Most of the château was at rest by the time Leslie slipped in silence from her room. She stepped into the long, shadowed corridor, expecting to see no one about. The other ponies would be nursing their exhausted muscles, quiet on their beds by now. The remainder of the harem would be resting, preparing themselves for the evening's dinner and festivities, and whatever else Prince Mir demanded of them.

Two minutes later, she found herself in the empty laundry room. Leslie had taken the servants' back stairway down to the ground floor, encountering no one along the way. There she had slipped into the large room, where industrial-sized washers and dryers were rumbling, as they often were in a mansion this large, with these many occupants.

Her adrenaline surge was in full force now. Half of her said, *Go! Quickly! Run!* The other half told her to wait, be patient, *be smart*, for her life hung in the balance. Timing was essential. Leslie figured she had one decent chance at escape, one opportunity to run. She did not want to blow it.

Ten steps down the hallway stood a back door, which led to the outside grounds. Out the door she moved, onto the shaded grassy knoll spanning the entire back of the château. Leslie's goal was to make it to the thicker woods, where she wouldn't have to deal with climbing the electrified fence. Unnoticed. The first leg in her escape mission.

Appearing as nonchalant as was possible—she knew CCTV security cameras were mounted in random spots around the grounds—she made her way toward the walking path. It was like a golf path that meandered its way along the edge of the château grounds, curving one way then another, leading eventually into the woods, where it emerged near the lake. Having dressed for the occasion, a jogger in her running suit, Leslie made a beeline for the paved path.

At the concrete edge, she broke into a light jog. Her leg muscles screamed their protest. Leslie reminded herself: *You're a jogger, out for a late afternoon run. Long distance. Not a sprint.*

Veering from the path as soon as she spotted the lake, Leslie knew her best chance was to move off the standard route. Two minutes later, she was brushing aside prickly branches of underbrush before emerging into a small clearing amid tall trees. It was not in her best interest to linger, so she kept moving. Another four minutes passed. Then another seven. She moved with the understanding the guards might already be scurrying about, having spotted her suspicious behavior on their monitors.

An airplane flew overhead, moving west. Heading from Brussels into France, or further on toward Spain. She was headed in a tangential direction, knowing there were a few distant farms situated on the roadway leading south, toward the river. If she could make it this way, staying inland, she might find shelter in a shed or some dank basement.

Leslie stepped through a thicket, imagining she could hear the babbling of a stream somewhere beyond the layers of shadow. The underbrush was heavy, slowing her progress. She paused and listened to the blood pounding in her ears. She was not free yet. Far from it. Could she ever relax again? Only when she was aboard a ship or a plane, away from Europe for good. Headed back to America. To safety.

Headed home.

Another few steps forward and she paused before the base of a cedar tree. No, it couldn't be! Not yet. She listened hard, and the forest around her turned quiet. There it came again, far off in the distance. The sound chased a chill up her spine. Leslie started forward again, moving now with a more fervent sense of desperation.

No longer jogging, she was running...running from the sound of what she imagined were determined bloodhounds.

***

Scrambling through the thick woods, Leslie heard another plane cruise overhead. It was flying low, a military cargo, she guessed. For a few moments, the rumbling engines drowned out the sound of the pursuit dogs, which seemed to be closing in by the second. She tripped over a thick vine, righted herself, listened for the direction of the barking. She knew she was close to civilization. A small town or farmhouse had to be coming up soon. If she could reach a country road even, flag down a motorist, she still had a chance at escaping.

Keep moving, Leslie. Don't stop!

She was gauging her direction by the lowering sun in the western sky, twinkling through the lush tree cover. Once it disappeared, she imagined her odds would improve. She would be almost invisible in her dark track suit, lost in over three-hundred acres of natural forest. But the prince's men were ruthless and drove jeeps and trucks and all-wheel-drive vehicles. They would have infrared night vision capability. Not to mention automatic weapons. For all Leslie knew, they had her surrounded right now, even as she fought her way forward through the woods.

She scraped her knuckles on the sharp quills of a rough Douglas pine, then paused again, listening. She heard the roar of an engine far off to her left, followed by a fierce voice barking orders in French. Moving opposite from where the sound came, Leslie attempted to make as little noise as possible while advancing forward. Without warning she slammed into a massive boulder. Only this granite object reached out and spun her around, wrapping tight arms around her. To Leslie's dismay, she realized the boulder was human.

"Hello again, Leslie," whispered the voice, rasping sandpaper in her ear. She felt one meaty hand cover her mouth and nose. She couldn't answer if she tried. "We keep meeting under such odd circumstances."

Leslie tried kicking at her captor's legs, his knees, stomping with the heels of her cross-trainers as she'd been taught in self-defense class. These had little effect as the man used his hulking arms to keep her pinned. Before she could manage to bite the fingers pressed across her mouth, she felt the jab of a sharp needle, as it pierced the flesh of her shoulder.

Then Leslie felt nothing.

CHAPTER 13

Atlanta, Georgia

Cale Van Waring did not hate flying in the way some people did. He did not fear heights. What he hated was the feeling of confinement. Trapped inside a long metallic tube, propelled through the skies at over five-hundred miles per hour. It was this claustrophobia, more than anything, which filled him with a dreadful sense of unease.

Having settled into his aisle seat in the final row of the plane—Delta flight DL70, Atlanta to Rome—he eyed the other passengers as they boarded. He counted a crew of seven flight attendants working the 80-percent capacity load. Cale caught the attention of a diminutive hostess who'd been assigned to the back section of the plane. Her name tag read "Lin." She handed him a bottle of water that she'd produced from the rear compartment of the serving cart, and watched Cale tap out a pair of pills from an orange plastic bottle. He swallowed the tablets, returning the container to the inner pocket of his windbreaker.

"Sleeping pills?" she asked with a smile.

"Antacids," Cale said, not embellishing. He had another half-filled bottle of prescription Xanax in his other pocket but wanted to hold off if he could. He removed his jacket.

"Can I ask you"—Cale glanced at her nametag—"Lin, are there any air marshals on this flight?" When she gave him a blank look, he added, "Reason I'm asking, I'm in law enforcement. A detective. Robbery-homicide."

This relaxed her. "I'm afraid not. Homeland Security is more concerned with people entering the country, than with them leaving." Cale decided it made sense.

She displayed a set of dimples, and he watched as she marched off down the aisle, touching the seat tops for support. Moments later, she was helping a man in a New York Mets cap with his stowaway. The tourist had long gray hair and a matching soul patch beneath his lower lip. He wore a simple button-down Oxford shirt, sleeves rolled to his elbows. The man stumbled a bit before plopping down in his seat, eight rows up from the final row.

Cale glanced across his row to gaze out the portside window. He felt relief at spotting a few empty seats in the last three rows. Having flown to Atlanta from Green Bay earlier, this was the second leg of his journey. The Georgia sun was still arcing in the western sky, the May temperature steaming outside. Cale reached up and opened his fresh air nozzle, cursing the narrowness of airplane seats. Designed for ten-year-old kids or dwarfs. For a few moments the panicky sense of confinement rushed him, but he managed to push it back.

Twenty minutes later, having risen above the clouds, he lolled his head against the headrest and allowed his mind to drift to the events of the past four weeks. Most of it possessed a dreamlike quality now, so Cale sorted through the sequence of events in chronological order:

The capture of Tobias Crenshaw; the discovery of Crenshaw's private house of horrors; and the rescue of his captured victims (Maggie included). The realization that a pair of victims remained unaccounted for and may have been murdered. Crenshaw deemed a flight risk, denied bail; followed by Cale's squabble with the Internal Affairs review board—this due to his ordering the break-in of an informant's home, along with his wounding of the suspect *without provocation*, during the arrest.

"He kidnapped and molested my fiancé," Cale had explained to the IA officers. "Same goes for the rest of his victims. He *beheaded* one of them, for Christ's sake! Two are still missing—at least that we know of. That's not enough provocation for you guys?"

The citizenry, these days, demanded police scrutiny, he was informed. Especially in a high-profile case, with the press looking over their shoulder at every turn. The entire department was under the microscope.

"What the citizens ought to be demanding"—Cale countered—"is for this sick bastard to be strung up by the gonads. Maybe then he'll tell us where the other two missing victims are."

"Look. We're not the enemy here, Cale," IA officer Andy Mertinson had stated.

"You're not, Mert? You sure as hell had me fooled!"

With a move lifted straight from some criminal defense how-to manual, Crenshaw was fingering a mysterious African thug as the mastermind behind the abductions. This same figure was also the murderer—so claimed Crenshaw—a Liberian who went by the solitary name of "Kinsella." The *true killer*. The ploy was so ridiculous it made Cale laugh. Yet they were required to take it seriously, on the outside chance it might be the truth. Agent Redtail had done his part: he had confirmed, via Interpol, how a man answering the name and description existed.

Now it was up to Cale to determine if this same man was relevant to the Chemist case.

So here he was, zipping through the clouds, headed east across the Atlantic Ocean. The plan called for his meeting in Rome with a man whom Agent Redtail had recommended: a mercenary soldier from the Czech Republic, a specialist who possessed a masterful knowledge of Europe. A man whom they could no doubt trust. *Hopefully*, thought Cale, trying to keep his skepticism in check.

A man whose name was Jacek Tumaj.

***

The passengers on board the airplane had settled in for the mind-and-butt-numbing journey. Cale felt his own eyelids becoming heavy. How easy it was to be lulled by the dull drone of the engines, the gentle sway of the wings, as they cruised above the candied clouds. He understood that at some point during the ten-hour-plus flight, he'd have to try and get some sleep. And he'd have to think about Maggie—what Slink had told him—although he had already compartmentalized the idea of her pregnancy, locked it away in a box buried deep inside his brain. He'd deal with it later, when proper time permitted. He couldn't allow what might be a rumor to interfere with his focus, or the purpose of his trip.

Cale decided he'd at least wait until the sun set to try and sleep. In the meantime, he focused on the flight crew as they continued to work the plane, silent as morticians.

Up the aisle he heard Lin rendering a polite reminder to a couple to please keep their fits of giggling to a minimum. Around them passengers had flicked off overhead lights and were beginning to close their eyes, listening to iPods, clacking at phones, or wearing sound blockers. Each row had at least a few occupants tapping on laptops beneath tiny cones of light.

For excitement, Mr. Mets Cap had created a mild ruckus earlier by attempting to order a "Double Jack Daniels on the rocks." This despite his beginning to show evident signs of inebriation. Marcus, a testosterone-challenged flight attendant, had attempted to smooth Mets Cap's ruffled feathers after he'd been denied more alcohol. He received some cursing and a nasty gender slur for his efforts at détente.

Marcus had walked away in a snit.

Just what I need, Cale thought. He'd been hoping for a peaceful trip, where he could gather his thoughts before meeting his contact in Rome. It meant no plane trouble, no flight delays, no terrorists. No drunken soccer hooligans. No snakes on the plane. An absence of any adventure in the slightest, thank you very much.

He hoped the drunk chose to sleep it off instead of becoming more belligerent.

Cale glanced at his watch. Nearing nine p.m. He had opted out of the inflight movie, something about cops versus Jamaican drug dealers, choosing instead to allow his mind to drift back to his seventy-minute layover in the Atlanta airport. He had called Maggie's number. Though he desired nothing more than to discuss her reputed pregnancy, Cale decided to hold off, at least until he had his facts straight.

Instead of her usual calm demeanor, Maggie's voice sounded excited. "Slink took me to the shooting range," she reported. "We just got back."

He conjured the image of his fiancé wearing sound blockers, in a professional stance, easing the trigger of the Kahr PM9 shot after shot. It caused Cale to smile with something resembling pride. At least she'd be safe while he was away. One less worry.

"Not quite up to Annie Oakley status, yet?"

"Getting there. How about we try me shooting an apple off your head? When you get back?"

Ouch! She was still upset at his decision to leave her at home. "I think not. Besides, you're mixing up your historical sharpshooters."

Maggie made a scoffing sound, and he could picture her rolling her eyes. They concluded the phone conversation like a pair of cooing teenagers. She told him she missed him already. Cale matched her sentiment by promising to call when he could, adding a hasty "love you" before hanging up.

He had managed to bite his tongue, mentioning nothing about the possible pregnancy. Cale had chosen instead to adapt the "ostrich" approach. Bury his head in the soil. Out of sight, out of mind. Besides, he reasoned, they would have plenty of time to address the issue when he returned—in less than a week, he prayed—from his trip.

***

As darkness enveloped the airplane, heavy and shroud-like, Cale felt his eyes beginning to close, the initial stage of dozing off. His peaceful repose, however, was interrupted moments later by the sudden clamoring of voices. He stared up the aisle, searching for the source of the ruckus. Lin was speaking tersely to the man in the Mets cap: "Leave him alone! Let him go—now!" Her gaze found the back row of passengers as if searching out Cale. "Or I'm summoning the air marshal!"

Without much effort, Cale discerned what was happening. Mr. Mets Cap had the flight attendant Marcus trapped in a one-armed headlock. He was employing his free arm to keep Lin a safe distance away.

"I'll snap his neck if you come any closer," Mets Cap snarled. He was positioned halfway into the narrow aisle, holding his prisoner tight.

Cale's seat belt was already unfastened, and he felt himself rise. In a half-dozen strides, he was right behind Lin. Around them several passengers had been roused from their somnolent calm. "Everyone stay seated." Cale kept his voice modulated, though making certain they all could hear. "I'm the air marshal. I'll take care of things here."

While saying this, he flipped open his wallet, flashing his police ID, wishing the captain hadn't forced him to turn in his golden detective's shield. In the dim light he doubted Mets Cap—or anyone else, for that matter—could discern the difference.

"Stay where you are, hotshot," sneered the aggressor. "Or I snap his neck."

Marcus was down on his knees, breathing heavy in the man's firm grasp. Cale noticed his eyes were bulging, his face sheened with perspiration.

"He's got a packet of powder inside his jacket," Lin explained, half turning toward Cale. "I saw him inhale from it minutes ago. He's stoned on something."

"Shut your piehole," snarled Mets Cap, cranking his arm tighter on the trapped flight attendant. "Else I'll shut both you and Twinkle Toes here up for good."

Cale stepped in front of Lin, shielding her with his body. "Look, sir, just let him go." His voice to Mets Cap was measured. "We'll take you in back. You can sleep all the way to Rome."

The man snorted. "Just what I want to do. I'm on holiday, dumbass."

"He's crazy—"

Cale cut Lin off with a hand wave. "You want to spend the rest of your holiday in an Italian jail? Is that what you really want?"

"What I want is for you to butt out. Whiskey-dick here won't serve me no more drinks."

The man's gray soul patch was covered with spittle. *Great*, Cale thought, *a drooling, drunken hophead*. Why couldn't he at least get a singing drunk? Or a crying drunk?

"Let him go, and we settle this clean...You don't, and you're facing serious charges, here." Cale realized he couldn't use the word "terrorist" out loud; not without creating a panic on board.

As if hearing a voice from somewhere, the man turned and looked opposite, far up the plane's narrow aisle, to where three other flight attendants were huddled in a tight gaggle. Mets Cap unceremoniously released Marcus, who dropped to the floor as if he'd been sucker punched. When Mets Cap's head swiveled back to face Cale, it was too late. Cale was on him like a linebacker, pulling the man into the aisle, falling upon him, pinning the drunk beneath his weight.

"I need to fly the plane!" babbled the drunk. "They want me...in the cockpit."

"Where we want you is out the door," Lin retorted, angrily. "Without a parachute." She was attending

Marcus, guiding him from harm's way, examining the extent of his injuries.

"Yeah, out the door," echoed one of the passengers.

Cale spied Mets Cap's iPod sitting on his vacated seat. He grabbed the ear buds and employed the cord to secure the drunk's wrists behind his back. Knotted them tight. He rose from his knees, pulling the man up with him. "You can all go back to sleep now," he proclaimed to the other passengers. "Excitement's over."

"'Ain't over till it's over'," slurred Mets Cap. "Boo-Boo Bear said that."

Cale issued him a withering look. *Drunks.* Withdrawing a handkerchief, he jammed it into the man's mouth until all he could manage were muffled sounds. Light applause spattered the rear section of the aircraft as he held his captive by the back of his neck, frog marching him toward the back row.

Lin cleared the aisle, stepping aside as the two men passed. "Do you need anything, Detective? Rope? Tape? Sledgehammer?"

"Nah, I got him." Cale pushed the man into one of the open seats in the final row. He sat down next to him, giving him a hard stare while pointing to the edge of his thick elbow. Mets Cap melted beside him, as if realizing that he had best sit still.

After a few long minutes, when the passengers had resettled, Lin arrived. She leaned in to where Cale and his prisoner sat and reported, "Marcus is fine. A bit shaken up. We're giving him brandy and coffee."

Cale nodded. When he glanced back at his prisoner, he was relieved to see the man had closed his eyes and was already fast asleep. Hopefully for six more hours.

He considered slipping him a Xanax or three, while he could.

Just to make certain.

CHAPTER 14

Château du Carthairs, Belgium

Blackness turned to hazy fragments steeped in gray. The odor of sweat and something bitter, like anesthesia, lingered in the dank air. Leslie guessed the smell was fear…and the fear was her own.

She remembered the prick of the sharp needle, remembered the forest, the large man holding her down. Now she was here, trapped, a prisoner again.

With a shift of her eyes, she could discern Prince Mir. He was at a workbench off to her left. She could see the other man—Kinsella, his name was—further across the room. He was sitting at a small table, as if in a restaurant. Neither man spoke.

Leslie attempted to talk, but a mere rasp came out. Her tongue was numb, and her mouth drier than old bone. But her senses were working, and her brain-fog was clearing away like morning mist.

The prince half-turned, speaking over his shoulder: "What I don't understand, Leslie, is *why*. You have things here girls can but dream of. A soft, warm bed to lay your tired head on at night. The finest meals. Clothing befitting a runway model."

He resumed his task, turning away. "And yet you choose to run away." Leslie could offer no response.

"I made you the lead of my pony team," continued the prince, without looking at her. "If only the others possessed half your talent." He shook his head as if in awe at her stupidity.

Thinking she could detect a faint odor of cooking oil, Leslie attempted looking about the room. But all she could see were shelves and the dusty ceiling, which faded away into the room's yawn of shadows. Where were they? The château basement? One of the outbuildings?

The prince approached her. He wore latex surgical gloves and held a long hypodermic needle in one hand. "While it is not to my usual culinary enjoyment, my African friend, here"—nodding across the room to the seated man—"belongs to a cult that enjoys the taste of human flesh. A practice he and his comrades partake of during their rituals. Somewhat the way you enjoy your turkey on Thanksgiving, I would imagine."

What is he saying? Leslie's mind shrieked, *Oh my God! This isn't happening!* She grunted, tried to squirm. He jabbed her with the needle and within seconds she felt nothing. But she could still see and hear, and Leslie realized this to her utmost horror.

The prince stared at her. "Our friend here is now going to slice an approximate five-inch chunk of flesh from your lovely buttock, my dear. He will fry the tasty flank in butter, olive oil, and a variety of spices." He paused. "Then he will sample your flesh, which he will no doubt enjoy."

My God, it's true, then. Leslie's thoughts turned to the memory of her friend, Mary Jane Moore. The other American girl from Green Bay, Wisconsin, who had been kidnapped and stowed inside the cargo vessel with her. Mary Jane had rebelled against Prince Mir, and then abruptly disappeared. Vanished without so much as a trace. The whispers, afterward, conveyed the gruesome rumor: the poor girl had been eaten alive.

But those were rumors, Leslie reminded herself. Spooky yarns meant to frighten the rest of them, cow them into submission. It couldn't be the least bit true! Still, she could not deny where she was at the moment, and what was happening. Was it *her* turn now?

"Your punishment for running away will be to watch Mr. Kinsella savor his tasty delight. If you behave properly"—and here the prince smiled his sadistic best—"he may be so kind as to offer you a sample."

Leslie allowed herself to be swept beneath the welcoming wave of darkness.

***

Above the Atlantic Ocean

Cale awoke from a two-hour slumber. Jerking his head up, uncertain where he was, he glanced around. The dim-lit interior of the aircraft provided little clue, but the highbacked seats, the steady drone of the engines, these all brought him to the present moment. He had been dreaming of something disturbing, the images dissolving like morning mist, before he could grasp hold of them.

If he had not been cognizant on waking, it didn't take long for Cale's awareness to snap him to attention. He was startled to see his "prisoner" sitting with ease in the seat across the aisle, eyes focused with the piercing clarity of a teetotaler. The man broke into a grin and extended a steady hand. In what Cale guessed to be a Czech accent, he said, "Detective Van Waring...Jacek Tumaj, at your service."

Cale gave the man a sharp-eyed sizing-up: both the New York Mets cap and scraggle of long gray hair had been replaced by an iron gray, receding, military-style haircut. Gone also was the soul patch. With hesitation, Cale extended his hand in greeting.

Jacek dangled the twisted cord in front of him. "I believe you wrecked my ear buds."

***

"I was fifteen," Jacek was saying with a shake of his head, "an excellent futbol player. Till I blew out my left knee. We hadn't any health insurance, living with my mother and two younger brothers. I limped my way to the military recruiting office. We were all forced to in those days. Required to sign up for three years of service. They were going to reject me as 'unfit.' I told them I'll sign for six years if they repair my knee.

"Here it is now, better than new," Jacek said, pointing to his left knee. "Except on damp nights, when it throbs—but ah, what is a little throbbing, eh?" He snickered, continued, "It took me four full months till I could walk again without a limp. Believe them, Mr. Packer, when they say the rehab is worse than the injury."

The man chuckled humorlessly and continued, "The military put me through training—this was the time of our Czech Republic's Velvet Revolution, so we were battling the Communists for control. And since we had no real war, I went in for further testing. They told me I had—what you call it, 'an aptitude' for strategy and firearms. So, they put me in military intelligence. I was trained first as a sniper, then afterward as a spy. Long trench coat, black hat, the whole works. We were mimicking the Bulgarians, I suppose. But it was useless. Pointless. The Cold War was over—the Communists were collapsing. I became bored with it all and wanted to go back to fighting. But we had no war to fight. I spent nine years total in the Czech militia then I left and began my life as a real soldier."

Cale was about to ask a question, but Jacek kept the backstory spinning.

"I worked for and with a number of subcontractor corporations. You may have heard of one of them: 'Blackwater,' they were called back then—their division in Europe. We did stints in Afghanistan, Somalia, Iraq. Then Peru and Kazakhstan. But it was still too much bureaucracy for me. Like being back in the military. Believe it or not, I am a free spirit. Like your Janice Joplin, eh? Though without the tits." He chortled and continued:

"I am too old now to be taking orders. I'm over forty. So, I formed my own small company. I have my own team, people I can trust. We take the jobs we choose. We work when we want, where we want. Most times in Europe. But very discriminating."

Cale nodded.

"And here we are, Mr. Packer. You and me. Two ships in the night, eh?"

After a few more hours of flight, hidden above the clouds and beneath the star-glazed skies, the airplane was beginning its descent. Turning to Jacek, Cale asked, "So what was with the act? The drunk passenger? The baseball cap?"

"Ah, that." Jacek grinned. "I was in your country visiting relatives. My nephews. A pair of 'bad Czechs,' I call them. That's where I was when I received the call concerning your little problems, eh? When I heard the details, well, no point shading it—I decided it best to check you out myself."

"So that's what this was?" Cale frowned. "Some kind of test?"

"I needed to know how you react under pressure, Mr. Packer." Jacek spread his open palms. "If you would have shot me...what can I say? Then maybe we don't work so well together."

Cale decided the man's story made sense on some level. Perhaps he was relieved that he had passed the Czech mercenary's examination. Though what it proved, he couldn't yet determine. "Can I ask you one more question?" he said, probing. "Who called you? Was there an FBI agent involved? Named Eddie Redtail?"

Jacek narrowed his crinkled eyes. "I believe that name came up. But an old friend, let's just say. A friend I owed a favor to."

"And this friend of yours? He has a name?"

"Yes," Jacek conceded. "Indeed, he does."

Twenty minutes later, with the morning sun peeking one eye above the horizon, they landed in Rome.

***

Château du Carthairs, Belgium

The room was bright. A cheery, pleasant atmosphere. The window sashes had been flung open and sunlight blazed in, casting golden pools of warmth across the maple wood floor. It reflected off the polished glass of the gilded full-length mirror.

She awoke as if in a Disney movie. *Snow White*, or one of the others, with birds chirping and dancing flowers blossoming everywhere. And seconds later, the memory rushed her like an attacker leaping from a dark alley. Leslie shot her hand down her leg, expecting to feel bandages or dried blood or pain. Or even worse. Instead, her skin felt warm and smooth and normal. Had it all been a dream? Some insane nightmare, precipitated by the strong narcotics she'd been injected with?

No. She didn't believe it. She had run. She had attempted to escape the château. This part was true. And she had almost made it. Almost. Until she'd been captured by the evil African man. As for the rest of it...

Springing from the bed, Leslie rushed across the room to the full-length mirror. She'd been an attractive girl all her life, and since she was little, the truth in mirrors seldom lied. Examining her smooth flesh, turning a circle, Leslie forced herself to look, to examine, to assess—to make certain that she was whole.

CHAPTER 15

Rome, Italy

The zippy brown Fiat eased through the exit from the airport before merging onto the boulevard. Ten minutes later, it slid onto the roadway headed away from Fiumicino Airport, the SP601, hugging the Italian coastline, headed south. Destination: the port city of Anzio.

Escape from the congestion of the city, Jacek informed Cale, was the main goal as he drove. Rome was too pedestrian, filled with tourists and natives alike, congested with everything from buses to cabs, from autos to motor scooters. Bicycles wove about, demanding respect; strolling tourists gawked and gaped, taking pictures of anything in sight. And the local drivers? *Dio Mio!* They drove as if they were racing the streets of Monte Carlo, each driver dreaming he had a chance of winning if only he could pass the bus on the right, the cab on the left. Insanity on wheels.

Once they cleared the sun-crusted rim of the city, a little past eight Wednesday morning, moving down the Pontine coast, Jacek proclaimed how he felt he could breathe again. Whether they were ahead of the pack, or trailing it, he wasn't certain. But he informed Cale they could now relax and enjoy the sights of the smooth Tyrrhenian Sea on the right, the balconies and porticos of congested housing on the left. As long as they avoided a fatal collision—a looming possibility, so it seemed—at any given moment.

"It feels odd," Cale commented, after a bit. "You driving on that side of the car. But on our normal side of the road."

"You'll get used to it, Mr. Packer," Jacek said, swerving to avoid a weaving Renault. "By the way, the phone you received at the airport? It's a Euro phone, full GSM tracking. Courtesy of your Homeland Security."

Cale was still shaking his head. "Your drunk act on the plane? I still can't believe TSA waved us through. I thought you'd be spending the evening in a jail cell."

Jacek executed a lane change. An Audi honked. He flipped the driver the bird. "All prearranged. I'm not so foolish as to mess with international air security."

"Arranged by who? By Homeland?" Cale watched Jacek nod in confirmation. He withdrew the new mobile phone he'd been issued, and a few other items they'd received, from his jacket pocket. He examined them. He pushed on the phone's power button. Fully charged. "Updated passport and travel visa," he said, approving. "I can't believe they can do things on such short notice."

Jacek chortled. "Full of surprises, your American government. But it's the kind of thing they are good at. This way they can monitor your movements anywhere via satellite."

Cale turned the phone over in his hands before pocketing it.

"They also explained to me about"—Jacek turned serious—"this man you are searching for? He is a human trafficker, no? A real bad apple." He shook his head. "A priority for all law enforcement in Europe. A United Nations mandate. No one wants to be seen dropping the ball, if they have a chance to break up a trafficking ring." Glancing over his shoulder, he made another lane change. "Homeland Security. Don't worry, my friend. They will watch over you like a big brother on your first day on the playground."

Cale was staring out the window, examining the sea port and busy harbor. Pleasure craft, sailboats and cruisers, working tugs, freighters, cruise ships, and ferries. They were all in evidence. Rome was an international port, and her shipyards were busy day and night.

"Good to know," Cale said, distracted, continuing to survey the scenery like a tourist. The realization that he had traveled a great distance in a short period of time was settling in. The fact his government was tracking him from afar provided no great degree of comfort. And despite Jacek serving as his European tour guide, he understood one grim fact: he was in international waters now, and a long, long way from home.

***

Upon receiving the call from the State Department representative, whereby the independent contractor terms the United States government was offering were laid out, Jacek Tumaj had done some sleuthing of his own. He phoned an old American acquaintance, Adrian Snowe, a former CIA spook with whom he'd had dealings in the past. Jacek wanted to get a read on the small city police detective who was on a mission to extract a bad guy located in Liberia, of all the godforsaken places! A man on the run from justice.

"And you've met him? This Detective Van Waring?" Jacek had asked of Snowe.

"A few times—yes. I don't live too far from Green Bay. So, our paths have crossed."

"And?"

Even though they hadn't spoken in a while, Jacek understood Snowe to be a man who kept his opinions close to the vest. Once a spook, always a spook.

"He's capable. Dedicated. So, I wouldn't worry," Adrian Snowe said, his voice flat. "If he comes recommended by Agent Redtail, then I'd trust implicitly in the man's character."

Jacek was silent, mulling things over. "How much babysitting am I going to have to do?"

"The man's a cop. He'll know how to handle himself," Snowe added. "You've been around long enough, Jacek. You know how these things work. Bon voyage."

He'll know how to handle himself. This was it, then. He would accept the job the American government headhunters were offering: to provide protection and assistance to this lone detective. To use whatever means were necessary to help him hunt down and arrest—as well as transport—a Liberian national named Kinsella.

Jacek now downshifted as the Fiat gasped for breath, moving with effort to climb an incline in the coastal roadway. They had their meager luggage crammed into the rear cargo space: the American's two bags, his own single. Not quite a bona fide load. He floored the accelerator and the car gained confidence. Jacek glanced at his partner beside him. Van Waring was busy studying a map of Italy. He watched the man yawn. It was coming up on nine a.m. Jet lag would soon be penetrating their bones.

The job appeared rudimentary enough. They had Interpol at their service, American intelligence and clout behind them. Most European law enforcement agencies—Jacek hoped—would provide them with manpower and support upon request. His team was already in place, so they were good to go. The difficulty would be in locating the suspect. Apprehending and transporting the man should be the simplest part of the mission.

The simplest part? Jacek caught himself smiling. It was the part that always seemed to blow up in your face.

***

Anzio, Italy

The city of Anzio sits seventy-two kilometers south of Rome. It is a resort town, famous for its historic point of landing during the WWII Allied invasion. A trio of museums bears memorial landmarks. Anzio is also the birthplace of two Italian notables: the infamous Nero Germanicus, and the even more infamous "Caligula" Germanicus. Both became Roman emperors, and both, as history has since revealed, were considered insane.

Something in the water? Cale wondered. He was reading the information in the tourist pamphlet as Jacek slowed the Fiat. The water off the coast was cerulean blue, with matching skies reflecting the spray of golden morning sunlight. The clustered houses and buildings were earth-toned in color, as if having risen straight out of the red clay soil. Cale was thankful he'd brought along his sunglasses. He could see how a person might fall in love with the area: the climate, the easygoing mood of southern Italy. He wondered how many homicide detectives were on the force in Anzio. A city of forty-five thousand residents. There had to be at least a couple of murders per year. An easy estimate, with Italians being famous for their quick tempers.

And, of course, people being people.

Jacek knew where they were headed, so Cale elected to sit in silence, taking in the postcard scenery as the landscape swept past.

They had moved down Via Ardeatina, entering Anzio without fanfare. "Right over there," said Jacek, breaking the silence and casting his eyes toward the beach, "is where the British first landed."

"Interesting," Cale said with a nod. The low, gray brick museum didn't look like much, but he was sure it held some unique war mementos. Too bad a guided tour of the area was not in his travel itinerary.

The harbor was filled with fishing vessels. A line of men on shore worked at untangling and repairing the fishing nets, as Anzians had no doubt done for countless generations past. With a few modestly tall buildings looming on their left, Jacek spun the Fiat around a corner. They moved off the coastal road, driving inland for a few blocks, into the city proper. The little car climbed another incline, then eased along past a marketplace, where locals could be seen selling fresh fruits and vegetables in outside stands. The air was humid and smelled briny from the sea. There was a whitewashed building beside one fruit stand that displayed a simple sign in English: "Fresh Fish."

A couple of restaurants zoomed past. Petrol stations. Kids on motor-scooters, which Italy seemed to breed like rabbits. A few minutes later, sailing in silence along the dusty, sunbaked streets, the muted color buildings flashing past like images from a Hollywood backlot, they turned into a wide parking lot. A silent warehouse loomed ahead, and Jacek pulled the Fiat up to a garage door. A halfhearted bleat from the horn. In less than a minute, the wide garage doors were swung open by a pair of inner inhabitants wearing gray overalls: one a tall, bronze-skinned man, the other a dark and petite female.

Jacek didn't bother to wave as he eased the Fiat into the cool and quiet darkness. Cale felt the doors of the garage swing closed behind them. To Jacek he said, "I'm assuming we've arrived somewhere?"

"Correct, Mr. Packer. We have arrived somewhere."

They exited the vehicle in the dimness of the inner warehouse. Jacek introduced Cale to the tall bronze man, whose kinky black hair was swept back in a Hawaiian ponytail. The man was introduced simply as "Pharaoh." Up close, Cale noticed the petite female with the smooth chocolate skin. She was beautiful. Her sharp cheekbones and almond-shaped eyes gave her an exotic appearance. A face that could no doubt stop traffic. She went by the name of "Cheetah." Cale decided it mattered little what Jacek's partners called themselves, as long as they were capable.

The pleasantries aside—with Cale grabbing his bags from the Fiat's trunk—Jacek led them across the warehouse to an area cleared of clutter. The space was designated for where they would congress: a tattered couch was aligned next to a pair of wooden-slat crates. A solitary lightbulb hung from a long extension cord, which was draped across a sawhorse. A white evidence board had been erected and leaned against a pair of large transport boxes. It looked steady enough.

"Ah, the comforts of home," said Jacek, flopping on the lumpy couch like a frat boy after a final. Dust mites trapezed into the air.

Glancing around, getting a feel for the length and breadth of the low-lighted inner warehouse, Cale said, "I take it you've lounged here before?"

Pharaoh remained silent, standing in the shadowed background, leaning against one of the building's inner support poles. Cale was surprised it didn't bend against the man's muscular stature. He watched the man flick a long switchblade open and closed, like a hood on a street corner.

"We did a job nearby. In Nettuno," Jacek informed him. He turned to Cheetah, who stood just inside the light with her arms crossed. "A year ago, wasn't it?"

Cheetah's voice held a hint of British accent as she said, "That's correct. Took down 'The Silencer.' Gave him up in handcuffs to the Italian *carabinieri*."

"And the local police couldn't capture this 'Silencer' by themselves?" Cale asked, looking from one to the next.

Jacek said, "It was the Germans who wanted him. That's who our contract was with. And to answer your question: No. The *carabinieri* had no clue he was even in Italy at the time. Planning some hit in Rome, if my memory serves." He glanced at Pharaoh, who nodded without speaking. Cale determined he must be the strong, silent type.

Cheetah strode away into the shadows and could be heard rummaging around in what Cale thought sounded like a junk pile. "Anyone for tea?" she called, rattling pots and pans.

Jacek issued Cale a shrug. "You're in Europe now, Detective. Might as well relax. I'll have a cup," he called over his shoulder, "and so will our guest." Cale consented with a shrug. Jacek continued, "This place fits our needs. We own it. Pay Italian taxes. It gives us unfettered access to Rome via the train. We've got bunks set up in the inner rooms, running water. The plumbing's decent. WC's across the way, if you're so inclined."

Cale glanced off into the dusty dimness of the place. His eyes were adjusting to the inner spaciousness, and he could begin to see shapes of larger vehicles, dark offices cubbied into the far wall. A few doors lead off to what he imagined would be an adjacent hallway of the warehouse's interior core.

Having seated himself on one of the wooden crates, he at long last began to relax. Cale hadn't realized how cramped he was from the car ride, how tired from the lengthy international flight. It was barely even midmorning, Italian time. He did the mental tabulations as to what time it would be in the States. He considered trying out the new phone. He needed to contact Maggie and Slink, provide them with his Euro-phone mobile number in case of any emergency on the home front. But with the time difference, it was still dark back home.

After Jacek returned from the WC—with Cale making small talk with Cheetah, and Pharaoh throwing in a few unenthused grunts—their team leader took his spot on the couch. He sipped from his teacup. "Now we get busy," Jacek said, his eyes cast in Cale's direction. "We know you're on a tight time window."

Cale had set his own cup on the cement floor beside his crate. "Good. All this sitting around is making me antsy."

"I booked you both on a two-a.m. redeye flight to Monrovia," said Cheetah crisply, doing a workable travel agent impression. "Air time is six hours. Direct flight. Your appointment with the minister of foreign affairs is at eleven a.m. tomorrow."

With arched eyebrows, Cale said, "We're flying again?"

"We're running down a Liberian national." Jacek chuckled. "First place we should look is Liberia, I should think."

"Didn't Homeland tell us the Liberian government wasn't too cooperative?"

"At first, they weren't. They changed their tune, when informed we were looking into a potential human trafficking case."

Cale nodded. "But still—"

"You didn't imagine the Liberian minister would come here, did you? Meet us in Italy?"

Cale massaged his forehead with two fingertips. "What I'm beginning to wonder is why we are here? In Italy? In the first place?"

"Ah. Quite simple," Jacek said. "We need a base of operations. A central location. Your target may not even be in his home country. And besides, we need a few hours to train you."

"Train me?" Cale's words echoed off the walls of the spacious warehouse.

"Of course," said Pharaoh, speaking up at last. The man's barrel voice caused Cale to turn, as if a circus elephant had suddenly spoken out loud.

"Train you to properly kill someone."

CHAPTER 16

Liberia, Africa

Colonel Tazeki Mabutu sat at the large mahogany desk in his private study. A few seconds after he had heard his computer "ping," he slipped in his decipher disc, applied it to the message, then sat back in his chair and allowed the electronics to do their work.

When the message at last flashed on his screen, he studied the words in contemplative silence. It was from Tobias Crenshaw—or rather the offices of his defense attorney. The message read, "Gave up Kinsella. Liberia. Plea deal." It was signed "Go Badgers!" The last—their private code—signified the message was, indeed, from Crenshaw, himself.

Tazeki reached for the delete key and watched the cryptic words vanish into humid air.

Though he had already foreseen the possibility of Crenshaw turning "stoolie," it was now time to assess his options with greater care. Pressing a button on the side of his desk, Tazeki spoke into the intercom. Two minutes later, his manservant arrived carrying a tray of refreshments. Without speaking, Kasim (wearing a crimson Nehru jacket) filled a generous glass with iced tea, placing the beverage on a desktop coaster. He departed. Tazeki took a long sip and welcomed the cooling effects of the amber liquid. Setting the glass aside, he opened a drawer and withdrew one of his two dozen secure—unregistered and untraceable—mobile phones.

Three calls later, he had the information he required. After punching in a text message, he waited a few long minutes. His right-hand man, Kinsella, was in Belgium at the moment, meeting with Prince Mir. He would give him enough time to respond on a secure burner phone of his own.

After another minute of waiting, he heard his newest phone chirp.

***

Brussels, Belgium

The muscular black man in the too-tight sports jacket stood in the ticket line of the Brussels International Airport. His plan was to book a flight to Monrovia, be back in Liberia by dinner time. When Kinsella's phone buzzed, he read the latest text message. Then, stepping out of the queue for privacy, he redialed the number. Colonel Tazeki Mabutu's voice sounded grim, measured, as if he were considering each syllable as he spoke. Kinsella informed him where he was.

"Change your plans," Tazeki said gravely. "Catch a direct flight to the States."

Kinsella stepped further from the ears of potential eavesdroppers.

"Something problematic has happened, I take it?"

"The news is confirmed," Tazeki said. "I want you back in Green Bay."

"Something to do with your old college friend, if I had to guess?"

"Crenshaw's lawyers have pushed the judge for a second bond hearing. If he agrees to provide the authorities with new information on his case."

"And this is troubling, somehow?"

"What's 'troubling,' is he has revealed *your* identity. We need to silence him. For good. Before he can reveal things that will…affect us. In a serious manner."

Kinsella considered the information for a moment. He was already tabulating the logistics of flying to Chicago—then driving up to Green Bay—on such short notice. Though he appeared the brute, he had always had a quick mind for mathematics. He understood the flight's real air time was between eight or nine hours. It was now Wednesday, almost noon. He would gain ample enough time flying west.

"The bail hearing is set for tomorrow morning," the colonel said. "You've got plenty of time, if you don't girlie about."

Glancing across the way, the large African spotted the check-in counter for four different American air carriers. "I'll let you know when I've made arrangements. Everything I need for the job is in Chicago."

"Fine," said Tazeki. "Brief me when you've got a plan." He paused. "And Kinsella, be discreet this time."

"A bit of sentiment?" The large man kept any humor from his voice as he began striding toward the American Airlines ticket counter.

"Nothing so maudlin," Tazeki said, dismissively. "But he *is* my old college roommate."

Snapping closed his phone, the large man lumbered his way through the maze of travelers. "Sis-boom-bah," he muttered beneath his breath.

***

Anzio, Italy

"Train me to kill someone?" Cale heard his words echo off the walls of the inner warehouse, sounding as if they belonged to someone else. "Kill who?" He was issuing Pharaoh a challenging stare.

Jacek was on his feet facing Cale, and he spoke with a genial wave of his hands. "Pardon my large friend, Detective. What Pharaoh is implying is self-defense. Hand-to-hand. Not the standard submission techniques you were taught—perhaps—at the police academy." He grinned. "*Verstehe?*"

Cale frowned. "I'm a homicide detective, Jacek. Fifteen years. I don't need to know how to kill someone. Not the way you might, anyway." He glanced at the three of them, holding their gaze. "If I need to shoot someone, I aim my Glock and pull the trigger. *Verstehe?*"

Watching as Pharaoh tossed Cheetah a smirk, Cale could only shake his head. Jacek spoke evenly: "We're all tired here, so how about this—we do a quick training session. Twenty minutes tops. Then we have ourselves a nice lunch. I know a wonderful little seaside bistro."

Lunch? What Cale wanted more than anything was to hop a flight to Liberia this minute. Bang on some doors. Talk to the minister there, find out the available information on their suspect. Follow some sort of *lead*. He understood this option was not feasible, however, and he had already committed to following Jacek's expertise. What harm could there be, he asked himself, in playing his new Czech acquaintance's little game? At least it would appease the man, make things more comfortable between them. Show them all he was a "team player."

Besides, wouldn't time pass faster if he kept himself busy?

"All right, then," Cale agreed. "So, where does this little exercise take place?"

Jacek nodded at Pharaoh, and the larger man moved across the center of the warehouse, beyond one of the parked equipment vans. Cale noticed that the man made almost no sound as he moved. A breeze in the night, a shadow, a soundless floating.

When the lights blazed on in the central area of the cavernous place, Cale could discern that a pair of large rubberized mats had already been laid down. Like wrestling mats set side by side. Christ! he thought. They've had this planned from the get-go.

Cale walked beside Jacek, and they moved across the concrete floor to the matted area. Cheetah followed a few steps behind, moving as silent as a shadow. Cale glanced over his left shoulder and she was five yards away from where she'd been, seemingly, an instant ago. He swallowed his obvious surprise: these were trained mercenaries, he reminded himself. Professionals. They made their living killing other killers. Silence and quickness were prerequisites. It went with the territory.

Feeling sheepish, Cale addressed Jacek: "You're right," he allowed. "It won't hurt to brush up on my field skills."

Jacek grinned. "That's the spirit, Mr. Packer. We all can use a few new pointers now and again. But let me forewarn you, these two"—a nod toward his partners—"are two of the finest hand-to-hand combatants in the world."

Cale looked at Cheetah, who grinned her dazzling white teeth and set of dimples at him. He swung his attention to where Pharaoh stood at the center of the mat, ten feet away. He locked eyes with the larger man in an unsmiling, prison yard stare. Cale had seen his share of crazy hombres over the years, locked up enough of them to fill his quota. He understood their code of manliness: you never glance away from a stare. To the hunter, it's a signal you're easy prey. He kept his focus lasered onto the black pupils of Pharaoh's dark eyes until his own eye sockets felt dry to the point of bursting. When the larger man glanced away, dropping to one knee to tie his shoe, Cale at last breathed. He blinked a few times, wondering if he had managed to pass his first test.

"How are you one-on-one?" Jacek asked him. "Be honest, detective. I want to get a feel for what we're working with here."

Cale recalled a tavern melee he'd been involved in five or so weeks back. A veritable bar brawl. He had never seen the punch coming, one that had purpled his eye and the uppermost half of his cheek bone. Maybe a professional pointer or two couldn't hurt.

"I hold my own," he said brashly. He moved onto the mat as Jacek waved him forward.

"Splendid." Jacek motioned Cheetah to the mat's center, opposite Cale. Pharaoh stepped back and sat Indian-style at the edge of the rubber floor covering. The petite black girl stood face-to-face with Cale. Her shoes were off, and she stood with her feet bare, her gray work overalls looking three sizes too large.

"No way!" Cale turned to Jacek. "C'mon. I'm not about to spar with a lady."

"Think about it for one minute, Mr. Packer. Do you think Cheetah would even be in this room if she couldn't kick any one of our asses? At any given moment?"

"How would...okay. I know you're right. I get it." Cale tried to sound apologetic. "I figured she's a whiz at computers or something? Or surveillance?"

"What I'm a *whiz* at," Cheetah announced, unceremoniously, "will be kicking your balls up into your throat. If you don't pay attention, you bloody wanker!" The flash in her eyes wiped away the smug expression from Cale's face.

Jacek clapped his hands together twice. He allowed Cale and Cheetah to eye one another—the lithe and diminutive female scowling—and position themselves in the mat's center, face to face.

"Time for a little demonstration," Jacek said. "Cheetah, slap him. Not too hard. And no ball kicking. Please."

As Cale shifted his eyes to Jacek, he felt the sting on his cheek, before he could take a breath. When he glanced back at Cheetah, it was like she had never moved. He could still feel the air shimmying, sense the blur of her quickness. All this before the sensation on his cheek even registered. His flesh felt hot and he imagined it was reddening. "I wasn't quite ready—"

"Again," Jacek ordered.

This time Cale was prepared, raising his arms to defend himself. He watched as Cheetah slow-motioned her hands through the air like a stage magician, before quickstepping and snapping one hand forward. Cale heard the slap on his other cheek as it echoed inside the warehouse. She was back in her stance again, before it registered that he'd been struck on his opposite cheek.

"What the hell?" He threw one cautious eye at Jacek, keeping the other nervously glued to his opponent. "Jesus—she moves...fast."

Jacek grinned. He spoke as if he were lecturing a class. "Now imagine if she had a blade in each hand. She would slice you to ribbons before you even realized you were bleeding."

Well, screw this! Cale decided. Without tipping his hand, he turned and charged his smaller opponent—a Ray Nitschke bull rush. But while Cheetah appeared stationary one moment, she stepped aside, as adroit as a matador, the next. Cale reached out with his futile left arm as he breezed past her, missing, landing on his knees, then shoulder, then chin. In cartoonish fashion, he let loose an audible "*Ooof!*"

Pharaoh was slow-clapping his hands, sitting at the edge of the mat with his legs crossed like some eighth-grade smartass. Cale shot him the finger. Pulling himself to his knees, he turned to witness Jacek's Cheshire smile.

"All right. Fun and games are over," Jacek said, soberly. "Let's turn the floor over to Ms. Cheetah. She will show you a few techniques in effective close-quarter combat. Then you may practice on me, or on Pharaoh over there. Your choice, Mr. Packer.

Cheetah?" Jacek nodded to his smaller partner.

Cale blew the air from his lungs. He rose and moved to the side of the mat, conceding that, like it or not, this was probably going to take a while.

CHAPTER 17

Liberia, Africa

On the beach outside the fortified compound—its high, whitewashed outer walls providing an effective sanctity—the rolling gray waves crested and broke thirty yards from the shore. They crashed with force against the jagged rocks of the shoreline, as if hellbent on destruction. The rainy season in Liberia made the land, the trees, the buildings and people, all appear colorless.

Staring out his window in the early afternoon, Colonel Mabutu decided the whole gritty world was cast in shades of gray. "Ashes to ashes," he said, philosophically, speaking to his reflection in the glass. He raised his glass of iced tea in mock toast, watched in the far-off distance as a large fin broke the surface. "Today, even the big fish are perturbed."

Back across the room, one of his mobile phones chirped, wresting him from his thoughts. The colonel moved to his desk and gazed at the readout. He answered in a clipped voice: "Yes, Minister. Agreed." He waited, suppressing his temptation to roll his eyes. "Should be no problem. I am pleased to oblige."

Hanging up the phone, Tazeki sat on his leather desk chair and smiled with smug satisfaction. It had been arranged. He would meet one-on-one with the American detective, at this same time tomorrow. The Foreign Affairs Ministry would not be involved. Better this way, he decided, calling to mind an old African proverb:

"The fewer eyes to witness, the fewer need to be blind."

***

Anzio, Italy

"Employing a gun—a direct head shot. Or a bullet to the central chamber of the heart," said Jacek, with a nod toward Cale. "Or using a sound suppressor...whenever possible."

Cale listened from the mat's edge, nodding, staying silent. Jacek stood at the opposite edge, across the mat. His two underlings, the giant man Pharaoh versus the diminutive, cat-quick female, were positioned in the center.

"Have you ever tried to garrote a man, Detective?" asked Cheetah, turning her head. "Piano wire or two hundred-test fishing line work best. But you still must control your target. He's going to fight, kick, slam himself backwards. He's not going to just sit there while you strangle him in silence."

Cale narrowed his eyes.

"And with a blade, you've got to slice the windpipe clean through." This was spoken by swarthy-skinned Pharaoh. "Otherwise, he'll let out a throaty gasp of warning. A wheezy rattle. Might anyway...Either way, it's still quite messy."

Whoa! thought Cale. He realized these people had just moved beyond the point of reading a suspect his Miranda rights. Nonetheless, the lesson they were giving him was sobering: this was not a game to them. It was life or death. It was the mental framework they functioned in. Their solitary rule? The Rule of Survival.

If they were to work as a team on this job—and he was, no doubt, the rookie here—then each was responsible for the safety of the other team members. In street parlance: they had each other's backs.

"Excellent." Jacek nodded to Cheetah in the center mat. She turned back to Pharaoh, her partner in their deadly demonstration. "Let's continue."

"Against a much larger opponent," lectured Cheetah, talking to Cale, "we use our superior quickness to 'chop down the tree.'" She issued Pharaoh a wink. "Never stay straight in front of your opponent. That's where he wants you." Then, utilizing near-blinding quickness—a millisecond, if Cale had to guess—she was beside and a slight bit behind the larger man. Her right foot snapped out fast as a switchblade, catching Pharaoh behind his left knee. The joint buckled and he dropped one-kneed to the mat, arms up in defense, cooly rolling away.

They're not faking this, Cale reminded himself. *This is not rehearsed.*

Anticipating her opponent's maneuver, Cheetah was already behind the man, moving in for the kill shot. As Pharaoh turned, his muscular arms levered for balance, she leaped in and raked swift fingernails across the front of his neck.

"Over!" exclaimed Jacek, adding a brisk handclap. "*Fini*. Pharaoh is dead."

"What?" Cale protested. "She just grazed him. Not any harder than she slapped me earlier."

"One difference." Jacek's lips held a smirk.

"One *big* difference," Cheetah echoed.

On the mat, Pharaoh did a front roll and came smoothly to his feet. The only sensation was the slightest quiver of air. Jacek waved Cheetah over to where he and Cale stood. Grasping one of her hands, he flipped it over, displaying her fingernails to him. Cheetah had overgrown the thumbnail of her right hand, as well as the forefinger and middle fingernails. The nails were hardened with what appeared to be enameled lacquer and had been sharpened to knife-like points. The strength of drill bits.

"Great for a silent kill," she said, with no sense of braggadocio.

"She means his larynx." Jacek said, before Cale could speak. "His voice box. In real combat"—a quick nod to Cheetah—"she just ripped it out. Slicing a few major arteries along the way."

Cale's mouth was dry, and he forced himself to swallow.

"And now," said Jacek, his grin wide and beckoning, "who's got a taste for fresh calamari?"

***

Château du Carthairs, Belgium

Another nightmare.

Leslie Dowd awoke from a midday nap, breathing hard. She'd been running, chased, trapped...and could remember no more. Her hair was disheveled, sweat on her forehead, but her limbs were all present. She was not maimed or deformed.

The bedroom was encased in shadow. The windows remained closed, drapes drawn, and she was just about to fling them open when the rapping sound came from her bedroom door. "Just a second," Leslie called, searching for her robe. She found it draped over the back of a chair. "Come in."

A key turned in the lock—she'd been a prisoner in her room since her ill-fated escape attempt—and the door opened. Expecting either a housemaid or nurse, she felt her pulse accelerate when the prince himself entered the room. He moved inside, watching hawkeyed as she sat on the bed's edge and gripped the collar of her robe against her neck.

Prince Mir took a seat on the edge of a Queen Anne's chair. He leaned forward, elbows on the knees of his pressed gray dress slacks. "Such a pity, Leslie," he said with a head shake. "Such a *waste* of your talent."

Leslie wanted to proclaim her feelings of disgust but held her tongue. Truth be told, it was by the prince's good grace she was even alive. Despite whatever selfish reasons he might have, she was breathing, upright, intact.

After her capture and consequent psychological torture—where the prince and his large African partner had threatened to consume parts of her cooked flesh—she had spoken on a near daily basis with His Highness. Theirs was a devil's pact. He had proclaimed his primary reason for keeping her in good health—minus any body parts—was the need for her talents in the upcoming pony girl competition. Leslie, in turn, had promised to compete in earnest. To help the prince's team secure the Winners' Cup.

In exchange, she would be granted the exceptional gift of "continued life."

The competition was now less than a week away. Leslie understood that any last-minute stand-in would seriously debilitate the Belgian team's chances of winning the prized—at least by the prince—400-meter pony girl race. Prince Mir had promised her, hadn't he, that if she performed to her capabilities, and she and her teammates emerged victorious, that all would be forgiven.

Leslie's attempt at escape would be expunged from her record, so to speak. And she had little choice but to believe him.

"You look somewhat peaked," remarked the prince. "It's not a virus, is it?" Alarm bells in his voice. "I'll send for my physician. Dr. Roen."

She wondered—sarcastic, bitter—if by "physician" he meant a real MD? Or did he mean a veterinarian? She kept the snide thought to herself.

"No need. The fresh air will do me good. Once I'm outside."

The prince rose, reassured by her words. "Very well," he said. "We're doing only a slow walkthrough today. Just to keep our pacing proper. Mr. Anselm wants your legs fresh for the competition."

Leslie nodded. She lifted her head as she heard a soft rap on the door. A dour-faced nurse in blue scrubs entered with her regular B-12 shot. *Equine health care at its finest*, she thought, watching His Highness make for the door.

He paused and turned before exiting. "After the workout," he said, "make sure you eat well. And get your proper rest later."

Leslie watched Prince Mir exit. She felt the nurse roll her sleeve up past her elbow, prepare to give her the injection, and found herself thinking:

"Someday," she told herself, "I will escape this house of horrors. Even if I die trying."

CHAPTER 18

Anzio, Italy

Lunch was held on the outside deck of a quaint local restaurant overlooking the marina. The cobalt color of the Tyrrhenian Sea painted a backdrop so blue that sunlight rainbowed off the waves in a spray of shimmering color. Gulls soared above the coastline, searching the azure surface for signs of an easy dinner.

They dined on fresh baked bread and broiled sunfish. No calamari, Cale thought, offering a silent prayer of thanks. He doubted he could endure any culinary adventures at the present.

After deciding on a bottle of Birra Moretti, Cale searched his pocket for his Euro phone. He left Jacek and his partners at their table and moved through the inside shadows, before slipping back out the front entrance. Standing on the shaded sidewalk, he punched his home number. Wednesday, one p.m. in Italy. He calculated seven hours earlier in Green Bay. Maggie would be up by now. Even showered.

"Remember to feed Hank," he said, after she answered. "Wouldn't want him withering away with me gone."

"Your journey hasn't dimmed your sarcasm," she retorted, playful.

Above all else, Cale had decided to maintain his regular tone. He didn't want to tip his hat that he knew anything about what Slink had revealed before his departure. Like a true stoic, he'd decided to deal with it all when he got home.

"Got here at nine a.m.," Cale said. "I've already met Jacek and his partners. We're making progress." He explained, further, who Jacek was, and how they had met on the flight to Europe. He chose not to elaborate.

Maggie sounded relieved. "I'm glad you're with someone who knows the lay of the land. Besides, I'm sure you can use all the able-bodied men you can get."

Cale decided against revealing how "able-bodied" Cheetah had handed him his ass on the grappling mat. "We're jetting to Liberia tonight," he informed. "Be there bright and early tomorrow."

"You sure this isn't some crazy bachelor trip you're not telling me about?"

"'Suspicion is the bane of romance,'" Cale quoted. "Read it somewhere, once."

"Some bachelor's handbook, no doubt."

He surveyed the scenery outside the restaurant. Cale was facing inland, and the congested buildings and houses appeared like toys crammed into the sides of the rolling hills. A teenager on a scooter buzzed past on the street. A pair of dusty taxis followed, then groups of students on bicycles. The hum and flow of daily traffic was salted by tourists at every turn.

Cale stayed within the shade of the building, shielded from the blistering midday sun. "I'll send you a postcard. Soon as I get the time."

"Just find your guy and come home, Cale. The sooner the better."

Maggie's voice held an edge that he couldn't miss. Was she hiding the fact they needed to have a serious discussion? Feeling guilty about harboring her secret?

The one Slink had revealed just before he'd departed on his flight? About her 'condition'?

"You feeling okay?" Cale asked, his tone even. "You sound a little nasal."

She was silent for a beat. "Touch of the flu this morning. No big deal. I'm—I wasn't going to say anything. You've got enough on your plate."

The flu? Wasn't it a codeword some women used for issues they were reluctant to discuss? Issues like being pregnant? Cale didn't want to give voice to his suspicion. Now was not the time. Still, the knowledge that Tobias Crenshaw had sexually assaulted Maggie continued to gnaw at his insides.

Was there a chance he was not the baby's father? He wondered. *That the true father is really Crenshaw?*

"I got a call from Slink"—she shifted the subject—"last night."

"What's he want? To borrow money?" Cale recalled his partner's car, how he'd last seen it rolling into the parking lot of the Green Bay casino.

"He says they're holding a bail hearing for Tobias Crenshaw. First thing tomorrow morning. Part of his deal for giving them the identity of the man you're searching for."

Cale felt his blood pressure climb. This soon? He hadn't set eyes upon their suspect, yet. Didn't even have a location for "Kinsella," for God's sake!

"Seems kind of fast-track to me."

"Slink figured you'd want to know," she said.

Cale pondered the news and decided there was nothing he could do about it. He hated the idea of Crenshaw being allowed his freedom, even if they did plan to keep him under 24-hour house arrest. Maggie was chatting in his ear, telling him news about Chloe and their detective agency project, but he wasn't listening. Cale's mind was in the courtroom, where Tobias Crenshaw was soon to be released. He cursed the high-priced lawyers who had managed to convince the judge that the Chemist—abductor, killer, sociopath, *rapist*—was no longer a threat to the local community.

It boggled the mind. Our wonderful criminal justice system at work, Cale thought, his guts twisting. An oxymoron if ever there was one. And the worst of it was, he couldn't shake the feeling that Crenshaw, somehow, was playing them all for fools. Had he managed to send Cale off on a wild goose chase? In search of a phantom human trafficker? While he, Crenshaw, did a celebrity stroll from the county slammer?

Shaking away the image, Cale glanced at his watch. He'd better get back inside: No time for discussing nagging little issues like secret, unplanned pregnancies. He wondered if it was him—not Maggie—who was avoiding the topic. No. He had to stay focused on his mission. This was not the time to become sidetracked by personal issues.

Those he could deal with later. When the time was right.

After saying good-bye to Maggie, Cale pocketed his phone. He retraced his steps back through the shadowy restaurant, emerging out into the blinding sunlight of the outside deck.

A blonde female in a brimmed hat had joined Jacek and his two partners at their table. She was sitting in Cale's former chair, her back to him as he approached.

"*Buongiorno*, Signore Packer!" Jacek said effusively, as Cale moved to rejoin them.

Their new arrival was garbed in a flowered sundress and sandals, dark sunglasses. Was she another one of Jacek's trained killers? Cale would not be surprised.

"Pull up that chair right there, my friend," Jacek commanded, waving his arm like an orchestra conductor. "Allow me to introduce you—this is Special Agent Amy." Cale reached for the woman's extended hand, gave it a tidy shake.

"Amy Fronteer, actually," she corrected with a nod, her eyes locked on Cale behind the dark lenses. "Homeland Security. ICE immigration. I specialize in human trafficking in Europe."

"Pleased to meet you, Agent." Cale pulled his hand back awkwardly. "Any friend of Jacek's…" He glanced at Pharaoh and Cheetah. "Well, you know the rest."

***

They had driven to the restaurant as a group, riding in one of the vans Jacek kept parked inside the warehouse. Pharaoh—a professional driver, so claimed Jacek—had done the honors. Agent Fronteer had arrived in her own car, a sporty white Cooper, and she suggested Cale hitch a ride with her on the drive back to the warehouse.

"So why the ruse on the plane?" he asked. "Jacek posing as a drunk? He's not in a ratty Rome jail cell, so I'm guessing you had to be in on that."

The ICE agent arched an eyebrow his way. "Jacek's idea. He wanted to 'field test' you, as he put it. See how you'd respond in a crisis. But you're right. I green-lighted him."

She kept her eyes on the road, watchful behind the dark lenses. "We had our own agents on board, Detective. The flight attendants and pilots were informed Homeland was conducting a security test. No one was ever in any danger."

Safe as a puppet on a string, Cale thought to himself. "And you're with DHS? For real? Not some Hollywood actress auditioning for the next season of *24*?"

"Real as it gets," she conceded, as if she'd told the tale a couple million times. "Straight to Langley by way of Brown University. Recruited to Homeland after Nine-eleven. Sixteen years in. Most of them in the field."

Cale's observation of her went unchallenged, as she focused on the Anzio streets. "Spent here? In Italy, I mean?"

Agent Fronteer nodded. "I'm the ICE Slavery and Trafficking Agent in Command. Central Euro Field Ops. Stationed in Rome. We're housed at the American Embassy."

Cale was impressed at her credentials yet remained puzzled by her presence. She glanced his way again: "You're wondering why I'm involved in your mission? The Liberian national? Wanted for questioning in a kidnapping case in Wisconsin?"

Cal stared out the Cooper's window as dusty buildings breezed past, all doing a shimmery dance in the sunlight's harsh glaze. He was feeling the effects of the Moretti, mixed with jet lag.

"You might say I'm curious."

Agent Fronteer spun the boxy vehicle around a corner. She drove as if familiar with the streets of Anzio.

"You're not a law enforcement agent while in Europe, Lieutenant," she said. "You're an ordinary U.S. citizen—like all the other tourists here. So, keeping an eye on you is in our interest."

"Much appreciated."

"Secondly, the subject you're searching for is an alleged international human trafficker. It flags him as a person of interest on our roster."

"In other words," Cale said, "you'll help me catch my bad guy? Hoping he leads you to some bigger fish?"

"In a nutshell." She smoothed a strand of wheat-colored hair behind her ear. She eased the Cooper through an intersection. "Human slavery has become the primary international problem of our era. Over five million sex slaves alone last year. It's far worse than terrorism," Agent Fronteer confessed.

"The bastards who operate in Europe, also move in and out of the States. The global problem of immigration has opened the floodgates. It's why we've got ICE agents stationed around the world."

Cale nodded and stayed silent. He was familiar with the grim statistics. He gritted his teeth and watched as Agent Fronteer turned into the warehouse driveway, before easing across the vacant, sunbaked parking lot. Cale noted how this part of Anzio was blessed with a dearth of pedestrians. The Cooper paused at the wide warehouse doors, which were once again swung open by Jacek's partners in their coveralls. A moment later, the automobile was swallowed by the shadowed inner space, easing to a halt alongside Jacek's dark van.

Before they exited, Cale turned to her. "One more thing, Agent," he said, staring into Amy Fronteer's green eyes as she flipped her sunglasses atop her head. "As you know, I'm a fish out of water on this." He paused for a beat. "It makes me wonder what kind of situation I've gotten myself into, here?"

Agent Fronteer opened the driver's door, swinging her tanned legs free. "No worries, Detective Van Waring. I'll answer all your questions in a few minutes."

CHAPTER 19

Liberia, Africa

Colonel Tazeki Mabutu had cleared his afternoon schedule. He'd cancelled his inspection of a parade troop—it was raining anyway—in downtown Monrovia, his country's capitol. Then he rescheduled a meeting with the Minister of the Interior. Tazeki could not be bogged down by trivial affairs of state. He had an important meeting scheduled for tomorrow afternoon. But tonight? Tonight, he needed to gather the forces of darkness he would require to assist him.

At the turn of the eighteenth century, the country now called Liberia, had been a far different place. Tribes of native warriors ruled the lands. Lush jungles blanketed the landscape, wild animals roamed free. The rainy seasons, followed by months of dry, unforgiving sunlight, brought along poverty and pestilence to the indigenous peoples, who dwelled in fern thatched huts or dung bricked hovels. And when they cried for relief, some respite from the drudgery of everyday survival, who did these natives call upon? The witch doctor, that's who. Known by a hundred different names, across millions of square miles of Dark Continent. The shaman; the sorcerer or sorceress; the *houngan* or *mambo* or *botono*. These natives—priests and patrons both—practiced the six-thousand-year old religion of their ancestors. They prayed to the creator being (*Bondye*), the lesser gods (loa), their deceased ancestors, as well as the mystical animal protectors. They worshipped the skies, the sacred moon, the jungle trees; they bowed before the water and wind, the sand and soil and mountains. And to all things relevant in their existence. If it was present in their lives, they found a way to incorporate it into their system of beliefs.

In the 1930s, one *botono* in particular elevated himself above all others. He was a friend of *Aida Wedo* and *Damballa Wedo*, a master of all loa (especially the petro loa, the dark gods). A leader of his own secret sect. This witch doctor's name was Njada, and he was the grandfather of Tazeki Mabutu.

Tazeki learned the dark arts of Vodun (African Voodoo) from his father, passed down from the great botono Njada, himself. Even as a young boy, he could call the petro loa down from the heavens, or up from the fiery earth, to "ride the horse": to possess a person's body, absorb his soul, and thus make him *nzambi*—a slave to the botono's bidding. Before the age of nine he had performed his first *angajan*—a pact with an evil loa, or spirit god. And he was to become only more proficient, as the years passed.

At this same tender age, Tazeki consumed his first meal of human flesh during a ritual. He sipped from his first cup of warm human blood. It had tasted wonderful. And for the young son of a shaman—a botono himself—Tazeki understood there could be no going back. Not after such a *sanctifying* experience. To consume a man's flesh, to savor his blood, was, indeed, to possess the man's very soul.

For all eternity.

Now Colonel Tazeki Mabutu, head of the Liberian military police, dark warlock of the night, stood on the open veranda of his oversized mansion, where it lurked in the midst of his fortified compound. The rains had finally let up. At least for a while. He stared out at the undulating seas south of Monrovia, the rolling waves as they flung themselves like desperate lovers against the crusted shore. Minutes ago, he had watched his men change guard. They were trained warriors, ever vigilant in their assigned duties. Tazeki could not help but feel protected, despite the terror-filled land in which he lived. And why not? He was armed with his talents as a botono priest; and his demon friend, his patron, Pazuzu—his true dark prince—was close by. He was surrounded by special forces military personnel, men adept at killing. What was there to fear?

So why then, Tazeki wondered, did this continuing sensation of unease seem to linger in the pit of his stomach?

He guessed at the answer: it was the American detective. The man responsible for stalking and capturing his old friend, his former college roommate turned criminal, Tobias Crenshaw. Now the lawman was coming his way, continuing his relentless pursuit. Searching for a pair of still-missing victims. And this made Tazeki quite uneasy.

The detective, they had been informed, was on the hunt for a Liberian national named Kinsella. The only thread he had—thanks to *fucking* Crenshaw!—to resolving his case. And Kinsella, as it stood, was a man whom Tazeki called "friend." His right-hand man, his most valued asset. Kinsella was his lieutenant, the man responsible for running Tazeki's trafficking operation in Europe. He was irreplaceable to the way the colonel ran his business. This American investigator, he decided—this dogged Detective Van Waring—could not be allowed to destroy an operation that had taken him over a decade to construct.

A most profitable operation.

Turning to stare back into the open doors of his study, to his desk where the charcoal-gray, pewter statue of Pazuzu sat, the colonel said out loud: "We shall size-up this American, Pazuzu. See if he deserves a rightful place on our chessboard."

The smirking figure of Pazuzu chose not to reply.

"And if he finds our little country not to his liking? Then we shall find him better accommodations, won't we?" Tazeki's tone was mocking, malevolent. He listened to the air between them.

"In the darkness, you say? Perhaps swimming with our squirmy little pets?" The colonel paused, thoughtful. "You are correct, as usual, Pazuzu."

Tazeki did not cackle like a fiend. Nor did he sneer in the fashion of a madman. Instead, with the night beginning to drizzle again, he strode back into the inner house like the high-ranking, jackbooted military official he was. Ever the gracious host, he commenced opening a tall closet, began gathering the items he would need.

Items guaranteed to impress their foreign visitor.

***

Château du Carthairs, Belgium

While the Liberian colonel was preparing for hosting his guest, three thousand miles away, in an opulent château in the Belgian countryside, Prince Mir Al-Sadar was cracking the whip. Or, rather, the riding crop.

His victim, in her latex equine gear, was trying her best not to whimper. Neither to let out a sound nor allow the prince to think he was breaking her will. After all, Leslie reasoned, he wouldn't risk marring her flawless flesh. Not if he wanted her to pass the judges' inspection come Saturday.

Still, no matter how much pain she felt, she understood matters could be worse. She was alive, wasn't she? Breathing? Still of this earth? Not being sautéed and roasted on a spit by some cannibals.

Hours earlier, Leslie and her trio of companions had donned their pony girl costumes and walked through the paces of one of the final rehearsals prior to this weekend's big event: the Belgian Fetish Festival. The highlight was easily the 400-meter sulky race. It was a competition Prince Mir's prized quartet was the odds-on favorite to win. One fateful trip around the oval track was all it would take. The teams, however, were judged on several merits, speed being only one factor. They were judged equally on style and showmanship, as well as by coordination and synchronicity. And on authentic attire. Attitude and obedience entered the final equation, as well. Pony girls must always—this was stressed by Mr. Anselm—be nothing more than ponies. The point of it all was to have as little human element as possible showing through the equine façade.

As the quartet's leader, Leslie had the teamwork part down pat. And the poise; as well as the athletics. But obedience? That's where she was lacking. Ever since her thwarted escape attempt, they had been watching her with unrelenting scrutiny. And His Highness was the worst. Where before he had seldom paid her much attention, now he was visiting her room at least twice a day, checking on her, asking questions, grilling her on the details of her escape: What had made her run?

Wasn't she happy here? What made her think escape would be possible? Allah be praised, girl, but she was in the middle of a foreign continent! Without a passport or visa.

Was she insane?

And on and on ad nauseam, until Leslie thought her head might burst.

Now here he was again, up in her room hours after the workout, forcing her to dress again in her outfit. Including the bit, including the uncomfortably inserted festive tail plume. Then making her kneel on the bed like some twenty-franc whore. Now whipping her with a riding crop, but one comprised of rubber-tips, so as not to cause welts or abrasions on her creamy flesh.

So clever was the prince.

Until finally, just now, the punishment stopped.

"You may relax," Prince Mir said, his voice strained and tight. A sheen of perspiration had broken across his smooth, caramel-colored brow, disturbing his otherwise calm demeanor. "We are finished for today."

Hearing the bedroom door close behind her, first then did Leslie allow herself to drop one shoulder to the mattress and topple over onto her side. She spat the bit from her mouth, her lungs panting from the torment. Tears streaked her cheeks and her face was flushed.

She recited the vow again—her private mantra—recited it mentally for the thousandth time: *Escape. Sometime soon. Or I will kill myself trying.*

CHAPTER 20

Anzio, Italy

"Human sex slavery."

Special Agent Amy Fronteer was standing in front of the group in the center of the warehouse, the large white grease board to her left, in what amounted to the war room. She had written the words in bold print at the top of the board. Below it she now wrote a figure as she spoke. "There are at present an estimated twenty-five million trafficking victims across the world today. A one-hundred-fifty-*billion*-dollar industry."

Allowing a few long beats of silence, for the enormity of her numbers to register, she continued:

"This is a dire problem, faced by every nation on the planet, and the fastest growing world-wide crime today. One that, sad to say, will become exponentially worse in years to come."

Jacek was sitting on the couch yoga style, the legs of his military camo pants crossed at the ankle. Next to him sat Cheetah in leggings and a knit top. Cale, in blue jeans, cargo shirt, and tan deck shoes, sat on a wooden crate. Leaning against a large metal support pole was Pharaoh, wearing military fatigues, and, just as before, from where Cale sat, he had difficulty telling which one was holding the other upright.

They had learned of Amy Fronteer's qualifications. That meant they'd also learned the *why* of her taking interest in their case. Trafficking occurred for the usual variety of reasons, the agent was informing them, briefing them for the past twenty minutes. Cale felt himself becoming antsy. Too much sitting around. First the lengthy overnight flight; and now this. He was wired, ready for action. On the other hand, might he be jetlagged? Enough to be uncertain where his head was at?

"Since the flood of immigration into the countries of Northern and Western Europe," Agent Fronteer was saying, "this problem has increased a hundred-fold. Part of the price we're paying for so-called 'globalization.'"

"Why don't any of these victims just leave?" asked Jacek. "Sneak out in the middle of the night? Vamoose?"

"Take your pick," the special agent said, her frustration evident. "Humiliation, dehumanization; or brutality, or cruelty, or death threats."

"Drug dependency," Cale added. "Their captors hook them into staying. They can't make it for long on their own, even if they try."

"That's correct, Detective," Agent Fronteer agreed. "It's a dead-end street if they attempt flight. If they try to find help in the narcotics underworld of any major city, they're spotted and returned to their captors. Often for a substantial reward. And the worst of it, their captors don't give a damn. If one of them become too much of a headache, they'll shoot them like dogs. Replace them with another truckload of victims. These girls—and in many cases young boys—are nothing more than cattle to them. Each one can be replaced in a snap."

The room was silent.

"Not to mention the passport difficulty, if they do manage to break free," added Cheetah, speaking from the couch. "The captors confiscate their passports, so these victims are helpless. They are unable to cross any international border."

"Except America," said Jacek, "where passports no longer seem to matter."

Agent Fronteer let his comment slide.

Cale felt his muscles cramping. He stretched both legs forward, keeping his arms crossed. "All right. This is all well and good, Agent," he said, prodding, "but in my own case, I'm looking for one *specific* man. One who might not even be involved in human trafficking." He looked at the others. "We won't know until we find him. Right?"

"*If* we find him," said Jacek. "Very, very large if." He remained frozen in his Buddha-like position.

"Our intel has been updated." Agent Fronteer spoke matter-of-factly. "While you all were horsing around on your mats over there this morning, we were searching for more in-depth information on your subject."

"With Interpol's help, no doubt," Cheetah stated.

"Correct." Agent Fronteer stared at Cale. "When Agent Redtail helped profile your unknown subject in your Green Bay kidnapping case—whom we now know to be Tobias Crenshaw—due to the serial nature of the crimes, the multiple victims, we furthered the probe on our own."

This came as news to Cale, and he returned her hard look. "I asked before," he said, "why would Homeland give a damn about a Midwestern city kidnapping spree?"

"We wouldn't. Normally. With no foreign nationals involved, it was outside our jurisdiction." The ICE agent moved across the room and took a seat on a wooden crate matching Cale's. "Until your case, relatively few

U.S. females have been abducted and trafficked internationally. A handful to Canada. Some through Mexican cartels. But that's it."

She searched their eyes for questions. None came. "But once the trafficker Kinsella's name popped-up, it changed the dynamics." She let this sink in.

"What your saying is, this Kinsella," Jacek said, looking one to the next, "being a known trafficker, allowed ICE to enter the game?"

Agent Fronteer nodded. "Our analysts reassessed your victim list. They were all attractive females, blond-hair, early twenties." Her green eyes found Cale's own. "Your fiancé, Maggie. We considered her abduction an anger attack, outside Crenshaw's victim profile."

"I agree," Cale said, frustrated. "If we hadn't gotten lucky, found her in time…" his voice trailed off.

"These American girls," Cheetah said, studying the grease board at the front of the room. "Since they're not typical trafficking victims?" She looked back to Agent Amy. "What are they, then? How do they fit?"

"The million-dollar question," Cale said.

Agent Fronteer rose, standing again before them. "You don't have access to our database, but I'll share this with you." She paused, as if searching for the proper words. "This sick slavery industry has gotten so broad, so diverse, that specialty niches have begun to emerge."

"Specialty niches?" repeated Pharaoh. He had been silent until now, so stoic Cale had forgotten the man was hovering in the nearby shadows.

"Correct. There are several high-end brothels and subgroups in operation throughout Europe. They cater to a more, shall we say, *select* clientele."

"Don't tell me," said Jacek, his look more coy than usual. "The fetish crowd?"

"Bingo." Agent Fronteer eyed them all. "They are a separate subculture unto themselves."

"And with prostitution being no big deal in Europe," Cheetah added, "these perverts fly under the radar. Whatever their sick fantasies might be."

Agent Fronteer nodded. "Just about anything goes in Amsterdam. As well as Berlin, these days. And other major urban areas throughout Europe. You can just about guess the rest."

The group was silent, mulling this over. Cale viewed them as front-line warriors in the fight, similar to the medical personnel who had first learned they could not contain the Ebola virus.

Reaching into her attaché case, the ICE agent withdrew a large manila envelope. She passed it to Cheetah, saying, "I put in a request to Interpol for listings—photos included—of five-star, pricey brothel operators around the globe. These came in just before lunch."

Cheetah opened the envelope. She withdrew multiple blown-up photographs, studying them one after the next. Passing them along to Jacek, to Cale, and at last to Pharaoh.

Agent Fronteer continued: "Three dozen of the world's major players in the private harem business. Many of them are also involved in the fetish trade. There's an overlap. Some are active in prostitution rings; others in arms or narcotics." The ICE agent surveyed them all. "Because our tip revealed the name 'Kinsella,' we retrieved the mug shot Scotland Yard had on record by that name. We cross-checked it. Ran whatever popped up through our facial-recognition software."

"And let me guess—" This from Jacek.

"You got lucky," Cale interrupted, his ears now perking up. He leaned over, studying the stack of photos Cheetah had passed along to them.

Agent Fronteer held up an 8-by-10 color glossy for them to see.

"This picture shows the man we've ID'd as this same Mr. Kinsella," She paused, with them all looking at the phot. "He's at a meeting in Belgium, with one Prince Mir Al-Sadar, who's a member of the Emer Saud royal family. The prince is a legitimate businessman, whose hobbies run toward the sexually racier side."

"Read pervert," Jacek blurted.

"He's a sex fetish enthusiast. One with way too much time on his hands, and enough oil money to purchase his own small country."

She handed Jacek the photo. The prince was conversing with a large African man, who loomed beside him. He angled it for Cale to see. The image appeared to have been taken with a telephoto lens. Behind a tree line, Cale imagined. A second photo showed the pair sitting on the rear patio of a luxuriant home, enjoying afternoon cocktails. After studying both photos, Cale handed them to Pharaoh, who extended one large paw from the shadows behind him.

Agent Fronteer added, "Our second hit came with this same African male—again facial-rec confirmed as Kinsella—standing in downtown Moscow. Conversing with a Russian general." She paused. "A man named Alexi Panterov."

"Another sick puppy," moaned Cheetah, giving her dark eyes a roll.

"We don't have much intel on Panterov. He might be new to the game. But we're on it." She took a breath. "What we do know, is he's retired and lives in a dacha somewhere north of Moscow."

"How about a Google search?" Cale meant it as a joke.

Agent Fronteer, however, failed to crack a smile. "We'll SAT-photo his residence. As soon as we confirm a verifiable address."

CHAPTER 21

Above the Atlantic Ocean

Flying backward in time was never a problem for Kinsella. He simply paid it no heed. He was a man who lived in the present, the now. No looking forward, nor back, just existing in the bubble of the minute. It was the Zen of how he approached life. But Kinsella was the furthest person imaginable from a philosopher. Instead, he was a brute. And a deviously attuned one at that.

As the airplane leveled its altitude above the Atlantic Ocean—Brussels, Belgium to Chicago, Illinois—Kinsella sat cramped in his seat. His thick forearms occupied both armrests of the window seat. No passenger beside him ever complained. As if sensing the aura of danger oozing from the man, they kept their mouths closed. And for good reason: the man known as "Kinsella" functioned as the bloody right hand of the botono, Tazeki Mabutu. The colonel was his partner, his leader. And if their past together was any indicator, his only friend.

Still, Kinsella was far from some mindless *nzambi*. He was his own man. There was no task he performed without reason. No haphazard killing, no bloodletting, no rape. What he did, he did for *the cause*. To please the loa or to please his botono. Whatever duties he carried out were all in Tazeki's master plan.

With his dark sport jacket folded across his lap, after a few minutes the large Liberian allowed his eyes to close. His head was on a courtesy pillow, the pillow tucked tight against the small window, whose shade he chose to keep open. Though Kinsella seldom remembered his dreams, the ones that did register in his consciousness were always about the past: his past, Tazeki's past, their past together as young lads growing up in the same village, fighting, as history recorded, the constant battle for Liberian liberation.

And in one such dream:

Twilight had faded. The African night formed around them in a quilt of blackness. The mountains in the background became vague and featureless, and the closer shapes of jungle trees and brush lost their form as well, rustling, swaying without pattern in the breeze. Creatures came out at night to feed, many of whom the pair of young boys knew best to keep a safe distance from. Sounds of low moaning often echoed in the distance; or the sudden shriek of night birds, hidden in the clinging darkness, sounded their alarm.

As she was on many such sweaty, cloud-scattered nights, *Lshne*, the African moon, was a spook-yellow eye staring down on the lush jungle landscape. The rainy season was past, and the sway of dry saw grass hissed and crackled. Insects thrummed in the underbrush. A diamond spill of stars sprinkled above the sparse cloud cover.

The two boys had been armed with traditional weapons—spears and cudgels, machetes and long knives—ready to do battle with large cats, whose stalking eyes peered through the broad ferns and shadowed branches. The pair moved forward, soundless, ever on alert for vipers creeping noiseless over the jungle floor. A python could suffocate a grown man in less than three minutes. A mamba's bite—100 percent fatal—could disorient in ten minutes, paralyze him in thirty.

On this night, however, the roles had been reversed: the lads had become hunters instead of prey.

Through the thick cover of underbrush, Tazeki and his friend—known as Nmanu back then—were spying on three white men who had set their camp in a clearing, not far from a stream off the river. They were sitting hunched around a fire, drinking from two brandy bottles. Rifles were set aside and leaning against an oversized chunk of granite. Brits, if they had to guess. Maybe Aussies. Or South Afrikaners, recruiting for the diamond mines of Sierra Leone.

The boys knew it mattered little: all blood ran red.

"Soldiers?" Tazeki had whispered, peering through the vines.

"Invaders," replied Nmanu.

Their village, consisting of twenty-three mud huts, was situated three hundred miles inland from the sea coast. Tazeki, though growing stronger in his powers, was yet but the son of a juju shaman. Still a village boy. In old African tradition, all boys must be sent out to exist in nature, not to return home until they had conquered a lion or a leopard, some beast of notoriety. First then would they be considered as men. First then would they be allowed to claim a female for a mate.

And here, on this warm and blackest of nights, what better way to advance across the precipice of manhood than to spill fresh blood, be it feline or human? For here loomed far easier targets than hungry jungle cats. These were drunken white men. And though they possessed modern weapons, they could not leap twelve feet into the air, nor could they eviscerate your organs with one swipe of razor claws.

For the pair of shadowed ghosts, armed with machetes and long knives, the slaughter had been efficient. Afterward, beneath the all-seeing eye of *Lshne*, Tazeki had sliced open one of the victims. He held the steaming entrails aloft, an offer to the loa he was calling. Shirtless, garbed in half-pants and leather moccasins, the two boys held their ceremony. It climaxed with their filling a drinking cup with warm blood, while the flank of one of the butchered men dripped fat over the fire pit.

It was Nmanu who was granted—by the young botono—the first long drink of blood from the sacred cup. And thus, it came to pass: Tazeki's young friend consumed his first soul.

Later, when they had dined on their fill of flesh and guzzled enough blood to satiate their unholy thirst, Nmanu had rifled through the men's belongings. He discovered the passport and ID papers of the man whose soul he now possessed: Arthur James Kinsella, United Kingdom. The boy Nmanu was now a man. And in his rebirth, he could assume a fresh identity.

From that day forward, he was known only by the solitary name of "*Kinsella*."

***

Liberia, Africa

It was dark outside the compound, the rolling waters calm but still rifled by the steady downpour. The botono, Tazeki Mabutu, was kneeling inside the Blood

Room on the uppermost floor of the main house. Doors closed, the candles flickered around him, shadows dancing on the walls where he had written a series of symbols in the Old Tongue.

He was by himself, eyes focused, naked as a skinned black cat.

The botono stared into the large, carved wooden bowl in front of him. He held the bowl in both hands, watching the fresh, warm blood as it swirled around the brilliant diamond.

It took but a few moments for the trance to come over him. Then, as if whisked away by a magic carpet, Tazeki found himself transported, and it was dark all around him. He likened it to deep space but without the planets or stars. He was a ghost, a silhouette, a specter in a mirror. He patterned his destination with his mind, his lone navigational tool. Set the coordinates, as it were.

And when at last he landed deep inside Tobias Crenshaw's damp and squirmy brain, the botono took a moment to study his surroundings. To assess his whereabouts. He examined the soft and undulating folds, the splashy blood, where it flowed and throbbed with sentient purpose. The echoing *lub-dub* rhythm of the heart below, pumping like a ship's engine.

He had been in this same place before. Years ago, when they had both been younger. And it had always served to frighten his old friend, as if he'd glanced in his bedroom mirror and seen Lucifer, himself, staring back with demonic eyes.

Satisfied, Tazeki murmured in a low, lipless voice: *"Hello, Tobias. Long time, no see."*

***

Green Bay, Wisconsin

Inside his cell in the isolation unit of the Brown County jail, Tobias Crenshaw's eyelids flicked open. His dream had been fogged with tendrils of crimson vapor swirling through his mind, the ghosts of his victims, bound and tortured, their rattling final breaths escaping bubbling lips. Beads of perspiration had formed across his brow. His lower back felt swampy.

Blinking one eye open, he searched his empty cell. He gazed at the vacant bed opposite his own. Something was not right here.

"Tobias," came the singsong voice, from the depths within his brain. *"Is this any way to greet your oldest and dearest friend?"*

"Damn it, Tazeki!" Tobias muttered out loud, the echo of his voice bouncing off the walls, floor, ceiling of his barren cell. "Get the *bloody fuck* out of my head!"

"Death is but a door, Tobias. Death is but a door."

The cackle of sadistic laughter. It rang through his mind, teasing the soft and gushy folds there, tripping, humming, traipsing as if a drunken imp had been let loose to frolic inside the rooms of his brain. On and on it went, into the night, and the mental voices echoed and screamed like the crazed cries of a thousand madmen, threatening to never subside.

In those tortuous, seemingly never-ending hours, Tobias Crenshaw, at last, understood one unnerving truth: He could no longer spend any length of time incarcerated. Not without having serious doubts about his own sanity.

CHAPTER 22

Anzio, Italy

The skies above the coastal waters of Anzio were shadowed in the west, and Cale imagined that if he looked hard enough northward, he could see the colors of nighttime Rome reflected off the low-hanging clouds. They had eaten carryout from a local diner Jacek knew, deciding to remain inside the warehouse as much as possible. Standard procedure for a band of mercenaries in a foreign land, whose desire was to maintain a low profile.

The plan called for their catching a couple hours of shuteye before heading to Rome for their 2 a.m. flight. Delaying the inevitable retiring to his bunk—consisting of a floor mattress in a cubby of a room off the central area of the warehouse—Cale decided to step outside for some privacy.

Jacek and his partners were busy at the computer, studying a Google map of Belgium. Agent Fronteer had requested a series of satellite photos of Prince Mir's château in the Belgian countryside, and together they'd all poured over them. A bit of reconnaissance, in case it was needed. Staring at shots of the opulent country estate had filled Cale with a sense of unease. The place was fortified with enough security measures to keep out the Red Army.

From his spot now on an abandoned crate stand in the empty parking lot, he watched a few vehicles cruise past on the street adjacent the warehouse. His mind wandered to the plan they had established for the following day: He would meet—along with Jacek, if allowable—with the Liberian minister of foreign affairs. Cale would show the minister the photograph in question, identify the man they were searching for: the Liberian national named Kinsella. The minister would hem and haw, but his country needed to remain on good diplomatic grounds with the United States. After a few protests, the man would provide information on the requested suspect. The minister would determine, it was hoped, where this "Kinsella" (the possibility of an alias remained likely) resided. With a military escort, they would visit the suspect's home, or his place of work. If he happened to be in prison, they would visit there, as well. If all went according to plan, and the man indicated his complicity in any fashion, they would have him arrested.

Cale understood that he was alone, for the most part, operating in an environment beyond his control. Nevertheless, he imagined that once they located the suspect, the best-case scenario would be the Liberian authorities taking the individual in for questioning. The rest, he hoped, would fall into place.

Employing Agent Fronteer's ICE connections, greasing the rails on the diplomatic front, Cale imagined the suspect could be remanded into his personal custody. He would proceed to escort the man back to the United States. To Green Bay, Wisconsin. There he would be questioned in the decapitation murder of Kimberly Vanderkellen, along with the string of abducted female victims; as well as his connection to Tobias Crenshaw, a.k.a. the Chemist.

If they were fortunate, the suspect would fast recognize the hopelessness of his situation. He would confess to the crimes, and that would be that. If not, well, the rest was beyond Cale's control, so he decided not to worry about it. First things first.

It was a little after nine p.m. now in Italy. That made it seven hours earlier in Green Bay. Cale punched in the numbers for Maggie's mobile, and caught her at home.

"Just checking in," he reported, realizing how robotic he sounded. Was it the military attitude of Jacek and his companions rubbing off on him? After they exchanged greetings, and a bit of small talk, he proceeded to update her on his progress. Cale informed her they had a few interesting new leads. When he inquired about her "flu-like" symptoms, she sloughed away his concern.

"I felt fine all day," Maggie said, dismissing his concerns. "Except for when I kept hearing about this Crenshaw mess. It turns my stomach."

"I can't believe a judge is letting him out. That's insane. The city's got to be in an uproar." Cale felt his anger smoldering beneath the surface. He had to push it aside. Thinking of Tobias Crenshaw's release from jail would only keep him tossing and turning when his own head hit the pillow.

"How's tomorrow looking?" Maggie asked.

"We'll be in Liberia most of the day. Dealing with politicians. So, who knows?"

She snickered. "I'll take the flu, any day."

"Speaking of which," Cale informed, "we had to get a dozen immunization shots. I never even thought about it before I left."

"They don't call it the Dark Continent for nothing." With a sigh, Maggie added, "Promise me you won't come back with malaria. Or Ebola. Or something worse."

"I promise. I find the bastard, bring him home. Those are my marching orders."

"They are if you know what's good for you." He could feel her smirk across the connection, before she turned serious. "I've got a few other things we need to talk about, Cale. But they can wait till you get back."

"You're not still mad about the trip, are you? Me going it alone?"

"I'm a big girl. I'm over it."

He nodded. "'Other things' it is, then. Care to give me a hint?"

"Nothing important." She was quick to brush it aside. "Just some stuff for the wedding. I don't want to bore you with details."

Cale fought away the image of her walking down the aisle in her white gown with a discernable "baby bump" on display. He had the sense to keep it to himself. They agreed to talk more when they had more time, when he wasn't fighting off jet lag. They exchanged "love you's" and rang off.

While he was bidding farewell to Maggie, the warehouse's back door opened, and Amy Fronteer appeared. She was cast as a ghost in the twilight, and seemed not to listen, as he ended his conversation.

"Everything copacetic on the home front?" she asked, in a quiet voice. She had carried with her a pair of opened beer bottles. She handed one to Cale.

"Mind reading, Agent?" he asked. "Another talent they teach you at Homeland?"

"Your tax dollars at work." She took a position leaning against the building and sipped from her bottle. "Call me Amy—please." She waited as he nodded. "Here's a question for you. What if he's dead? Kinsella? You just pack up your bags? Fly back home?"

Cale had considered the possibility a hundred times already. The problem—if such proved to be the case—was that he required some sort of verification. Solid proof from someone in a position of authority.

"There goes my Roman holiday, I suppose," he quipped, taking a casual sip of beer. "I verify his status. That's my mission. But you're right"—he shrugged in the shadows—"I'm a one-trick pony on this. I find my man, I bring him home. End of story."

The ICE agent nodded. "Wouldn't be an entire waste of time. At least you'd know. And at least the families would have some bit of closure."

They spent the next ten minutes discussing the latest report Agent Fronteer had received on the men in the photographs with Kinsella: the Emer Saud prince and the Russian general. Cale was having a difficult time taking the shadowy figures seriously. In his mind, both of the men's connections with his suspect—if indeed there were any—sounded like something out of a Tom Clancy novel.

He shifted gears. "So, how'd you get involved in this stuff? The human trafficking thing?" When she failed to reply, he prodded. "Always had a soft spot for the underdog? Helpless victims in need of rescuing? That sort of thing?"

She smiled without humor. "It started back when I was in college, I suppose." Another pull from her bottle. "I was twenty, home for the summer from school. I lined up a job in one of those small computer stores. Sales, repairs, general stuff. I was a total geek. Figured if I majored in computer science, I'd always have a job, in this day and age."

"Logical." Cale was a guy who knew how to plug in the computer, keep clacking away until he got where he wanted to go. To him a "hardware crash" meant a box of wrenches falling on a garage floor.

"I've got a sister, seven years younger," Agent Fronteer continued, "so this was back when she was thirteen. A vulnerable age for any girl."

"I've seen girls that age who could make Lady Gaga blush."

"Touché, Detective." She rolled her beer bottle between her palms, eyeing him. "Anyway, when I was home that summer, Lisa—my sister—was walking with one of her friends. Coming from the mall or something. A car pulls up in broad daylight—we lived in Ohio, right—and some freak jumps out and grabs for them. Lisa dodges him. But her friend—Tess—freezes. The scumbag grabs hold of her and tosses her into the backseat, kicking and screaming, and drives away."

Cale rubbed the back of his neck. He studied the ICE agent's features in the shadows. She possessed a sharp nose he hadn't noticed earlier. He could hear the steady thrum of moving traffic coming from blocks away. From the seashore, a bell clanged soullessly.

"They catch the guy?" he asked, imagining he already knew the answer.

"That whole summer they searched for Tess." Agent Fronteer relayed this in a somber tone. "Each night for weeks, the local TV news described the futility. By

August, the whole investigation had died to a whimper. No news; no body found—nothing."

Cale stayed silent, breathing in the salty night air.

"I didn't want to return to school in the fall. I guess I was afraid to let Lisa out of my sight. My family, we wanted her to stay inside, not go anywhere." She shook her head, hearing voices only she could hear. "I went back to Brown. Changed my major the first day back to law enforcement. And added prelaw. I planned I'd end up the DA one day, back in my hometown. I'd keep working on Tess's cold case until it burned me out enough to forget."

"Some cases you never forget."

She raised the dark bottle and took a long drink.

"Instead, Langley came calling?" Cale prompted her, taking a swig of his own.

"Good old Langley." Her silence spoke volumes. "I wonder if anyone ever turns them down. The rest, as they say, is history. I worked in the field, and when the human sex slavery problem kept growing globally, well, I guess I found my niche."

"Still looking for Tess? After all these years?"

"And all the other missing Tess's out there."

They were silent for a long moment.

Cale finished his beer with a final swallow. "Can I tell you something, Agent? Something personal?" Her silhouette nodded in the shadows. "At least you don't look like a spook," he amended. "Except for right now. In this light."

Amy Fronteer feathered a smile, thankful for the small compliment. By then the shroud of darkness had settled around them, and Anzio took her first yawn of the evening. Cale held open the door and together they disappeared back inside the warehouse.

***

Cale's sparse room off the main floor of the warehouse appeared to have once been someone's office: the shelving, the metal file cabinet standing in the corner, a large desk pushed against one wall. He was able to close the door, in case he desired privacy, and the mattress on the floor appeared solid enough. The blankets were clean, courtesy of Cheetah. Not quite the Ritz Carlton, but he'd make do for the next couple of hours. Cale doubted that he'd fall asleep anyway. The image of Maggie filling out her wedding gown would choke away any chance of that. And before long, Jacek would summon him. With their meager travel items in hand, together they'd catch the train back to the airport in Rome.

Cale lay upon the mattress in the dark, arms crossed behind his head. He tried to scrub his mind of thought. There'd be enough time for thinking of killers and madmen and pregnant brides during the six-hour flight to Liberia. What he needed now was to erase everything from his mind, to meditate. A least until it was time to depart.

As he drifted into a half-sleep, what Cale could not know was that the man he sought was jetting above the nighttime waters of the Atlantic Ocean, cruising at an airspeed of five-hundred-fifty miles per hour. The old adage tells us: "What you don't know can't hurt you." In this case it was true, for Cale was oblivious to the fact that his suspect—the deranged psychopathic killer, whom Tobias Crenshaw had fingered—was *en route*, via Chicago, to the city he called home.

Straight toward where Maggie was now. Along with the rest of Green Bay's unsuspecting citizenry. Like a denomination of innocent lambs, they were all blissfully unaware of the wolf who would soon be arriving at their doorstep.

CHAPTER 23

Rome, Italy

Despite the late hour, Fiumicino International Airport remained a beehive of activity on a Wednesday night. Both tourists and travelers were filled with nervous energy, prepared to board the long metal tubes that would whisk them to their desired destinations.

The armed security guards eyed Cale and Jacek with interest, as they were escorted by an airport official, who helped them skirt the regular security checks. This was accomplished courtesy of Agent Fronteer. She had notified TSA and convinced the Italian authorities both men were traveling diplomats. The official brought them straight to their boarding gate, for the 2:00 a.m. redeye flight to Monrovia, Liberia.

They had their tickets in hand, which Cheetah had preprinted when she'd booked their flight.

"Remember," Agent Fronteer had reminded Cale in earnest, "keep your phone powered on at all times. We'll be GPS-ing your location."

"Gotcha."

"And if you wind up flying back to the States, I'll know you succeeded in your mission. So best of luck, Detective." Turning to Jacek, she added, "Look out for him. Remember, this isn't some make-believe at Euro Disney."

"Ah, Agent Amy"—Jacek feigned a hurt expression, puppy dog eyes—"remember who you are talking to here. I am the best, am I not?" He shot Cale a wink.

Agent Fronteer gave the Czech bodyguard a shake of her blond hair. "It's what you keep telling me, Jacek. Don't prove yourself wrong."

Cale was garbed in the creased, no-iron dress slacks he'd packed for the trip. Rubber-soled cop shoes and a button-down shirt. His effort at looking presentable for the Liberian foreign minister. Jacek, for his part, had on creased dark Dockers pants and a cargo shirt. Functional footwear. As he was not on any sort of "official" business, it mattered little what he clothing he wore. He decided, however, against camos or anything military looking. Nothing too "provocative" in an unstable country like Liberia. Still, his choice of attire was based on being prepared for whatever crisis might involve the man he had been assigned to protect.

"*Arrivederci*," said Jacek, issuing Agent Fronteer a crisp military salute.

"Me too," added Cale.

On board, sleep-challenged travelers were preparing for the flight, sorting through travel planners, conversing on mobile phones, rifling through luggage. Laptops and iPods were in evidence. Jacek carried only a small duffel bag containing a few personal items and both his mobile phone, as well as his fancy Iridium SAT phone. Cale had his own mobile in his pocket—guaranteed by Agent Fronteer that it would provide coverage from Liberia. He carried nothing else but a hardcover binder, which held the photographs and necessary documents he would need to present to the government officials.

They settled in the middle of coach class. The Air Italia flight appeared about halfway filled. Apparently, Liberia in the rainy season was not a prime vacation destination. Many of the passengers were dressed in colorful African garb, a reminder for Cale he was not in Wisconsin anymore—land of blue jeans and green and gold Packers sweatshirts. He decided gaining a little international culture wouldn't hurt. And judging by the number of empty seats, they'd have room to stretch out once they were in the air. He glanced around from his spot in the window seat, eyeing a handful of passengers. Both he and Jacek were traveling unarmed, and the thought afflicted Cale with a mild sense of vulnerability.

Twenty minutes after takeoff, Jacek reached into one of his shirt pockets. He handed Cale what looked to be a sturdy penlight.

"What's this for?" Cale examined the object with suspicion. He was learning that with Jacek, you never could be certain what tricks he had up his sleeve. Was the innocuous penlight what it appeared to be? Or was it a Swiss Army knife, akin to the fancy switchblade Pharaoh possessed? Something out of Ian Fleming?

"A gift, my friend," Jacek said without ceremony. "In honor of your trip to the Dark Continent."

"A light for the dark, Jacek? You truly are cleverer than you look."

"Waterproof. Never know when it'll come in handy."

"No hidden compartments?" Cale slid the penlight into his pants pocket.

"Sometimes a cigar is just a cigar, eh?" Jacek cut his eyes toward Cale. "Always so suspicious, Mr. Packer. I want you prepared, is all. Like your American Boy Scouts."

"Prepared for what?"

"The unexpected. A good rule to follow." Jacek tapped his wristwatch, a playful glint in his eye. He held up his wrist for Cale to observe. "My watch here. I seldom travel without it."

"Great. If I lose track of the time, I'll know who to ask."

Turning, Cale stared out the airplane's small window. Nothing but lavender sky and teal-blue clouds, as far as the eye could see. Wonderful, he thought. *The unexpected.* Just what he wanted to hear on the way to godforsaken Liberia—land of lions and hippos and snakes that would kill you for looking at them crossways.

CHAPTER 24

Liberia, Africa

The six-hour flight had been smooth sailing. They chatted a little, but for the most part chose to rest with their eyes closed. When the morning light shifted from its smoke gray to a purplish haze, and they broke beneath the cloud cover, Cale was able to distinguish the Atlantic Ocean as it stretched forever to the edges of the horizon. Inland, the lushness of greenery, the winding rivers, the foreboding might of the occasional mountainous peaks. While these appeared cut from a fairytale book, the landscape was cast in a colorless palette of browns and muted earth tones and blends of dull metallic. The rainy season summoned all the joy of a funeral. Not to mention, they were visiting a country torn apart for a century by war and strife. The movies from Cale's youth—lurid tales from the Dark Continent—tripped through his head: savages beating the brush on tiger hunts, mad elephant stampedes, giant crocodiles leaping from the rivers and snapping men in half. These images remained until he saw his first car-congested freeway. The sorry sign of twenty-first-century life.

Roberts International Airport in Monrovia left much to be desired. The runways looked to be carved from the flat surrounding fields, complete with pot holes and dirt pits and encroaching weed beds. Cast straight from some central city urban renewal project. The only thing missing were a graveyard of tombstone-like high-rises, and painted gang graffiti. The plane's landing on the narrow strip of concrete was a bit uneven, but the bounce smoothed things out. The realization they were, indeed, in Africa, was quick to hit home.

Welcome to Liberia, the country created for post-Civil War African American slaves and their descendants. Cale had learned this tidbit by reading a historical reference to the country before boarding the flight in Rome. It gave him a brief overview, at least until he'd become bored with the politics of the story. He cared not a hoot about the long-term struggles and internal strife of the country's indigenous inhabitants. Like an Old West sheriff, his primary concern was for one man. Once he had his suspect in handcuffs, he'd hop on the plane and giddy-up back for home.

So much for adventure in the lush tropical forests. So much for blazing sunsets. He had about as much interest in a safari as he did in wearing pantyhose.

After they were done taxiing around in what Cale guessed to be a circle, the plane eased to a halt. Rising, gathering their carry-ons, the passengers progressed toward the plane's single front exit. Jacek had warned him ahead of time to be ready with his passport, travel visa, and whatever other necessary papers would be required to pass through customs.

The terminal at Roberts International looked like a Midwestern U.S. terminal out of the 1950s, with a long, slanted roof that bore an angular overhang. The steady rain was pelting the metallic sides and roof. It sounded like a constant thrum of tiny BBs striking home. Traversing down the plane's steep exit ladder, careful of wet footing, Cale watched as a covered military jeep came zipping up to where the airplane was parked. The jeep skidded to a halt on the damp concrete. It intersected with where the passengers were deplaning, and a dark man in a tan military uniform jumped from the front passenger seat and hailed them.

"Mr. Van Waring?" the shave-headed man called, raising his eyebrows. He reminded Cale of a football player who had gone soft since his retirement.

Cale gave the man a wave and a nod, and the officer motioned them over to the jeep. The other passengers ahead of them were beelining for the terminal, trying to avoid getting too drenched, attempting to squeeze into a single door, luggage and all.

"Please, sir," the officer called. "Right this way. We are your ride to the embassy."

Cale gave Jacek a glance, and the Czech arched one eyebrow his way and shrugged *Why not?* A military escort in a land of revolution? It made sense. The American government may have even greased the wheels on the diplomatic front. Together they moved toward the jeep, and their host held the door open for them. They climbed into the backseat, with the military officer hopping into the passenger-side front seat and closing the door against the steady rainfall.

Inside the jeep, the officer turned. "I am Sergeant Ditt, Liberian National Police." He motioned to the driver, "This is Sergeant Wanto." The man driving was a slenderer version of his partner, and he gave a slight nod as Ditt added, "May I have your passports, please?"

Cale followed Jacek's lead and fished his passport and travel visa from his binder. They handed their papers to Ditt in the front seat. The man gave them a quick perusal, frowning a bit as he examined them.

"Is there a problem?" asked Jacek, his voice steady. He had both hands on the leather duffle bag in his lap.

Ditt pocketed their papers in the inside pocket of his military jacket. When he turned back, he said, "I need to see your other vaccination papers, as well."

Jacek said, "You have them. Stamped with the visas."

"The American embassy provided for our necessary shots—" Cale protested, before Jacek held up a hand to silence him.

Ditt issued them both a look of concern. "We need to check for the yellow fever, you know? A requirement. You must also have H1N1 vaccination these days to enter Liberia."

Cale stared hard at Ditt, then back at Jacek. Without any argument, Jacek asked, "How much?" His stare was fixed on the Liberian sergeant's profile. "How much to get either the vaccination, or the papers saying we've had them?"

Ditt shared a quick glance with his driver before turning back to them. "It is not a matter of money, sir. It is the law here in the people's great country of Liber—"

The chirp of a phone stopped the man in mid-speech. The sergeant reached into a different pocket, withdrew his mobile phone. He answered, nodded, listening to someone. Cale hoped it was someone with half-a-brain, someone who might clear up the confusion.

While this was going on, in the backseat Jacek turned to him. "Fear not, Mr. Packer. Allow me to handle the diplomatic concerns of our wonderful hosts."

Cale rolled his eyes.

Ditt was saying into his phone, "Yes, sir. I understand." He snapped his mobile closed. When he swung his head back around to them, he was smiling. "A change of plans," the sergeant said, displaying some relief. "We are to take you to the residence of Colonel Tazeki Mabutu, instead of the embassy."

"But our meeting was scheduled with the foreign minister," Cale protested. The jeep was already moving, swinging around in a circle on the damp runway, Sergeant Wanto not choosing to waste further time, it appeared.

"This is much better," said Ditt amicably. "The Colonel, he is a powerful leader in our country. Strong juju. Mighty, mighty fist." He held one fist up for them to see. "He says to forget about H1N1. Forget about all your worries."

"What I'd like," Cale said, pressing his point, "is to meet with your foreign minister. Not some military flunky."

"No offense," Jacek amended, shooting Cale a dark look.

Ditt's flash of teeth again. "Colonel Mabutu is the man you want. You shall see this when you meet."

"And why is that?"

"Quite simple. He knows this man you seek—this gentleman of yours—who goes by the name of Kinsella."

It would take them approximately thirty-minutes to reach the residence of Colonel Tazeki Mabutu, they learned. Sergeant Wanto navigated them across the expanse of the airport, onto a maintenance road, then minutes later onto to a mud-caked roadway. A right turn would take them back toward the city of Monrovia. Instead, they took a left, away from the shore. A few twists and turns later, they were heading down the central avenue of a shantytown suburb. The roadway was paved but uneven, sporting numerous crests and potholes. Detroit in the springtime, Cale imagined.

Traffic was sparse in the rain, and Ditt left the driving to his partner. All was silent, but for the steady rhythm of the jeep's slapping wipers.

"Your Colonel Mabutu, said Cale, breaking the quiet. "Did he say where he knows this Kinsella from?"

"No matter where, sir," Ditt said, agreeably. "The Colonel is *machismo*. A *nyani*. A strong-arm figure in this country." He paused. "He commands the elite military unit. It is his job to ensure peace and stability inside all of Liberia."

Cale decided it was the best explanation he'd get. "Your Colonel sounds like someone who can help us," he said, diplomatically, shooting Jacek a glance. His partner opened his palms as if to show he had no concern.

"Yes. Colonel Mabutu will explain to you all things. As soon as we arrive at his compound."

"His compound?" The shift in Jacek's gaze speared the men up front. "This Colonel? He doesn't live in a normal residence? Like everyone else in your country?"

Sergeant Ditt shared a glance at his driver, and the exchange wasn't missed by their passengers. "The Colonel's family became wealthy many years ago," the sergeant explained, as if revealing some clandestine state secret. "Investing in the diamond mines. Because of the wars, they stored all their wealth in Swiss banks. Colonel Mabutu lives in a guarded home. His soldiers are his family now. They protect him with their lives."

"And this compound of his? Not too far away, is it?" Jacek kept his voice steady. "Inland? Shoreline? Where are we headed, to be exact?"

"Not too far outside of Monrovia, my friend. South of the city. Along the shore."

"How far south?"

Ditt half-turned to them in the backseat. "Not far. We will be there in a jiff-jiff."

CHAPTER 25

Green Bay, Wisconsin

It was amazing, Maggie marveled, how a single tiny strip of plastic might grab a chokehold on her future. But there was no getting around the fact.

The morning was lining up to be hectic. First, she had Hank's appointment at the vet for his shots, and her furry companion did not travel well. *What cat does?* After that, she had errands to run, then plans to meet Chloe for lunch to go over the final details on the real estate site for the new detective agency. Perhaps when all the running around was finished, and they opened their doors for business, they might even land a client or two.

As she now drove west, navigating across the Mason Street bridge, the morning traffic was sparse. Hank was making growling sounds from the cat carrier on the passenger floor. Her phone chirped, and guessing it was her sister, Maggie answered, "Hey, girl, what up?" Her best street-hip imitation, done while she turned the volume down on the NPR show she'd been listening to.

"What up?" She recognized Slink Dooley's sarcastic tone. "Please tell me you're not cornrowing your hair these days."

"Not quite," Maggie said, not missing a beat. "But you bringing up the option is giving me instant street-cred."

She could feel Slink's smirk. "Since when is proper street-cred on an attorney's list of ambitions?"

"If I'm going to be a private eye, I'll need whatever cred I can get."

"There's some truth in that."

Maggie guessed if Slink were calling, it meant he possessed the latest inside information on Tobias Crenshaw. Hopefully the judge in the case had come to his senses, decided the kidnapper of six innocent females—and the murderer (alleged) of at least one of them—needed to remain incarcerated. So what if he was cooperating with authorities. He could cooperate to his heart's content from his jail cell.

"How about Cale?" Slink asked. "He fluent in Italian by now?"

"He might know *ciao*," Maggie allowed. "And maybe order spaghetti. That's about it. But it shouldn't matter—he's headed to Liberia today. Meeting with their minister of something or other."

"Glad it's not me, if politicians are involved." Slink hesitated, as if carefully choosing his words. "You're not still mad at him, are you? For going off on this trip?"

"I'm over it. It's just...he's so damn bullheaded sometimes. I still think I could have helped him with things over there..." Her voice trailed off.

"Tell me about it. We've been partners over ten years, so I've seen the bullheaded side." Slink paused for a beat. "Can't blame him, though. He thought you'd slow him down. Worrying about you on foreign soil is stressful.?"

"Sounds familiar."

"He might be dealing with some dangerous hombres over there," Slink's tone put him—no surprise—on Cale's side of the debate. "Going alone was the smart play."

"I get it." Maggie swung her Mazda through a sharp left turn, causing Hank to growl in protest. "I told him I expect his rear end back here by next week."

Slink shifted topics, explaining the reason for his call: Crenshaw's judge had decided to release him, after all. He was being transported to the county courthouse for a processing hearing. After posting bond, he'd be placed on house arrest.

"It's one of the reasons I'm through practicing law." Maggie couldn't disguise the disgust in her voice. She could no longer deal with the inequities of a legal system, where criminals appeared to have more rights than law enforcement. She didn't need to tell it to Slink. She'd be preaching to the choir.

With a promise to keep him updated on Cale's progress, whatever she heard, she ended the call. Maggie stared down at Hank's dour face in the carrier. "Don't worry, pumpkin, we're almost there." She received another growl in response.

Twenty minutes later, after dropping Hank off, then driving to the pharmacy, she was headed back home. Maggie had been ill again that morning. This time she couldn't con herself into thinking it was a flu bug. Although she'd never been pregnant before, never even late with her period, it didn't take a genius to recognize morning sickness for what it was. She'd been in denial for over a week now. It was time to confirm her fears. Time to find out for certain.

One way or the other.

As she navigated back across the city, Maggie was calculating the probabilities in her head. When was the first time she'd felt the nausea? How many weeks had it been? Before her frightening ordeal with the juvenile criminal—Juan-Julio Sanchez—she had been religious about taking her birth control pills. After her sexual assault in the juvenile detention center, however, she'd been in a state of shock, locked in the throes of dark depression. For a week post-Sanchez, she had walked around like a zombie, or a war veteran suffering from PTSD. Maggie had a hard time remembering, during those confusing, trembling, incoherent days, if she'd taken her pills or not.

Then her even more frightening nightmare had transpired—she'd been drugged again and kidnapped by Tobias Crenshaw. Held his prisoner for over four, six, however many hours. Sedated, in a semiconscious stupor for much of the time. It was Crenshaw's modus operandi to sexually assault his victims. Maggie had little doubt he'd done the same to her, before beginning his cat-and-mouse game with the police.

This had all taken place before Cale had located—with Chloe's help, of course—and rescued her. And had eventually led to the Chemist's capture.

She'd paid little heed when she missed her period two weeks ago. Maggie had written it off to the stress of all she'd been through. But it was now four weeks since her assault, and she'd been experiencing morning sickness the past few days. She had made love with Cale a dozen times, she calculated, since recovering from her ordeal. Such being the case, Maggie decided the suspected fatherhood pool was down to two possibles:

Her fiancé, Cale Van Waring. The man she loved.

Or Tobias Crenshaw—kidnapper, rapist, sociopath. Likely even a murderer. Now incarcerated. At least for the next few hours, anyway.

Having worked as a state's public defender for the past ten years, having witnessed firsthand the sad, disappointing, unfair, anything-can-go-wrong side of life, Maggie harbored no illusions that this episode would come out the way she hoped. *No one ever said life was fair.*

She understood, further, from many cases she had handled, that prenatal paternity could not be determined via a CVS test until about ten weeks post-conception. When the time came, she would be forced to make some Hobson's choice. Would Cale, regardless of his being the biological father or not, still support her through her crisis? Who could predict how another person might react? Especially under such life-altering and awkward circumstances? How would she, herself, react if the shoe—hypothetically—were on the other foot?

Maggie wasn't sure. Was it fair to even ask Cale to make such a choice?

She didn't know the answer. The truth was, she didn't know any of the answers. And even if she did, she decided it was not in her best interest to beat herself up with what-ifs.

Climbing the stairs of her house—their house—Maggie made a beeline to the bathroom. She was tearing open the e.p.t packaging, flinging pieces of instructions and cardboard aside as she moved. She pressed the bathroom door closed, even though she was alone in the house. She had learned a lesson the hard way about imagining you're always safe in your own home. Her nightmares, in fact, were still haunted by Tobias Crenshaw lurking in the shadows of her bedroom.

Maggie shook the image from her mind, concentrating instead on the task at hand.

In the mirror above the sink, she stared at her flushed reflection. She watched herself as she held the tiny strip of plastic in her fingertips.

My God, she thought nervously. Did it really all come down to this? A tiny strip of plastic? The sour taste of uncertainty rose in her throat, and she realized she was holding her future in her fingertips.

CHAPTER 26

Liberia, Africa

The military jeep navigated around the outskirts of Monrovia, with Sergeant Ditt acting like their travel guide. He pointed out the vast rubber tree plantations as they swept past in the drizzle. This suburb, those buildings, all as if he were giving them a tour of downtown Paris. Prior to their departure, Cale had checked the five-day weather forecast at the airport. Rainy and eighty-seven degrees. Humidity at 99.8 percent. The forecast read the same for each day. He regretted not bringing along a few more shirts, but their plans had not anticipated an extended stay.

"Interesting city, Monrovia," said Jacek, staring out the window at trash heaps, tarp-covered shacks, decrepit bombed out buildings. Stray dogs and goats. "I read it has a nice seaport."

Ditt turned from his passenger seat. "Correct, my friend. A very large seaport. Huge deal. Big, big ships."

"But we're headed south, you said. We won't see the port. Correct?" Cale had little interest in sightseeing or history lessons. His focus was on capturing his prisoner. He wondered where in this country of swamps and flatlands, mountains and jungles, the man might be hiding. Was Kinsella even aware he was wanted as an international fugitive? What if he happened to be some peace-loving goat farmer tending his herd? Innocent of the crimes he'd been accused of?

"That's correct," Ditt said. "We are heading south of the city."

Cale matched Jacek's stare out the window. It was midmorning, not many people about. Tarpapered shanty homes drenched by rain, wooden planks for sidewalks, sporadic running water and decrepit public outhouses. A half mile later, they saw what looked to be a wayside picnic area, with two large tents and matching trailers bordering them. A pair of mud-spattered jeeps stood blanketed with canvas covers, keeping them somewhat dry. A stenciled sign in English read "United Nations Peacekeeping—Hospital Facility."

"The UN keeps a presence in Liberia," Ditt informed them. "Since the fighting ended in '03. They assist with food and fresh water, inoculations against diseases."

"A humanitarian bunch." Jacek conveyed this with sincerity. "Some of the finest people I've met."

"Too nice for their own good, sometimes." The sergeant shook his head.

"Meaning?"

"Meaning they treat the bad criminals, as well as the poor." Ditt raised his chin for emphasis. "I see no rationale in helping out a person who might later put a bullet in your brain."

"This happens much?" Cale asked.

"Not so much. Not since the revolution ended. Still, it happens."

The enclosed jeep continued to skirt the periphery of Monrovia, its suburbs of shanty-typed dwellings fading in the distance. More thick vegetation, more rubber trees. They were progressing west along a battered and muddy road, until the wide expanse of ocean appeared once again before them on the right. Dull and gray in the distance, as if her foul mood had been brought on by the inclement weather.

Twenty-minutes later, after numerous twists and turns and switchbacks in the road, their driver pulled up before a gated seaside compound of tall whitewashed walls. The jeep entered the blunt driveway and Sergeant Wanto rolled down the window as the guard approached. The guard was garbed full-military, an assault rifle strapped over his shoulder. Black beret. He leaned in and studied both Cale and Jacek in the backseat. Ditt flashed their passports, indicating he'd cleared his guests at customs. The gates swung open a moment later and the guard pulled back and watched them pass through.

Sergeant Wanto aimed the jeep toward the inner main house. It was a magnificent structure, a three-storied central building with matching double-story wings flanking each side. Tall French windows with balconies. A giant pillared front entranceway. It appeared more palatial than a mere residence.

A toothy smile from Ditt: "Colonel Mabutu is a man of great stature. You will no doubt enjoy his presence."

"No doubt." Jacek's voice held a serious pitch. "May we have our passports back? If the Colonel cannot help us in our search, we'll be returning to the airport in short order."

"I'm afraid not, Mr. Tumaj." The sergeant said this with concerned eyes. "You and Mr. Van Waring are on official business in our country. Liberian law says we must hold your passports until you choose to depart." A wan smile. "However, I will have them placed in a security file at the airport. This should expedite things, in the unfortunate case you choose a hasty retreat from our wonderful homeland."

"That's not standard—"

"It's okay, Jacek," Cale interjected. "I doubt we'll need our passports during our visit with Colonel Mabutu."

Jacek relented with a shrug, saying, "You're the boss."

Ditt exited the front of the jeep as both Jacek and Cale opened the rear doors. The rain had let up some, but the sky was slate gray over the ocean, and dark clouds threatened like a gang of bullies. Cale took the opportunity to examine the inner area of the compound. It was a veritable fortress, from the looks of it. There was a trio of interior buildings, and he saw a pair of military guards enter one of them. The second building appeared to be a guest house; the third was possibly a maintenance building, if he had to venture a guess. The twin guard towers at the corners of the front wall were ominous, and he spotted men with sniper rifles stationed in each.

"The Colonel must have some enemies," Cale said casually. "That the reason he lives in Fort Apache, here?"

"You make a joke, eh?" Ditt arched his eyebrows.

"Sort of."

They were approaching the broad front steps of the main entrance, Ditt in the lead. "Colonel Mabutu is a military leader," the sergeant said. "Our land has been riddled with war for so long, that each person seeks whatever defensive position they can afford."

"Looks like he can afford a very safe one." Jacek was examining the tall pillars and solid brick masonry of the structure.

"Some men require more safety than others. But this place," Ditt flicked a dismissive hand, "is mostly for show. The Colonel has other means of protecting himself."

What these "other means" might be, the sergeant chose not to elaborate. Before Ditt could ring the front door chime, the giant oaken double-door swung open. They were met by the stare of a dark eyed servant clad in black slacks and a crimson Nehru jacket.

"These men have an appointment with the Colonel, Kasim," Ditt explained. "They are expected."

Kasim bowed and opened the door wider. Before they entered, however, Jacek turned back toward the sergeant. "Just wanted to thank you, Ditt," he said, extending his open hand, "for a wonderful tour of your fabulous land."

As the officer extended his hand to shake, Jacek pulled the burly man into his chest for a warm embrace. When they separated, the sergeant's face showed surprise. "Oh. Anytime, Mr. Tumaj." Ditt stepped back, his smile skittish, and he nodded to them before bowing. He then skipped down the steps, taking his leave.

"One question," called Jacek, causing the sergeant to turn back, his head shining with moisture. "How do we get back to the airport?"

"Colonel Mabutu will arrange for your return." Ditt opened the door to the jeep. "Good luck with your search. And as we say in Liberia, you have an amazing day."

Kasim was still waiting with the door opened wide behind them. As Jacek turned, he whispered to Cale, "Amazing day, indeed." He rolled his eyes.

They entered the interior of the opulent home with Kasim closing the door behind them. After pausing inside the elevated foyer, gathering their bearings, they followed the servant as he led them into a spacious open front room. It was cool inside, well-lighted, tropically pleasant. The open ceiling stretched at least two floors up, highlighted by a massive, rotating paddle fan, which was constructed of lacquered jungle ferns.

"The Colonel will be with you in a minute," Kasim said, his English accent straight out of Oxford. "May I offer you a refreshment? Coffee? Tea? A brandy?"

They decided on iced tea, and Kasim directed them to a long oxblood leather couch in an area designed for waiting. He slipped away in silence to procure their beverages.

Jacek seated himself while Cale strolled the room, interested in examining the array of African artifacts, which hung from the walls and provided the room's decor. Battle shields and crossed spears and fertility masks. A magnificent rhinoceros head stared down at them, flanked by a pair of snarling tigers. There were paintings of battlefields and framed photographs of African sunsets and of steep, cascading waterfalls.

Jacek set his duffel bag at his feet and withdrew his Iridium SAT phone. He slid the object into the pocket of his pants. He pulled a newspaper from the spread of magazines that covered the granite topped coffee table in front of the couch. "Hey, *USA Today*," he said, waving the multicolored newspaper in the air. "Yesterday's date. Must have a damned good delivery service."

Cale issued Jacek a bemused look. "What was with your new friend there? Ditt? Pretty chummy hug for a guy you've known about twenty minutes."

"Seems like a nice enough gent."

"Still, local custom or something?" Cale continued giving him the eye.

Jacek reached beneath his cargo shirt, extracting something from his waistband. "If you call pilfering our passports back a 'local custom.'" He flashed the items for Cale's benefit. "Like you Americans say, 'No harm, no foul.'"

"How? I was watching you the whole time."

Flipping open the newspaper, Jacek leaned back and crossed his legs at the knee. "Old saying, Mr. Packer: 'The devil's hand is quicker than a bishop's eye.'"

"Shakespeare?"

"Jacek Tumaj."

Kasim reentered the room carrying a circular tray containing a pair of tall glasses and a fat, clear pitcher of auburn tea. "Colonel Mabutu will be with you in a bit," he said, then disappeared as quiet as a spider.

Not more than three minutes had passed when a pair of tall double doors opened, and a man emerged. Their dark-skinned host wore a patterned African shirt over a pair of pleated dress slacks. Short and wiry, his smile appeared genuine as he approached. "My friends, I am Tazeki Mabutu, at your service."

They shook hands. "Come into my study, please," offered the colonel. His guests followed him through the room's eight-foot entrance. Kasim appeared as if from out of nowhere once more, closing the doors behind them.

CHAPTER 27

Colonel Tazeki Mabutu's private study was decorated much like the front room of his home, an opulent display of African artifacts: war headdresses, thatched shields, crossed long spears, *tanbu* drums, a variety of knives. Tall bookshelves were filled with volumes of leather-bound tomes. A collection of ceremonial masks peered out emptily at the room. These were interspersed alongside several photographs of a younger Mabutu in military garb. The pictures showed him shirtless, arms around other soldiers in his unit, brandishing his scoped rifle and grinning from the battlefield like a hyena.

"Our country," stated the colonel, taking one of the spears from the wall, examining it, "is a land carved by war, bathed in bloodshed."

Cale and Jacek stood facing the man, rendering him their attention. "Much like my own, under the thumb of the Communists," Jacek reported. "I am Czech. The Russians kept our people beneath their bootheels, treated us like savages...No offense, Colonel."

Mabutu flashed his too-white teeth. He replaced the spear on the wall. "None taken. I am confident if you search any dictionary under the word 'savage,' Mr. Tumaj, you will find the face of a Liberian."

Casting his gaze across the walls, viewing the room's decor as if he were in a museum, Cale told himself: *This is some spooky African shit.*

The colonel's dark-eyed stare encompassed the room. He turned his head back, issuing them both a flat look. "What some visitors might think of as spooky African artifacts...well, I like to think of as our cultural history."

Cale's eyes narrowed, and he told himself: *No way! Did this guy just read my mind?*

The colonel failed to glance in his direction. Instead, he turned crisply and began striding toward his oversized desk.

"But, gentlemen, let us get to the point of your visit." The wiry military man spread one arm, indicating a pair of chairs positioned in front of the desk. They were tight-armed wooden chairs, set close together on a patterned, hand hewn rug. Jacek and Cale sat on the designated chairs, as propriety dictated.

"I take it you've been briefed, Colonel," said Cale, getting down to business. "Regarding our purpose? The reason we're here today?"

Seating himself behind the mahogany monstrosity of a desk, rolling his chair so he was not blocked by the screen of his computer, Colonel Mabutu clasped his hands in front of his lips. "You are in search of a countryman of ours. Correct? A presumed outlaw? Who goes by the name of Kinsella?"

Cale felt his hopes surge. This man was a ranking military officer. He would not play the time-consuming diplomatic games most foreign affairs ministers were known for. Recognizing him as a fellow law enforcement agent, Cale prayed the colonel might expedite things.

"That's correct," Cale said, encouragingly. "Do you have any information on this man's whereabouts?"

The colonel pondered the question. When he stared back at Cale, his dark eyes brightened. "You are in luck today, Detective. I know of whom you speak. In fact, I knew him many years ago, back when he was known only as Nmanu."

Cale leaned forward. Time was at a premium, and he trusted the colonel recognized how far he had traveled, sensed his urgency.

"Allow me to tell you a story," said Colonel Mabutu, his voice modulated, deliberate.

Cale felt his teeth grind but decided he would listen to what the man had to say. After all, were they not guests in his home? Or compound? Or whatever the hell he chose to call it? Glancing at Jacek, he noted his partner's serenity, as if the man hadn't a care in the world. Cale decided to take his cue from Jacek, force himself to relax.

"Are you familiar with the term *'botono,'* Detective?" The colonel glanced at them both, as if rendering the visitors an equal opportunity at the answer.

Cale caught himself staring at a few objects on the colonel's desktop. He noticed an animal paperweight: a fierce-looking, upright, red-and-white little badger. Bucky Badger? It seemed implausible the colonel should have in his possession a Wisconsin mascot, in this faraway land. The man must have a fondness for animals of many different shapes and sizes. Besides, it was evident from his walls he enjoyed collecting things. He had most likely been given the item as a gift, Cale reasoned. Or purchased the statuette in his travels. He shifted his focus back to the present and considered his guest's odd question.

"Some sort of animal?" Cale answered. "A monkey, maybe?"

Tazeki Mabutu smiled. "A *botono*, in our language, is a shaman. A holy man or healer who practices the people's religion of Africa. Vodun."

"Voodoo," Jacek said, for Cale's benefit. "And by 'botono' he means a witch doctor."

Cale tried to swallow his scoffing sound. "I have to tell you, Colonel—"

"I know what you're thinking: pins in dolls, hexes, spells and trances, pounding jungle drums." The colonel's smile was self-effacing. "After all, who believes in *spooky* African shit?"

Cale decided—once again—not to take the bait. Instead, he asked, "And all this has what to do with Kinsella? Are you telling us he's some sort of voodoo priest? Something along those lines?"

The comment deepened the color of the colonel's face. "Far from it. Kinsella was a member of the revolutionary force, years ago," he said. "A man who fought with the army of Charles Taylor. When he learned the truth—the *real truth*—learned of the lies, he fought *against* Taylor and his band of evil jackals."

Jacek had been thoughtfully absorbing the exchange. "What you're saying, Colonel, is your friend Kinsella is someone not afraid to recognize change? And to adapt?"

"I suppose one could argue for this."

Cale decided he'd had enough of the word games. They had to cut to the chase. "I don't mean to be rude, sir, but do you happen to know where this man is? Right now, I mean?"

Jacek rose from his chair and strode in easy fashion over to the far wall, began to study the decorative artifacts hanging there. "Pardon me," Jacek said, turning back, "but we've been on a plane for six hours. Then your officer's bouncing jeep. I need to stretch my legs."

Watching his partner, Cale noted how the glare from the bank of broad windows had turned a heavier shade of metallic. Raining again outside, a steady thrumming. In the distance, the waves crested with force, before rushing to the shore and flinging themselves like scorned lovers against the sharp, rocky barrier.

Colonel Mabutu watched across the room as Jacek set down his duffle-bag. He took down an African lance, which was adorned with colorful osprey feathers. Upon examining the object, he returned it to its rightful place on the wall.

To Cale, the colonel said, "I understand this is difficult for you, Detective. So many miles from your home."

"If you don't know where this man, this Kinsella is, isn't this something your foreign minister should have informed me over the phone?" Cale's words dripped with frustration.

The colonel, however, ignored him. His eyes instead were lasered on what Jacek was up to, watching hawk-like as the man moved to the fireplace. Jacek grabbed a female shrunken head from the mantel, began examining it close, in detail.

Colonel Mabutu called out: "Something catch your eye, Mr. Tumaj?"

"An interesting head. It doesn't appear as weathered as many others I've seen. Is she authentic?"

"You ever heard of a man named Prince Mir Al-Sadar?" interrupted Cale. "He's involved in purchasing human sex slaves. Keeps a private harem of females." He was attempting to rope the colonel back to the conversation. "A member of the Emer Saud royal family, I believe?"

The colonel ignored Cale's words, speaking instead in a clipped tone to Jacek. "Rest assured, she's the real thing. I believe she is—or was (a soft chuckle)—a missionary." He paused. "The price one pays for trying to convert the heathens, one supposes. I found her in a small village in Gambia."

Jacek replaced the object back on the mantle. "Every head tells a story. So, the saying goes."

"A pity she cannot reveal her own."

Cale glanced at his watch. Nearing 11 a.m. local time. He studied the colonel for a few long beats and decided he could detect something—a serpentine quality, if he had to describe it—lying just behind the man's hooded eyes.

"Prince Al-Sadar, did you say?" Colonel Mabutu turned, giving Cale his full attention. "I might have heard the name once or twice."

He reached near his computer and grabbed the pewter-colored ceramic idol. It appeared weathered, scuffed about the edges, ancient-looking. He held it in his hands, examining it, saying, "I regret that I'm unable to provide much assistance, Detective."

Cale watched as the man studied the fifteen-inch statue, as if he might be seeing it for the first time. It possessed an enigmatic expression, as if matching that of their host. Cale felt a shiver work up his spine. "You rub his belly for good luck?" he asked, cynical, knowing the comment expressed little humor.

Colonel Mabutu set the statue back atop his desk. "His name is Pazuzu. Sumerian king of wind demons.

And no, I have little need to rub him—as you insultingly put it."

"So, what about this Prince Al-Sadar?" Cale pressed. "We've seen photographs of him and Kinsella together. Are they partners? In some slavery or human trafficking arrangement?"

The colonel showed amusement at the question.

Jacek began moving across the room, headed back to where Cale sat in the chair.

Cale could sense a discernable dip in the room's temperature, and turning toward Jacek, he spotted a sudden look of concern on his partner's face.

"Detective," Colonel Mabutu said, his frown blossoming into a near demonic expression. "You are asking questions I have no intention of answering. On top of that, your uninformed accusations will soon be the least of your problems."

Cale turned back to the voice, watching as the colonel leaned forward. The man was reaching beneath his desk.

"Sorry you feel that way," he told the colonel stiffly. "That last part almost sounded like a threat—"

"Cale!" Behind him, Jacek shouted: "Get out of that chair! *Now!*"

CHAPTER 28

The warning came too late.

Before he could move a muscle, the floor gave way beneath him and Cale found himself falling into empty space. The chair he'd been sitting in was traveling below him, along with the fancy embroidered rug. Jacek's empty chair was tumbling a fraction behind, above him, and together they had all dropped through the sudden gaping hole in the room's floor.

Stretching his arms out, Cale sought purchase on the walls as he descended. He smashed an elbow, then a shin against the sharp stone. The walls were cool and slimy, and the smell of briny seawater rose up to greet him. Dropping, he heard Jacek's warning shout echo from above as he plummeted down the gaping tunnel. It was cut off abruptly, as above him the trapdoor snapped closed. Cale found himself engulfed in utter blackness.

Falling, falling, falling...through humid, briny salt-tasting darkness. Dropping through the tarry air, the sound and crash of the sea nearby came rushing up at him. There was water below, Cale could sense. The ocean? A pool of some sort? How deep could it be?

As he plunged, he could feel the arms of the chair he'd been sitting in and thought for an instant he might employ it to cushion his fall when he crashed through the wet surface below. No matter how deep it was, Cale's brain reminded him, water was better than rocks. One of the chair legs, however, brushed against the jutting stone wall of the cavern, and now the chair was alongside him, like a companion, both of them free-falling together through black-shadowed space.

Cale tucked his legs up beneath him as best he could, wrapping his forearms around his head.

An instant later, he cannonballed into the water with a crash. Submerged, he realized he had not gone down too deep. The falling rug—thank God—had landed below him first and dissipated the water's surface. Cale nevertheless floundered, searching to locate his bearings in the inky water. The second chair had landed somewhere with a crash, and he realized his good fortune that it hadn't bludgeoned him from above, crushing his skull.

Cale lifted his head above the surface, gulping for air. He spun around, dogpaddling, trying to see anything at all in the cave or grotto, or whatever the hell this was. He was treading water and hadn't felt anything close to bottom, so he was clueless as to how deep the pool—if that's indeed what it was—might be.

No point in shouting for help, he decided. Only two people knew he was down here: the man who had purposely sent him here; and the second, Jacek, who would be doing his best to avoid a similar fate.

Please, God. Cale offered up a silent prayer. Let him still be alive.

Searching inside his pants pocket, he fished out the penlight Jacek had given him. Alive or not, his new friend might still prove a lifesaver. Cale flicked on the small beam and at once the dark rocks and water were illuminated. He'd been right. It was a cave; or a deep high-ceilinged cavern. And now he could determine its dimensions.

Cale felt something brush against his leg below the water's surface. Seaweed? The leg of the floating chair? He concentrated, instead, on his light beacon. Whether the cave was man-made or a natural formation, he couldn't determine. The forty-foot-high walls were slippery, sharp, black rock, covered with condensation. It would take an expert climber to attempt their ascent; and to do so would require ropes and pitons, a harness and a sturdy hammer.

Cale had none of these.

The pool, if he had to guess, was about forty meters in width, oval-shaped, and filled with briny seawater. It refilled with the tides. He was trapped, it seemed, in an underground, rock-lined grotto.

Just wonderful. Cale's adrenaline-infused mind was summoning one horrific thought after the next: *My own Davy Jones' locker.*

Flashing the penlight around again, examining the rocks where they met the tepid water line, Cale noticed a shadow dart at the penumbra of his light. Once again something brushed between his kicking legs. Perhaps it wasn't seaweed, after all. Focusing the light more intently, he studied the pool of water he was floating in. A dark form swam past. Then another, and a third, fourth and fifth. Were they large fish? He couldn't quite tell.

Something cool and slimy grazed his forearm.

Remembering his blind descent down the upper opening, Cale now felt a dull throbbing pain in his elbow; and a similar pain in his leg, where he'd been slammed against the rocky sidewall. While nothing felt broken or dislocated, he guessed the injuries might be bleeding below the surface. Attracting whatever sea creatures happened to be swimming in the pool here with him.

Cale spun around in the water, kicking, keeping his head afloat. His light spied one slimy fish as it slid toward his chest in the blackness: *Christ!* he thought. It was prehistoric, and it was not a fish—*It's a fucking eel! My God! I'm in a whole nasty pool of them!*

The toothy creature veered away at the last second. Cale trained the penlight beam on the edges of the pool. He spied the second chair, which had fallen through the tunnel behind him. One leg had smashed against the rocks, lodging itself tight. The water was lapping up to the chair's exposed seat, and Cale could tell it was not floating, but rather wedged in a crevice against the rocks.

He began paddling fiercely toward the chair, feeling the slimy creatures part before him in the ripples as he moved. He was at the pool's edge when he felt a nip at his left calf. "Son of a bitch!" he cursed, aroused by the pain of razor teeth piercing the cloth of his pants leg.

Placing the penlight between his teeth, Cale reached for a lower rung of the chair. It didn't come loose. The entire chair didn't budge. It was stuck tight—he hoped—trapped by the rocks. A second bite nipped against his shin and he yanked his leg upward. He felt another eel slide against his hip, then another against his thigh.

He had to get out of the water.

Grasping the solid back of the chair, Cale tested his weight. He had no other options. Time to go for broke. He lifted himself from the water, raising upward, balancing one knee precariously on the chair's seat. His arms felt like rubber, shaking as adrenaline coursed through his body. He pulled his other leg up, the injured one, and in the arc of light caught sight of sharp teeth as an eel tugged at the leg of his pants. Cale levered himself upward, half-standing on the chair's angled seat. His right hand held the wooden back. He slammed his left fist down on the eel, again and again, until he witnessed the slimy creature release and slide back into the water without a splash.

What Cale saw next all but stopped his heart. The eels were a teeming swarm in the water mere feet away. Dozens of them. A hundred. They slipped over one another like a brigade of greasy night crawlers, or maggots grappling over a clump of dead meat.

My God, he thought, *I was almost their dinner.*

Careful of his footing, he placed one sodden shoe on a six-inch wedge of nearby rock. Not much purchase, but it served to take some weight off the chair's precarious position. With his left hand, Cale felt along the damp wall until he could lodge his fingertips into a crack in the granite. He shone the penlight up to the ceiling. A good thirty feet to the top.

He swept the beam back to study the black pool once more, where the eels had settled, cruising shadows beneath the dark surface, waiting, as if in some ritual of anticipation.

Cale thought gloomily, *Now what?*

***

Watching stunned as his friend was swallowed by the sudden hole in the room's floor, Jacek could hear his shout of warning still echoing off the walls. Now he viewed—awestricken himself—the open trapdoor as it snapped back into place. The polished wooden surface of the floor, where minutes ago they'd sat side by side, appeared seamless.

Despite his impulse to rip apart the floorboards and descend after his partner, Jacek had the presence of mind to keep moving. His cat-quick reflexes brought him alongside the large work desk, staring into the icy eyes of their tormenter. When he saw Colonel Mabutu sitting in his highbacked swivel chair, pointing the barrel of a German Luger straight toward his chest, Jacek froze in place. He was a mere five yards from the round black eye of the pistol.

"What the hell's going on?" Jacek growled. "What did you do to my friend?"

The colonel was not grinning. The weapon's thin barrel didn't waver. "You're entitled to your questions, Mr. Tumaj. But I'm afraid that's the last one I'll hear."

Before Jacek could respond, he felt the cool wire slip over his forehead and down across his neck. His impulse was to slam his elbow backward into whoever's ribs he might find, but years of training reminded him it was better to reach up and slide his fingertips between the taught wire and tender flesh of his throat.

Too late for either move.

The man controlling the wire was an expert—had somehow slipped behind him, silent as a cobra. This realization gripped his heart with icy fingers. Jacek became aware that if he moved more than a few centimeters, in any direction, the sharp piano wire would slice through his windpipe cartilage and carotids.

He heard the wooden handles clack and felt the wire tighten even further.

The colonel, without lowering his gun, said, "Kasim is well-trained with just how taught to play his instrument. Now, Mr. Tumaj. Slow as you can manage—for you understand the consequences—please drop to your knees. One at a time. I will tell you what your future holds."

Employing the utmost caution, Jacek bent his right knee and lowered himself. His hands were at his neck, though he could manage not even a fingertip inside the wire. His eyes were wide to the point of bursting. Until...he inched down to the ground with his second knee.

Behind him, cool and expressionless (he guessed), Kasim held the garrote's handles in place. His hands were expertly crossed, could administer the ultimate twist of pressure in an instant, if required.

Colonel Mabutu first then lowered his gun and set it on his desktop. He faced the pewter statue standing two feet away. "What's that you say, Pazuzu?" His chuckle was dark and macabre. "Who can truly say?" He paused, the air thick, the rain spattering against the banked windows. "Of course. I'm quite aware how much the mess will stain the antique floors."

The man was certifiable, Jacek decided. Talking to spirit ghosts. Surrounded by maniacal killers in a sadistic, dysfunctional land...on a continent comprised of tribal warlords and blood-thirsty animals. Somehow, it failed to surprise him.

Turning to Jacek, the colonel said, "Pazuzu suggests you offer any prayers you might have learned in Sunday school."

Jacek, his face flushed like a bruise, managed to gasp: "Tell your ugly friend...that I have an old Czech saying for him—"

"Oh? How quaint."

"Fuck you all..." he rasped, "and the donkeys you rode in on!"

Colonel Mabutu's lips twisted in a scalding grin. Jacek noted how much he resembled the laughing hyena depicted in his wall photograph.

"That's what I enjoy," the colonel admitted, "an eloquent goodbye speech." He nodded to Kasim. "Feed his putrid body to the jungle dogs. With all this rain, they deserve a nice warm meal."

PART TWO

SEASON OF THE WITCH

CHAPTER 29

Green Bay, Wisconsin

Maggie stared at the plastic e.p.t readout. *Positive*. Just as she guessed it would be. She tossed it into the wastebasket. Out of sight, out of mind. If life were only that simple.

She moved from the bathroom, breezing through the bedroom. Downstairs in the closet, from the upper shelf, she removed the box containing the leather holster and the Kahr PM9 that she'd received from Slink Dooley two days earlier. She withdrew the holster and weapon and set them on the kitchen counter, along with the full box of ammunition.

A hundred different options ran through her mind. Whatever it took to lose yourself, to deal with your problems. Problems like a positive pregnancy test. Problems like not knowing who the father of your growing fetus might be.

She slipped the holstered weapon and ammo box into her purse. Leaving the house, phone in one pocket, Maggie moved across the apron of the driveway. Sliding onto the warm seat of her Mazda, she performed a Y-turn and eased down the driveway. She flicked the AC on and proceeded to check her phone for messages. It was too early for Cale to have called. With his nighttime flight and meeting with the Liberian authorities, she wasn't surprised. And anytime politicians were involved—she knew from experience—your chances of expediency became exponentially diminished.

On the brighter side, perhaps he already had his suspect in hand? Was already interrogating the "real killer"? As fingered by none other than—*gag!*—Tobias Crenshaw, himself.

The father of your baby, her mind chided, twisting the knife.

Cale would call when he could manage it, she decided. Punching her phone's speed dial, she reached Chloe at the beauty shop. "Hey," she said, forcing a smile, "you got time to do me a favor?"

"My day's as open as the Great Plains," Chloe said, joking. "So, anything involving male underwear models, kinky sex or alcohol, is fair game."

"How about a pissed-off cat with an attitude?"

"Ouch. Not what I had in mind."

Maggie explained how she was running late, how her precious pet would be finished at the veterinarian's sometime after eleven. They knew enough to give him sedatives. Hank's reputation and ornerier-than-thou attitude preceded him.

"Pretty please," Maggie cajoled. "I'll even buy you dessert for lunch."

Chloe relented, as they both knew she would. Before doing so, however, she made Maggie promise to join her in touring a vacant old house—another one!—which her sister had her eye on. That is if they were still serious about starting their own detective agency.

"I thought we already had a location?"

"I was going to tell you. It fell through."

With her schedule cleared, Maggie navigated the Mazda through the morning traffic. She was headed across the bridge spanning the Fox River, the broad flat waterway that split the city in half. She was headed toward the far west suburbs. An industrial park that held a brick and gravel company, a construction business, a heavy equipment dealership.

Further up the road lay her destination: Paulsen Brothers Gun and Ammo Shop. It was a family owned business, which she had learned sold hunting equipment, along with all types of other weaponry. They also had three private target ranges. The one in the basement was designed for pistol shooters.

Maggie had decided to forego the police shooting range. She'd visited it as Slink Dooley's guest two days ago and didn't want to burden him with being responsible for another visit. This range was open to the public and Slink would not have to accompany her or sign in for her to use it.

Pulling into the asphalt parking lot, Maggie checked her purse, making certain she'd remembered to bring the box of ammo. The pregnancy test reading had left her both scatterbrained and a bit frazzled. Her gun was there, cool and shiny. Along with the ammo. She loved how the PM9 fit snug inside her purse. It was the perfect weapon, as far as she was concerned, and she intended to register it in her own name as soon as she had the chance.

Just as Maggie was reaching for the Mazda's door handle, her phone rang. She checked the readout, hoping it wasn't the vet with complications.

Slink skipped his usual joviality and got straight to the point. "Like we thought, it's a done deal." Maggie knew at once what he was talking about and let him continue. "They'll fit him for an ankle bracelet, round-the-clock surveillance, the whole nine yards. But in about an hour from now, he'll be walking the streets a free man."

"What about the press? It's going to be a circus when a murderer comes whistling out the front doors of the courthouse."

"Word has already hit the streets," Slink said, frustrated. "In fact, I'm headed over there right now. Captain wants as much security as we can muster—just in case."

Maggie realized she'd been holding her breath. The city's most notorious serial criminal was on the verge of freedom. What kind of country were they living in, if they let an animal like Tobias Crenshaw waltz free from jail?

"You sure you're all right?"

"Nothing we can do about it, so I'll have to be." She let her breath out slowly. "I'll let Cale know when I speak to him later."

Slink rang off with a promise to call her if anything changed. Any last-minute appeal, for instance, which could keep the Chemist in lockup.

"Fat chance," Maggie said aloud to herself, as she slipped from her car. She walked toward the front entrance of the Gun and Ammo shop. She couldn't wait to begin blasting away at her target, even if it was mere cardboard.

It was Tobias Crenshaw's face she'd be picturing each time her finger squeezed the trigger.

***

Blam.

The sound, muted by blockers, reached her as if from far away. Maggie steadied her outstretched hands, just as Slink had taught her. She locked both elbows, head turned a fraction, fixed one eye on the front sight, exhaled, squeezed. *Blam-blam-blam-blam.*

In the dim and dingy distance of the firing range, the dark silhouette of the man swayed with an infinitesimal jerk. Why, she wondered, did things always have to be such a soap opera with her and Cale? If she were inside a church, and not in a basement firing range, she would lift her eyes to the heavens.

She wondered why things couldn't ever be simple between them?

Blam. Blam.

Maggie ejected the seven-round clip and inserted a fresh one: a six-rounder.

For the past three months, her relationship with Cale had been growing tense. An undercurrent of indecision seemed to color their every emotion. Each little comment and joke they said, every time they went somewhere—each kiss and cuddle. It had gotten to the point where she understood that she had to decide: was he either in it for the long haul? Or wasn't he? Maggie was thirty-three years old, now. She needed a commitment. Did they want to settle down together? Get married? Start a family? If so, then Cale had some decisions to make.

Making matters worse, Cale had been stressed to his limits by his work: the past six months of trying to hunt down and capture a serial kidnapper. Followed by the continued attempt to locate a pair of victims who remained missing.

The Chemist was behind bars now—for how long, it remained to be seen—and she and Cale were making wedding plans. But as of this morning, well, it was all threatening to blow up in Maggie's face. Cale was off in God-Knows-Where, Africa. And now, they were learning that Tobias Crenshaw was being released from jail.

Further, did she mention she was pregnant?

Blam. Blam. Blam.

Cale's reaction to this news would be anyone's guess. Even in a normal situation, it would be stressful, Maggie allowed. But this whole thing seemed anything but normal. Quite the opposite—if you added to the mix that the biological father may be a murderer, as well as a rapist.

How could she blame Cale—Maggie wondered this, in all honesty—if he wasn't being supportive of her pregnancy? Especially considering the circumstances? Despite her desire to begin a family, if she were honest with herself, she'd admit to having great trepidation, as well. As the situation now stood.

Why couldn't things ever be simple?

Blam. Blam. Blam.

Maggie set down her pistol and removed the sound blockers. She pushed the button that caused the silhouette to jerk and begin sliding toward her on its motorized rotors. When the target reached her, she examined the tiny black points where her bullets had struck. Not perfect (it was only her second day of practice, after all), but not bad either. A grouping of five shots total, right in the target's neck. Not the standard kill area, as law enforcement agents were taught. But deadly, nonetheless.

Satisfied, she turned and studied the remainder of the target area basement. The range had ten shooting lanes, and nine of them stood empty.

Alone in the silence, Maggie could feel the tight grip of unease building. It was coming—she knew—from a place deep inside her chest, an emotional and visceral location.

A place called her heart.

***

Driving her Mazda through the noontime city, Maggie reached for the phone inside her purse, which sat on the passenger seat. She pressed Chloe's number. She wanted to check and see how her little pumpkin was doing.

"He's fine," Chloe said. "Slept all the way home in the car."

"So, all your worries were for naught," Maggie said lightly. "You didn't lose a hand or an ear."

"It's you I'm worried about. I'm getting some very intense vibes." Before Maggie could respond, her sister launched into a staccato of: "Did you hear they're releasing Crenshaw? The sick bastard! What are they thinking? Are they insane? It's all over the radio and social media."

Maggie groaned. "Slink already told me."

"They've scheduled some press conference at the courthouse. I've got the TV on right now. Nothing yet. Everyone's milling around there like a herd of cattle."

"I'll call Slink and find out what's going on. Lock up the house when you're through. Please."

"Will do. By the way, have you heard from Cale? I forgot to tell you earlier, I had this weird dream last night. Something long and slimy was after you."

Just great, Maggie thought. As if she didn't have enough problems, without long and slimy things chasing her?

"Nothing today. But I'll let you know when I talk to him."

Agreeing to meet for lunch at one p.m., Maggie hung up her phone. Making a left turn, she accelerated the Mazda into the lane now heading toward the bridge. She pressed the button for Slink's number. He answered on the second ring.

"I'm at the circus right now," Slink reported. "Outside the friggin' courthouse. Reporters all around. Like they're releasing Charles Manson or something." When she didn't comment, he added, "Maggie, if you were thinking about it, *Do not come down here!*"

"No worries. I'm meeting Chloe for lunch."

Promising Slink they'd talk later, she ended the call. Maggie had no intention of going anywhere near the courthouse. She'd spent too many years inside the building as it was, enough to know she didn't relish being around the stodgy old place again anytime soon. Her time as a public defender was history, the past. A memory in the rearview mirror.

With Slink's stay-away warning fresh in her ears, the Kahr PM9 warm in its holster, safe inside her purse, Maggie watched with wonder as her car—with a stubborn mind of its own—nudged itself over into the right-hand exit lane.

The thought struck her like a bolt, hitting home on some subconscious, limbic level: Did she desire one final glimpse at the father of her baby? Was she that sad and desperate? Her rational brain shouted back: *No way! Hell, no!*

With neither a wish nor conscious effort on her part, Maggie watched the Mazda glide down the exit ramp. It was the street that would take her to the one place she had little desire of visiting right now:

The downtown courthouse.

CHAPTER 30

The area around the East Side entrance of the Brown County Courthouse had been cleared of regular traffic. A trio of sheriff's deputies stood watch over the gathered media members, who formed a loose semicircle at the base of the broad steps. Cameras and mobile phones, digital recorders, boom mics and plain old-fashioned notepads—these were part of the electronic arsenal that awaited the arrival of Tobias Crenshaw and his attorney.

At the periphery of the crowd, Detective Slink Dooley gazed in awe at what was transpiring around him. The event was snowballing into much more than the brief, two-minute statement that Tobias Crenshaw's attorney had requested.

Slink noted the arrival of a group of familiar faces. They were men and women, wives and mothers, teens and students, all of whom comprised the stone-faced members and supporters of MOMD: the Mothers of Missing Daughters victims' group. They were escorted to a position stage left of the courthouse steps. There they would await the chance to glare icily at the man who had caused their families more sorrow than they could ever have imagined.

Slink noticed Cynthia Hulbreth standing amid the group of thirty protesters. Jeans, hoodie and sunglasses. *Poor Cindy*, he caught himself thinking. She had been through hell, held captive for weeks, tortured at the hands of her kidnapper, Tobias Crenshaw.

He wondered why they were even having this bogus sideshow. Similar PR events seemed to draw the crazies from the woodwork, much the way restaurant dumpsters attracted vagrants. Why couldn't Crenshaw have just slipped out the back door like the coward he was?

The street in front of the courthouse had been sealed off by city patrol cruisers, which sat positioned at the intersections, lights flickering. The officers were outside their vehicles directing traffic away from the scene. One block in the other direction, cars and SUVs of all makes were pulling into a church parking lot. College students, curious onlookers, gawkers and gapers, individuals who simply enjoyed a crowd—they had parked and were advancing on foot in a steady stream. What were they hoping to see? Some sort of confession from the man? Or something even grislier? Some Jack Ruby moment?

The arrest of the Chemist, along with his employing a fentanyl drug mix in his abductions, was an emotional hot button for the community. And you couldn't rule anything out these days, Slink understood. Not with human nature being what it was; and not when public anger had remained bottled up over a year. Since the manhunt for the unknown serial kidnapper had begun.

The sky above had turned overcast, a haze of sun trying to peek through the low-hanging cumulus. Slink's phone buzzed. The readout said "Maggie Jeffers." "Please tell me you've got a flat tire," he pleaded. "I'll do anything to get out of here."

"Just pulled into the church lot. Did I miss anything?"

"What about 'stay away; did you not understand?" Annoyance colored Slink's tone. Most times he wouldn't care, but he promised Cale he'd look out for his fiancé.

"I was driving. Couldn't resist. Sorry."

Slink watched people drifting in from different directions, moving with haste to get to the event in time. The department ought to be selling tickets. They'd pay for a dozen new radar units. "I'm south. Over by the Channel 11 news van," he said into his phone. "Left of the main steps, as you approach."

After hanging up, Slink cursed beneath his breath. He wandered a few steps forward, scanning the crowd. On the main stage—the courthouse steps—he watched as a sheriff's deputy emerged, followed right behind by a man in an expensive dark business suit. Behind them came Tobias Crenshaw, a sympathy cane in one hand, limping along like the deputy from *Gunsmoke*.

"What a load of crap," Slink muttered out loud.

***

Kinsella stayed hidden behind the bulk of his high-end BET video camera. He had on a company windbreaker and a baseball cap pulled low. A faux newscaster stood beside him—one of his Chicago men—to complete the ruse. He doubted Tobias Crenshaw would notice his presence. Why would he? There was no reason for Crenshaw or anyone else, for that matter, to suspect he was even in the States at the moment.

The camera's viewfinder functioned as the sight. The housing held the body of the weapon and trigger mechanism. The nine-inch microphone extension, complete with foam cover overlaying the sound suppressor, housed the weapon's barrel. Accurate to eighty yards. Soundless and unencumbered, with the element of complete surprise, Kinsella guessed he could fire a half-dozen 9mm rounds before anyone realized what was happening. For this job, it wouldn't take anywhere near that many.

On this day, beneath the hazy, clouded skies above the courthouse, he would need but one shot. Two at the most.

So it stood now with Kinsella aiming the camera's viewfinder at the attorney, where the man stood speaking on the courthouse steps, reminding him of some yappy upright poodle. The mouthpiece was not the target, however, and Kinsella shifted the camera ever-so-slight...until the chest of Tobias Crenshaw came into clear focus. He raised the viewfinder and zoomed the crosshairs upwards, onto the center of the man's forehead.

With the lawyer blabbing away, he exhaled slow air from his lungs. He understood the sound emitted from his camouflaged weapon would sound as innocuous as clearing one's throat. He released his breath and pulled the trigger.

At the same instant that the man toppled backwards, out of the viewfinder's sight, a pair of popping noises had sounded. The echoes caused many of the occupants on the courthouse steps to turn their heads or jump in startled surprise.

Kinsella recognized the *pop, pop, pop* of gunshots when he heard them. He peeked his head from behind the camera to survey what had occurred, the direction the trio of shots had been fired from. They came from off the right wing of the courthouse lawn, it appeared, judging from the crowd's initial reaction. But before he could determine anything further, all hell broke loose.

***

Maggie never managed to reach Slink Dooley. As she'd been working her way through the crowd, she had spotted Cynthia Hulbreth—one of Tobias Crenshaw's victims—and witnessed the young woman's outstretched hand pointing at the courthouse steps, fifteen yards from where the attorney was speaking. Then the gunshots had sounded. The crowd had around her erupted in chaos, screaming, shouting, running panicked from the area.

Maggie had observed, terrified, as officers and a few citizens wrestled Cynthia Hulbreth to the courthouse lawn. She watched as they pried the handgun from her grip. When an officer asked if anyone witnessed what had occurred, Maggie was quick to volunteer. The officers took her name, then insisted that she best accompany them to the station to provide a written statement.

Five minutes later, she found herself in the downtown Adams Street station, sitting at a gray-haired sergeant's desk. Around them uniforms were moving with purpose, the entire station abuzz over the tragedy that had just occurred. The entire department was on alert, in crisis mode. The sergeant was asking Maggie something, requesting she hand him her driver's license for ID purposes…and his voice snapped her from her fugue state. As she reached inside her purse for her wallet, her heart leaped into her throat. In the tumult that had taken place, Maggie had forgotten about the Kahr PM9, which was sitting there like a live rattlesnake, atop her day planner.

How could she be so stupid?

She looked across the desk at the sergeant, whose sharp-eyed stare was now sizing her up. Attempting to smile away the misunderstanding, Maggie felt one of her eyes twitch, and her face felt numb. The man likewise tensed, his own neck tendons growing taught against the fleshy skin.

"It's not what you think, Officer," Maggie protested. "I can explain."

"Stay right where you are, ma'am," the sergeant said, now rigid in his chair. "Very slow, very slow... Could you please set your purse down on the floor?"

She did as he asked.

"Now back your chair away from your purse."

Maggie was about to protest again, but from behind her came the voice of a second officer. "Problem, Sarge?"

The older sergeant kept the calm in his voice. "Officer Splawski, would you mind taking a look inside this lady's purse?"

Maggie watched in disbelief as the younger officer's fingers withdrew the Kahr PM9 from her handbag, holding handle-end with two fingers, as if it were a turd. He sniffed the weapon's barrel and his eyes grew wide. "It's been fired."

Maggie cast her gaze between the two men. Two little words popped into her mind, fired as if from a cannon deep in her chest: *Utterly Hopeless*.

***

The chaos was over. Minutes ago, people had been running, screaming, ducking, tripping over one another in effort to flee the area. Slink had earlier used the metaphor, jokingly, of a circus. He recognized now how right he'd been. Only it was a circus of panic and confusion. As if a large, toothy animal had somehow broken loose inside the big top.

Circus Bizarro World.

Glancing around now, the scene reminded Slink of some ground zero scenario. Minutes after a bomb blast. Even the sound of trailing sirens in the background supported this sensation. The ambulance had come and gone, carting the gunshot victim—Tobias Crenshaw—away. Still alive, the EMTs had informed Slink, but clinging to life by a thread. Shot in the head. Brain dead was the most probable prediction.

Slink was stooped on the sidewalk now, conversing with one of the crime scene techs, as they were already beginning to arrive. Officers had completed cordoning off the area with yellow crime scene tape. Slink's phone sounded, and he glanced at the readout. He excused himself, stepping away beneath an elm tree near the curb.

When the shots were fired, and the media event had dissolved into something resembling a fire in a Chinese theater, Slink had wondered, briefly, where Maggie was. But since the first time they had met, he had understood one thing about the woman who had become his best friend's fiancé: Maggie Jeffers possessed a strong survival instinct. She would have sought cover at the sound of gunfire. She was no doubt already home by now, safe and sound. Out of harm's way.

Into his phone, Slink said: "Hey! Where are you? Are you all right?"

"You're not going to believe this. I'm down at the station."

"Our station? You're kidding me—what the hell for?" When silence greeted him, Slink felt the chill of disbelief closing in on him. "Maggie?"

"They think I shot Tobias Crenshaw."

CHAPTER 31

Liberia, Africa

Though his fingers sought purchase, still Jacek could not manage to insert a single digit inside the piano wire biting into the flesh of his neck. Kasim was a professional and understood the amount of tension necessary to apply to the garrote. Enough to trap his prisoner, keep him hanging on the precipice of death.

"Best to move with caution, Mr. Tumaj," Colonel Mabutu instructed. "Less painful for you this way."

"Go to hell," managed Jacek, his forehead sweating. He struggled to maintain his balance.

"I have a boatload of friends already there." The colonel did not smile. He turned back to his desk, flicked his computer screen on, waved a dismissive hand to Kasim. "Get him out of here. This final act is boring me."

Kasim moved a few degrees left behind Jacek. With the wooden handles of the garrote in his hands, he raised his prisoner to his feet, then steered him toward the room's tall doors.

"One more thing," gasped Jacek, managing to halt their progress. His desperate eyes flicked toward the colonel still at his desk. "What did you do with my friend?"

Tazeki Mabutu swiveled around in his chair. "Do you enjoy classic American movies, Mr. Tumaj? If so, then you'll understand when I say your detective friend 'sleeps with the fishes.'"

The colonel's hollow laughter followed them as they eased through the study's doorway and into the home's vaulted outer room. Moments later, they were moving down the length of a narrow corridor. Jacek walked carefully, a slight backward lean to relax the tension on the wire. Kasim allowed this, shadowing behind his prisoner, permitting the man enough play to breathe and continue forward.

They passed through a stylish, broad-windowed kitchen area, the outer glass sprinkled with rain, and Jacek was uncertain of the direction he needed to proceed in. When he hesitated, Kasim said, "Forward. We're headed outside."

Progressing down a second hallway, Jacek searched for anything he might use to surprise his captor. To free himself of the wire. Kasim was a professional, however, and would not allow this to happen. He kept his focus on his prisoner while guiding him toward their destination.

Jacek knew shouting was pointless. They were in the devil's lair—each man in the colonel's hip pocket. He doubted he'd receive support from the armed military men working the outer grounds. Quite the opposite. They would enjoy nothing more than putting a volley of bullets in his torso.

No other servants appeared. At the end of the hallway they paused, where shallow steps led to a supply area. Across the room, Jacek spied a door leading to the backyard of the main house. He scanned the stored supplies inside the wide room: a long-handled spade, a sickle, a coiled garden hose on the floor. Any of these might prove a weapon in a desperate situation. When he hesitated, Kasim issued a clipped whisper into his right ear: "Take the steps. Very slow. Then we move through the door."

Jacek rasped a comment and his tormenter made a *shushing* sound. "Save your tongue. You may talk when it's time to lose your soul."

Fumbling for the door handle, Jacek led the way, and they moved outside into the humid midday air. The sky was filled with ash-colored clouds, but the rains had subsided to a paltry drizzle. Birds called from the dense jungle beyond the tall white walls of the compound. The air felt swollen with purpose.

"Head for the back wall. Follow the path in the grass ahead of you."

Jacek spotted the worn grass where it had been depressed. The path led to the rear outer wall, and together they moved in a macabre parade. He imagined the tower guards monitoring their progress. He wondered if others might be viewing the CCTV monitors, whose cameras were designed to cover every angle and square meter inside the compound.

Thirty-seconds later, they had reached the back wall. It stretched ten feet upward. "There, at the seam," Kasim said, controlling Jacek's head so he stared forward at the otherwise blank surface of white stone.

Along the seam, he spotted the barest outline of an exit door, its hinges painted to match the alabaster masonry. Jacek reached one hand forward and lifted the small latch. The door popped open with a *snick*. Prodded by Kasim from behind, Jacek stepped with care through the opening in the wall. A worn, soggy footpath spread in both directions. He gazed ahead at the dripping ferns and broad leaves, the thicket of jungle ready to engulf them whole.

"To the left," said Kasim firmly. "Then right. Between the trunks of those two rubber trees."

Jacek advanced forward on the uneven path, his footsteps depressed in the squishy terrain. The pressure on his neck was intense, the wire threatening to slice the reddened flesh. "Why not kill me back at the house?" he rasped. "Why walk all the way out here?" Silence from Kasim.

Jacek stepped forward, as the man directed, easing his way between the trunks of the rubber trees. Rain seeped from the uppermost branches, a few waterlogged leaves from the underbrush tickling his face. They progressed deeper into the lush vegetation. After two dozen paces, they reached a modest clearing. The killing field.

"Stop. Kneel down. Right here," Kasim ordered. A bird screeched from somewhere. In the distance, the rolling waves crashed monotonously, sounding a steady death knoll against the rock-encrusted shoreline.

"Why (gasping)...this place?"

Kasim guided the wire, forcing Jacek to his knees.

"The night animals will make short work of your body. No burial needed."

Although no order was given, Jacek reached both hands up behind his head. He interlaced his fingers in the fashion of a man facing a firing squad. "You said I could...speak." His teeth were bared in a grimace, his head angled back, the wire chewing on the tender flesh of his neck.

Kasim twisted his wrists and Jacek felt the killer's hands tighten the handles of the garrote.

"Brief," was all the assassin said.

***

The green moray eel thrives in oceanic salt water. It enjoys seclusion in the rocky caves and crevices found up and down the African coastline. It is considered reclusive but will display a nasty temper if harassed or threatened in its habitat. Along with small eyes and a superb sense of smell, these creatures possess wide jaws and razor-sharp teeth. They can grow up to five feet in length and relish the taste of raw fish and fresh mammal blood. The moray secretes a protective thin mucus layer, highly toxic, over its smooth skin. This provides the creatures with their famous slippery feel.

From his perch on the rocks—one foot on the treacherous stone, the other on the seat of the trapped wooden chair—Cale could not have cared less about the eel as a species. What he did care about was how his muscles were cramping, and how the deep pool of water inches from his feet was thick with the swarming, toothy creatures.

There was blood already in the water. His blood.

The only thing Cale could surmise, regarding the carnivorous little bastards, was: when it came to a fresh meal, they seemed to learn fast. Mabutu's swimming pets had no doubt gained their knowledge from experience. He would not be surprised to discover a pile of polished bones at the bottom of this tepid pool.

Human bones.

And Cale discovered he had other problems, as well. Wet, hungry, shivering from his dip in the water, despite this being Africa, hypothermia was a definite concern. Realizing he was safe—for the time being—where he stood on the rocky ledge, he turned his thoughts on how he might free himself from this precarious predicament.

Jacek, where are you when I need you, buddy?

As far as his bodyguard went, Cale decided he should expect the worst. He was on his own, and the realization was far from a comforting thought. Weapons? He took a quick inventory: he had the penlight—waterproof, thank God—and it was turned off now. His desire was not just to save the battery, but also to provide a less visible target for the creatures nipping—literally—at his heels. In his pocket, he had his mobile. That was it. Cale wondered if his plunging into the pool might have rendered the phone useless. He pulled it free. The orange power button was still steady. A positive sign. He pressed the numbers nine-one-one out of habit and listened for a dial tone.

Nothing. Tried 9-9-9. The Euro variation. Zilch. He tried "zero" for the operator. Same result.

What did you expect, moron? You're trapped inside a granite cave, at the bottom of a solid brick mansion. In bumfuck Africa!

The light from the phone's screen cast an eerie green glow around the walls of the cavern. At the edges of the pool, the water made a soft lapping sound. Cale closed the phone, deciding to employ his items only as needed. The penlight and phone provided at least a modest form of comfort, if little else. What was there to see down there anyway? Shouting, he'd already recognized, would help little. Nor was making a swim for it a viable option. As for other weapons, he guessed he might yank the chair free, if he could locate a more suitable place for his footing. He could smash it against the rocks and employ one of the sturdy wooden legs as a club. Still, he doubted it would provide much help against the brigade of hungry eels, which lurked just below the surface.

In a matter of hours, hunger would begin to gnaw at him. *At least I might whack one of the suckers.* Cale's thoughts were turning darker by the minute. Sushi for dinner. Who cared if he wasn't Japanese.

He stared up at the top of the cave, the pitch blackness there. Not even the faintest suggestion of light could be discerned from where he guessed the trapdoor to be. He listened for any sound, hearing the dripping water as it echoed off the craggy walls. Nothing more. Cale adjusted his foothold to ease his cramping muscles. His fingers sought a new grip on the damp, cool rock.

What he felt most like doing was shrieking at the top of his lungs: He hated the dark; he hated confined spaces; he hated insects...and I despised fucking eels! Yet it was pointless. He was a stoic detective, after all. He would not be reduced to the level of a babbling schoolboy. How about singing the blues? He considered a few of his favorite John Lee Hooker or Magic Slim tunes but decided they would, at best, turn him even more melancholy. Not a good frame of mind when you're clinging to the final vestiges of hope. Clinging by your fingertips.

Every time he caught himself wondering if the cavalry might be coming, the adage his father had drilled into his skull as a young boy kept taunting him: *"God helps those who help themselves."* The saying proved the antithesis of "playing the victim." It meant—to Cale, anyway—that when you've exhausted each possibility, every means of solving your problem, only at this time would providence step in and lend you a hand.

And even then, it came with a qualified *maybe*.

With the cloying fingers of darkness closing in around him, a coffin-like absence of light, Cale thought of Maggie. God how he loved the little way her nose crinkled when she laughed. And the way she always said "interesting," when he'd finished telling her about some case. It confirmed that she cared about what he was saying. But now, stuck here in the dark, Cale wasn't thinking about the good times they'd had together. Not the laughs or the lovemaking, and certainly not their future together. Instead, he couldn't stop thinking about one thing: her pregnancy.

Am I the father? Or is Crenshaw?

For any number of reasons, it made him feel worse than he already felt. And this amazed Cale, considering the circumstances. How was feeling more miserable than he did even possible?

***

"We're a lot alike, Kasim. You and I."

Kneeling on the loamy jungle ground, the fingers of both hands laced behind his head, Jacek was attempting to delay the inevitable. He hoped for a miracle of some sort but understood how improbable the odds were. Further, he doubted either begging or praying would render him much comfort. "We both work for important people—we kill for them." Jacek managed a breath. "You're an expert with...a garrote. I could your talents...on my team." Gasping it out while he choked.

Behind him, close, Kasim barked a laugh. "What could you possibly have to offer me? I work for the most powerful botono in Africa."

"You mean *witch doctor*, don't you? Good old bone-in-the-nose?" He rasped out the words. "A chicken-wringing...charlatan?"

The assassin replied with a mere snicker.

"One thing you should...realize. Don't think you...led me out here, Kasim. If you think so...you've got it *bass-ackward*."

Kasim squeezed the wire tighter.

"I wanted y-you here...away from the...guards—" Choking, Jacek sputtered the words out. "In fact...I'll give you a...a token of my...good faith."

"You are quite mad."

"My watch. Take it... And come work...for me."

Kasim leaned in closer. "Your stinking watch? How amusing."

"It's a nice...watch."

Jacek worked his hand over his wrist as if to remove the shiny timepiece. Kasim, he imagined, would be focusing his eyes on the silver-plated dial, just as Jacek was pressing the tiny setting-knob into the round metal frame.

The *trigger*.

A clear jet of muriatic acid shot forth as if fired from a squirt gun. It splashed into Kasim's face, his eyes, down his neck, searing his flesh as it splattered. The assassin's hands flew from the garrote handles to cover his singed flesh, and he screamed, gasping, horrified.

Jacek sprang up from his kneeling position. He spun around while grabbing the loose handles of the garrote. He slipped the wire from his neck, then circled it around Kasim's own neck, where the man lay curled in a fetal position, writhing on the rain-sodden ground.

Jacek snapped the wire tight and the assassin's pain was erased in an instant.

CHAPTER 32

Slipping the crimson Nehru jacket over his soggy shirt, Jacek wound the wire around the wooden handles. He tucked the weapon inside one of the inside pockets. Time was running out, he understood, so he did not hesitate as he departed the clearing. He retraced his path back through the thick underbrush. When he reached the door hidden in the compound's outer wall, however, he continued past. He was headed in the direction of the crashing waves, toward the roadway, which ran along the front of the fortified grounds.

Mindful of the security cameras perched atop the outer walls, Jacek kept hidden a yard deep inside the thick vegetation. He understood he was playing with house money. By all counts, considering the amount of time that had passed, both he and Cale should be dead by now. As things stood, Jacek understood he might have one slim chance to rescue his friend.

He decided he had better make the most of it.

Withdrawing the mobile SAT phone from his pants pocket, he hit the power button and searched for a signal up between the drooping tree branches. Nothing. He decided he would have to move onto the path near the outer wall of the compound, where the vegetation was sparser. The light flashed green and he hit a speed dial key. When Pharaoh answered with a grunt, Jacek spoke in rapid French, setting up a rendezvous for an extraction.

"Can you confirm the hot spot?" Pharaoh asked, instantly alert.

"Negative. I'll be on the move. You'll have to GPS my position."

"I'll coordinate with our pilot. Transport's going to take a number of hours, though."

"Roger that. I'll contact you when I'm ready."

Ending the call to his team member, Jacek attempted a long shot. He rang the number of the new Euro-phone Cale had been issued, hoping that if his partner was still alive—even if severely injured from his plummet through the floor—he might answer.

The SAT's display indicated NO CONNECTION. Keeping the phone powered on, for Pharaoh to fix his position via satellite, Jacek slid the phone back into his pocket. He heard the roar of a vehicle approaching along the road. The risk being spotted was too great, and Jacek darted back inside the cover of thick vegetation.

The *whoosh* of wet tires blended with the crash of the breakers against the shoreline. Concealed by tree trunks and broad ferns, he watched the silhouette of a gray Audi touring car as it swept past, headed away from the compound. Though the windows were tinted dark, Jacek guessed the colonel was inside, headed off to wherever his business might demand. The man would feel comfortable, of course, leaving his heavily guarded fortress in the hands of his capable servant, Kasim.

Former servant, Jacek reminded himself, though he failed to rally any satisfaction. He imagined some large cat, or pack of dogs, once they'd caught the scent in the rain, would drag away Kasim's body to where they could better feast.

Better him than me.

The timing of the colonel's departure could not be more advantageous. It offered the one rare opportunity he might have of rescuing Cale. *If he's even alive.* And if good fortune remained in their favor, together they might punch a one-way ticket out of this most unwholesome of places.

***

The drizzle continued. Moving through the soggy foliage, imagining snakes and leopards and spiders the size of his fist, Jacek wove his way back until he located the entry point where Kasim had forced him into the jungle. Eyeing the wall opposite the narrow footpath, he located the door, which remained invisible to any casual observer. He crossed the path, pressing his body flat against the wall, a perched bat. He searched inside the dead servant's jacket pocket for a set of keys. Found nothing. He flipped the latch, hoping his luck remained, and the door opened in the way they had used it to exit.

So much for Colonel Mabutu's elaborate security measures.

Adopting Kasim's rigid manner, Jacek closed the door and began striding across the soggy back lawn, headed toward the rear entranceway of the main house. He hoped any disparity would go unnoticed on the video monitors he was certain the guards were watching. With his wet hair and the rain blurring the camera lenses, the ruse just might work. For how long, was anyone's guess. With the colonel away, he prayed the guards would not be as diligent as they might otherwise be.

Inside the house, after drying his shoes, he moved in silence across the kitchen area. He retraced his path back down the long length of hallway. He paused outside the doors of Colonel Mabutu's private study, one ear pressed to the wood. No voices, no movement inside. In the manner of a cat burglar, Jacek opened the door and slipped into the room. Closed the door behind him. No lights. The haze outside the bank of windows had deepened to battleship gray in the rain.

The room was empty. Glancing about, Jacek noticed the pewter statue of the demon god, which had earlier sat staring at him from atop the desk. The statue had given him the creeps then—its smug expression and beady, glinting eyes. It continued to stare at him now, seeming to follow his steps as Jacek crept across the room.

A new piece of colorful, hand-hewn rug had been laid across the floor, concealing the surface of the trapdoor. With his foot, he swept it aside. Jacek examined the floor panel for seams, careful not to press his weight on the central spot—no desire to be devoured by the same dark mouth that had swallowed Cale whole. Rising, he made his way to the oversized desk and examined beneath the surface. The colonel had been reaching for a hidden trigger, just before Cale disappeared.

Jacek discovered the tiny metallic thumb and flicked it forward. With a *snick* the trapdoor sprang open, a dark opening where solid floor had just been. Grabbing a long spear from the wall, Jacek knelt beside the hole. He cracked the spear in half and worked until he was able to lever it inside, wedging it along the edge enough to keep the trapdoor from snapping closed again.

Aiming his own penlight into the darkness, he could discern the figure of a lone man perched precariously on the rocks, clinging as if crucified there. He was adjacent a pool of black water. "Mr. Packer," Jacek called down, "like most cats, I can tell you find no pleasure in the old swimming hole."

"Christ, Jacek! Quit dicking around! I'm losing my grip here." Cale's voice echoed from below, sounding warped with exhaustion.

Jacek performed a quick survey of the room. Nothing of use. He then recalled the storage room off the kitchen, where the coiled garden hose had lain. In a flash, he was there and back, moving as silent as Kasim at his best. Kneeling beside the opening once more, he removed Kasim's Nehru jacket. He began to unravel the long hose down into the ebony pit.

"Wrap your foot around the hose," Jacek ordered from above, his voice still rasping. "Coil it. Like a trapeze artist."

"Last time I saw a circus, I was eight," protested Cale. Nevertheless, he did as instructed.

It took fifteen long minutes—close to an eternity—to hoist him up from the dank, wet coal-black pit. Cale was like dead weight, and Jacek was forced to brace his legs against the giant desk—two turns of hose wrapped around his midsection—to accomplish the task. The mahogany desk slid a mere eight inches along the floor, a testament to its bulk.

With close to inhuman effort, one final mighty heave, and Jacek watched as his partner pull himself *up-up-up* through the opening, inching an elbow, then knee, thigh, then hip...and at last the rest of his limp body...before heaving himself onto the room's wooden floor. Cale moaned, too tired to speak. From his back, he stared up at the ceiling.

Exhausted as much himself, Jacek remained flopped in a sitting position, his back pressed against the lower surface of the tank-heavy desk.

"Next time," Jacek gasped, unwinding the hose from his waist, "I'd suggest being a bit more careful."

"Next time. I'll pull on the hose, you drop into the pit." Cale forced himself to an unsteady knee, then to his feet, hunched over. They studied one another, each amazed at finding the other still alive.

They were living on borrowed time, Jacek knew well enough. They had to move. He took a survey around the room for their weapon options: the long spears and war clubs and arrows would be little help when facing the security guards with AKs, MAC-10s, and sniper rifles. He remembered the colonel's Luger. Could it still be in one of the desk drawers?

"Where did Mabutu go?" Cale asked, flicking his eyes about the room. He shook out the cramped muscles of his limbs, moved to the broad bank of rain-streaked windows and peered outside.

Rifling through a desk drawer, Jacek frowned. "He left. In his car. Who knows for how long." In the lowest drawer on the right, he located the Luger. It was the old P08, held eight 9mm rounds. He checked the clip: full ammo, ready for action. He slipped the weapon in his waistband. Thinking it might work to their advantage, he put Kasim's jacket back on. He stared at his duffel bag. It contained the SAT phone charger-dock and a few other items.

Examining the hole in the floor, Jacek decided they had best snap it back in place. The items his duffel bag contained were nonessentials and would serve at best to slow him down. Unzipping the bag, he dropped it down into the dark hole and heard it hit the water with a splash. The weighted bag would fill with water, he knew, and fast sink to the bottom. Lost forever. He fed the long hose through the opening, where it likewise disappeared into the darkness. Freeing the long spear from the trapdoor, he set it back on the wall where it had been.

Back at the desk he reversed the toggle switch, and the trapdoor snapped back into place. After pushing the desk over to its original position, Jacek slid the patterned floor rug into place, where it once again concealed the seams of the opening.

Across the room at the side wall, Cale was examining a nine-inch-long blade. Knife in hand, he moved over to the fireplace mantle. He grabbed the shrunken female head and stared at the shiny, lacquered features.

"We don't have time for collectables," Jacek said, pointedly. "Come on. We've got to get out of here."

"Who did Mabutu say she was? A U.N. worker?" Cale was squinting across the room at him. "Nice jacket, by the way. I'm assuming the servant—"

"Is no longer with us." Jacek didn't elaborate. Instead, he added: "She was supposed to be a 'missionary worker.' I believe that's what he said. Let's get going. Now!"

Jacek watched Cale come back across the room toward him, the shrunken head still in his hand. The man's clothes remained damp from his plunge into the dank water of the pool, and his shoes squeaked on the room's wooden floor, as he made his way back to the desk.

Peering out through the cracked door, Jacek turned back to the room. When he spotted the pewter idol now in his Cale's other hand, he rolled his eyes. "Bloody Americans. You and your souvenirs. Serves you right if you get a bullet in your ass."

Voices were hailing from a distance. The guards outside? Jacek guessed one of the men might have at last studied the CCTV feed, spotted his amateurish imitation of Kasim. If they were discovered, they'd be shot on the spot like dogs.

Cale removed his wet shoes. They slipped without sound from the room and out into the open central area. After easing the tall doors of the study closed behind them, Jacek led the way again down the dim length of hallway. Quiet as shadows, they headed toward the rear of the main house.

CHAPTER 33

In the oversized kitchen of Colonel Mabutu's mansion, Cale and Jacek raided the refrigerator. They understood that time was short, but energy was a necessity. Who knew when they might have the chance to eat again? Despite the sound of voices in the front courtyard, no guards had stormed into the residence with weapons drawn. They had a few safe minutes—they hoped and prayed—to consume sustenance, rehydrate, and plan their next move.

They wolfed down bread and roast beef Jacek had discovered in the refrigerator. Glancing around the kitchen, Cale wondered why there were not more servants in a house this large. It was odd that Kasim was here alone during the daytime. He imagined there had to be cooks and housekeepers and laundry maids in the colonel's employ, but thus far, the huge house remained steeped in silence. Mabutu had driven off, and it was anyone's guess when he'd be back. Armed guards were on patrol, surrounding the place. So as things stood, they were trapped inside a fortress.

It might as well be a prison.

While they refueled and gathered their strength, they took the time to assess where they stood. Cale demanded answers to a number of questions that had arisen since they'd arrived.

"The Colonel," he whispered, as they slipped down a hallway leading to the back exit, "said he knows Kinsella. From years past. But what was with that crazy witch doctor business? What was the word he used?"

"'Botono.' In African dialects, it means *sorcerer*."

Cale shot a look at Jacek. "And this *botono* is supposed to be who, exactly?"

"My guess? It's the Colonel, himself. But who knows?"

Cale decided his partner looked ridiculous wearing Kasim's Nehru jacket, but held his tongue. "Did he say anything? After I disappeared? About Kinsella or Prince Mir?" After a pause, he added: "The trafficking business?"

Finishing the last of his sandwich, Jacek said, "Nothing relevant. We don't know much more than we did before we arrived."

"Except for one thing." Cale's tone turned harsh. "The Colonel is one sadistic bastard. Who drops people into a pool filled with hungry eels?"

"A man who knows he can get away with it."

They descended the steps leading to the storage area. Cale cleared a spot on a shelf and set down the shrunken head and a carving knife he'd grabbed. Then the pewter statue beside them. Withdrawing his phone from his pocket, he checked the power level. The device remained dark, no signal. He had been hoping to check for messages, but the dunk in the black waters of the pool had shorted the circuitry.

"How about trying the land-line phone?" Cale asked.

"Too risky. Traceable."

They still had Jacek's SAT phone. At least it was something. Jacek explained how he'd contacted Pharaoh earlier, and a hasty rescue was in the works. Yet it all hinged on their escaping the compound and making their way to an arranged rendezvous point.

Through the windows, Cale could see that although it was midday, a hazy purple veil had settled over the soggy back lawns. The gloomy weather made it appear as if dusk was near. So much for the splendor of African sunsets, he thought ruefully.

Jacek's plan was less than elegant. Then again, they understood their escape options were limited. It was pointless to call Agent Fronteer, to have her alert the Liberian authorities that an American law enforcement agent was trapped inside their country. Colonel Mabutu *was* the Liberian "authority." He would no doubt concoct some story portraying them as invaders, out to harm his country. He would order them shot on sight. The colonel would claim he was acting for the good of Liberia.

End of argument.

No. Calling the cavalry was a low percentage play, they decided. It would not only reveal their position, but also that they remained alive. It was decided that they were best left to their own devices, and Cale understood that putting his faith in Jacek was the smartest play they had. He hoped the man could get them the hell out of Dodge.

With hostile soldiers patrolling the compound, and the solid outer walls serving as a barrier—CCTV monitors at every corner—making a sprint for the jungle was tantamount to committing suicide. The sniper rifles remained positioned in the towers. Even if they did manage to break free, they would be hunted down and shot like curs. Their bodies would likely end up back in the eel pit. Nothing left but a clean pile of bones, identities erased from the face of the planet.

Jacek's plan, instead, called for a bit of deception.

"Shouldn't we wait until dark?" Cale asked. "A better chance of escaping unnoticed?"

Jacek shook his head. "The Colonel may be back any minute. We've got to move while we can."

Cale was staring at the steady drizzle, uncertain of the wisdom of venturing from their dry sanctity. "Say we make it past the walls. Then what?"

"We run like hell through the jungle."

"That's your plan?"

"Beggars versus choosers, Mr. Packer. You got a more brilliant idea? This is a good time to share it."

Couldn't they sneak out the front door? Cale wondered. Slip into the arms building? Slit a couple of throats like Cheetah had taught them? Grab Kalashnikovs? Shoot it out with the guards? O.K. Corral revisited?

Cale pondered the odds of this scenario: Two men against a dozen trained Liberian soldiers. No doubt handpicked from some elite death squad, the way Army Rangers or Navy Seals are chosen. The odds of their surviving a firefight were not in their favor. Even further, weren't most soldiers in this country already hardened to killing and warfare? Temperaments forged from decades of armed upheaval? A century of bloody struggle for liberation?

Cale decided to remain quiet. If it weren't for Jacek's miraculous escape from Kasim, he'd still be standing on his tiptoes, on the verge of becoming dinner.

"What about weapons?" he asked, hopeful. "Can't we grab something from the Colonel's study?"

"You have the knife, there."

"Besides that."

"Long-handled spears? Thatched shields? I'm certain the guards, after their laughter subsides, will find us inventive, if none-too-intimidating." Jacek lifted the Nehru jacket to reveal the Luger tucked in his waistband. "This was all I could find."

Cale searched around the storage room. He grabbed a long-handled garden hoe, which he discovered leaning against a wall.

"Please," said his partner, pulling a face. "That might work if we're members of the rabble in search of the Frankenstein monster."

Cale put the hoe back against the wall. Spotting a canvas sack, he tipped it upside down. A hundred carpenter nails spilled on the floor. He placed the shrunken head and the statue inside the satchel, spun the top, knotted it. With the knife, he indicated the sack: "Think the Colonel wants these back? Enough to make a deal?"

Glancing at the weapon in Cale's hand, Jacek said, "Better leave that."

"I've got to have something."

Jacek's look at him was tight. "You're leaving here a prisoner. How realistic will it look with you brandishing a knife in your hand?"

Cale untied the neck of the sack and dropped the long blade inside, before knotting it again.

They could delay no longer. Jacck fished inside the Nehru jacket pocket and withdrew the garrote, glanced at his watch. He steered Cale in front of him, positioning them both at the cusp of the doorway. "Showtime," he said, his tone serious.

Cale tensed as the wire was slipped loosely around his neck.

Out the door they moved, into the drizzle. Cale played the role of prisoner, marching ahead, progressing down the rain-slicked path. With one hand he gripped the wire at his throat, while the other kept hold of the canvas sack.

Jacek walked behind him, erect, mimicking the movements of Kasim once more. When they reached the back wall, with jungle grime seeping down the white walls like runny mascara, they halted. Jacek coached Cale on flipping the latch and the door swung open. They proceeded through the opening in the wall and closed the door behind them like proper schoolboys. This done, Jacek relaxed the garrote and directed Cale through the opening in the jungle growth, between the tree trunks. The exact spot where Kasim had led him an hour before.

"Where's his body?" Cale whispered, glancing around the clearing. He could see a runny pool of crimson still staining the leaf-covered soil. Sprays of arterial spurt.

Jacek looked around. "Gone," was all he said. The killing field.

Pocketing the garrote, Jacek held a finger to his lips for silence. They listened in the distance for calling voices, for engines revving, for any sign they had been spotted and were being pursued by the colonel's guards.

No whistles. No sirens could be heard. Nothing but the rhythm of the waves as they crashed against the nearby shore.

CHAPTER 34

The cargo ship *Kwensana* sat docked in the port harbor of Monrovia. There she awaited her final load of goods, before setting course for the United Kingdom. After tonight's voodoo ceremony—the third in the past week—the last dozen young virgins would be loaded aboard.

At daybreak tomorrow, the *Kwensana* would lift anchor and set off. The dingy, coal-charred vessel's blunt horn would *blaaatt* a few times, until she cleared the harbor.

No delays. No impediments along the way. No surprises. Just business as usual. A simple matter, where all proper hands were greased, and each individual along the chain profited.

For Colonel Tazeki Mabutu, the afternoon had been filled with meetings. First, with the foreign secretary. Then after that he'd receive an update from Health and Services on the Ebola crisis. Stable for now, he learned, but for how long was anyone's guess. The off-and-on rampages of the disease had proved a boon for local voodoo and witch doctors across the land. Superstition, Tazeki understood, was good for business. When the U.N. doctors and medical people could not provide a cure, the locals turned to ancient remedies from the mambas and houngans, the traditional experts they trusted—the way Africans across the continent had done for over three thousand years.

Tazeki Mabutu strode to his gray Audi sedan and, closing his umbrella, slipped into the backseat. He waited for his driver, Sabu, to catch up and take his usual place behind the steering wheel. While Tazeki waited, he stared out the window at the moored ships and steel-gray waters coloring the Monrovian harbor. As the rain cried against the windows, his mind drifted ahead to the ceremony that would take place tonight.

Tazeki had everything he required prepared ahead of time. After all, whatever he needed was at his command. He was a powerful *houngan*, a botono, and people averted their eyes and whispered when he moved among them. His government position, in fact, could be considered a masterful disguise. One that allowed him to mingle with the rich and powerful elements in the country (however few they were). Tazeki understood his true power—his calling—lay in his ability to practice vodun. And he did so with his left hand, the Latin root of which was *sinestra*. Sinister.

His expertise was in summoning the "dark" loa to do his bidding.

His thoughts rounded back to that morning's events. Tazeki had chosen to dispose of the two visitors, the American detective and his mercenary accomplice, with due diligence. Without having to rely on an ounce of magick. And without Pazuzu's aid. Each man's body would have been consumed by now: either by the razor-toothed eels or the ferocious jungle pack dogs. The bones would return to the earth, the rich loam of his ancestors, seasoned by the spill of fresh blood. How fitting.

Six times a year, for the past eight years, Tazeki had held a voodoo ceremony in an inland country village. He called it the "Ceremony of the Virgins." The trafficking business—children, in particular—was profitable not only for him but for his country. For all of Africa, in fact. In a continent ravaged by war and poverty, by starvation and dehydration and unending viral epidemics, many of these children were destined for fatal disease or death by the time they reached puberty.

Thus, Tazeki reasoned, wasn't he doing them a favor by setting them free? Long ahead of their predestined pain?

Truth be told, there had developed a competition among the country's tribal elders to have Botono Mabutu bless their village. To keep it free from the countless ills that were cast down upon them. In exchange for a full year of protection, these wise elder leaders begged the botono to hold a ceremony, whereby they would be pleased to hand over a dozen healthy young "gifts" to him, as payment for his blessings.

Few Mafiosi thugs selling neighborhood "protection" ever had it so easy. Tazeki barely had to lift a finger, and these superstitious yokels were tripping over themselves to preserve virgin girls for his taking. It was how he'd made a fortune in the competitive international human slavery arena over the past decade—selling young African maidens into the clutches of Northern and Western Europe. All with the corrupt EU's blessing, of course. For it fell in line with their "global diversity" master plan.

And who could blame Tazeki for accepting the profits he reaped? The worldwide demand for his commodity was seemingly endless. He, point of fact, did not make the rules. He employed them to his advantage, however, similar to any clever businessman who dealt in a desired product.

What did it matter, Tazeki reasoned, that the young girls had to turn twenty tricks a day in some grimy flat in North Berlin? It was a quid pro quo tradeoff. A favor for a favor. At least they'd gotten out of Africa, where a life of pain and poverty and suffering was otherwise inescapable.

***

It was late-afternoon now, and the rains showed little signs of letting up. The skies remained dull and swollen as the shark-like Audi town car pulled up to the front gates of the compound.

His security guards watched eagle-eyed as the iron barriers eased open. Minutes later, Tazeki was climbing the broad steps to the main house. He opened the front doors, surprised that Kasim was not there to greet him. Then again, Kasim had no doubt had a busy day himself.

Striding through the grand foyer, his boots clacking officiously on the polished wooden floor, Tazeki noted that just a handful of lights were on in the residence. The gloom outside made this more evident. It was of no consequence, however. Often the lack of illumination was soothing, preferable even.

After showering—one must be cleansed to summon the loa—and dressing, Tazeki would be flown by private helicopter out to the Bomi territory. There, in a small mining village, inside a mountain cave protected from the persistent drizzle, he would perform his third "virgin" ceremony that week.

The botono would summon the dark loa—Ofumba this time, he'd decided—to ride a "horse's" back, to offer protection to the village. A military truck would be waiting afterwards, and his men would supervise the loading of the young "gifts." They would be driven to

Monrovia and loaded aboard the *Kwensana*. After the reception of this precious cargo in the U.K.—thirty-six virgins in total—the sum of three hundred thousand American dollars would be wired to Tazeki's private bank account in Switzerland.

A sweet deal if you could get it.

Swinging open the tall doors of his study, he reached for the wall switch, flicked on the lights. The spacious room lit up as usual, undisturbed. Striding forward, he noticed his trap door in the room's floor remained closed. The new woven rug was in its proper place, just as he'd left it.

Seating himself at his leather desk chair and loosening his collar, Tazeki pressed the desk button for his intercom. "Kasim!" he barked. "I need you in here."

As he spoke, his eyes scanned the room. Everything seemed in order, his paintings and precious African artifacts appeared undisturbed on the walls and desktops and curio cabinets. But wait! The American girl's shrunken head...it was no longer atop the fireplace mantle. And something else—a long spear's handle appeared cracked, splintered. His eyes searched around, more intent now, for his longtime friend and mentor, Pazuzu. Also absent.

The rains had streaked the bank of broad window glass, and the sea rolled and crested, the monotonous sound of crashing waves reaching him like a lover's distant moan. Rising from his desk, Tazeki's eyes surveyed the four corners of the room, the wet bar, the mantle again, the tops of every desk and table and surface in the place. No sign of either object.

Rounding on his massive desk, he pressed the intercom button again.

"Kasim!" he shouted, his anger rising. "Get in here at once! And bring Pazuzu with you."

CHAPTER 35

Any cop will tell you that if it's utter boredom you're seeking, you can't beat a good old-fashioned stakeout. Cale had been on too many stakeouts in his life to count. Most of them occurred years ago, back when he had worked narcotics and vice. This one, however, was different. Most often stakeouts involved sitting in a vehicle, safe and out of the elements. Not being outside in the rain, attempting to steal one.

They had progressed through the jungle, which bordered the mud-caked road leading away from the compound. Heading northeast, they'd kept the ocean to their backs, traveling for a good mile before they paused. They hadn't seen a truck or a civilian vehicle for the past ten minutes. They were trying to avoid military jeeps, as they guessed there might be an APB out for them by this time. Two Caucasian men traveling on foot, likely armed, dangerous and deadly. Shoot to kill. Ask questions later.

Direct orders from Colonel Mabutu.

Confining themselves to the shadows as best they could, they had continued to move another half mile inland. Forever mindful of snakes, of wild dogs, of large jungle cats, even of creeping spiders and other insects. Anything that could bite. Behind them the ocean stretched to the black horizon, and roiling gray clouds loomed above, as if summoned by some dark witch stirring a caldron.

On their earlier drive with Sergeant Ditt, they had noticed a pair of jeeps parked at the U.N. mission tent-camp. Jacek decided a stolen jeep might provide their best chance for escape.

They were now hiding across the roadway, in a thicket of underbrush. A few birds trilled, and an occasional small animal rustled about in the bushes somewhere behind them. Cale felt a shiver traverse his spine, despite the humid eighty-nine-degree heat. Though in proximity to the capital city of Monrovia, there was danger lurking everywhere—slithering snakes, venomous spiders, mosquitoes, tsetse flies. This was still Africa, after all. To the big cats they were little more than an upright meal. An old joke popped into his mind: *All I've got to do is run faster than Jacek!*

For the past fifteen minutes they'd been on the stakeout, and Cale was unable to discern any movement from the camp, itself. It appeared as if they'd closed operations for the day. An occasional vehicle swept past on the road, *whooshing* through puddles of rain. Of the five vehicles he'd counted driving past, two had been Liberian military jeeps. Searching for them, Cale decided grimly. He wondered if they would ever be free of this godforsaken land. It was like being trapped in some circle of Dante's Hell.

The U.N. tents, braced by solid poles, stood empty in the fading light, like a fair the night before it opened. Adjacent to the tents stood a pair of long motor homes. These served as base camp for the United Nations workers who were bringing food and medical care to the unfortunate shack-dwelling suburbs outside Monrovia. On the side far-opposite, a rubber tree forest stretched into misty dullness, seeming to go on forever.

What struck Cale most was the absolute sense of quiet. Despite the capital city of Monrovia being mere miles away, there was no nearby highway to create a constant hum of flowing traffic. Just the silence, accompanied by the dripping rain and white noise of steady drizzle. Except now for the distant radio or CD player sounds...playing scratchy rock music, which was issuing from inside one of the camp trailers. Cale could discern a bluesy rock tune: some 80's group, rhythmic and distracting. He imagined the U.N. workers needed to unwind after a long day of administering bottled water and inoculations. Walking around in Ebola masks and hazmat suits.

Turning toward him, Jacek whispered: "Remember our ride? In from the airport? I commented to Sergeant Ditt about the port at Monrovia."

"Yes. Many big ships. So?"

"I'm hoping he also remembers. It's where they'll concentrate their search for us. My guess, anyway."

"There and the American Embassy." Cale exhaled. "I'm sure they've got the place surrounded by now."

Cale swiped a mosquito from his forehead. In spite of the drizzle, the temperature hadn't let up. There was nothing resembling a cool breeze, especially now that they had moved inland, away from the ocean shore. Cale's clothing was soaked and sticking to his skin, and he added another profound affirmation to growing list: he despised the rainy season.

Between the drizzle and low cloud overhang, the fading daylight, it felt as if twilight was upon them already.

"We can't afford to wait any longer," Jacek said, his tone serious. He gave Cale a thumbs-up, then crouching low, he scampered away across the road. Seconds later, he was slipping into the shadows beside one of the pair of jeeps, which were both covered by canvas rain tarps.

Cale watched as his partner disappeared beneath the waterproof covering and up inside the enclosed cab. He imagined the faint glow of Jacek's penlight as he labored inside, working beneath the steering column, pulling free the jeep's wires, attempting to hotwire the ignition.

Just as he was about to slip across the road as well, Cale noticed the approaching headlights. He held his spot, clutching the sack in one hand. He prayed the vehicle wouldn't slow and enter the U.N. camp. It sluiced past in the rain, a dark military SUV. It swept past with the swish of wet tires, never slowing, and Cale watched the vehicle's orange taillights shrink in the distance until they vanished.

Hearing the jeep's engine cough to life was his cue. In a crouch, Cale splashed across the muddy roadway, arriving at the covered jeep, where he grabbed the rear section of the canvas cover and lifted it free. He performed the same task all around the vehicle, thankful Jacek had the sense to keep the headlights off. Tossing the cover to the sodden ground, he slipped into the passenger side, where Jacek already had flung open the door. Cale closed the door behind him, soundless as possible. Jacek let out the clutch and the jeep spun a half circle, back tires churning clumps of mud as it bounded onto the narrow, half-paved road. First then, as they accelerated away from the tent camp, did his partner flick on the headlights.

Glancing at Jacek in the closed cab, the man was grinning as he drove, and Cale realized his partner was humming "Season of the Witch," as they sped away through the gloomy African twilight.

CHAPTER 36

Creeping in like a brazen thief intent on stealing what was left of twilight's gray gloaming, the African night took no prisoners. From out on the water, the lights of the compound glowed warm and serene. Half-palace, half-prison, the giant walled enclosure gave the illusion of safe harbor.

Inside the fortress, however, the truth was being exposed.

Tazeki Mabutu was enraged. His anger was multiplying by the minute. He had kicked away the new rug, and from his chair he now reached beneath the desk and flicked the tiny metal latch. He heard the trapdoor in the floor of his study spring open. The odor of seaweed and salty brine rushed into room like demons freed from a hell pit. Moving around his desk once more, he shone a flashlight beam down into the gaping dark hole in the floor. Nothing moved. No sound but the usual irregular dripping. No figure was lurking there, holding on for dear life. The detective, he imagined, was long dead by now. Gone. Eel food.

Back at his desk, Tazeki pressed the button that snapped the trapdoor back in proper place. Silence then, save for the monotonous crash of waves against the rocky beach outside. Tazeki's dark eyes swept the room, as if unable to comprehend Pazuzu was not there.

"Don't worry, old friend," he spoke to the shadows, "I'll find out where you are. If it's the last thing I do." And to accomplish this task, he understood he must locate the missing Kasim.

Tazeki pressed another button on his intercom. "Boto, get in here now." Rising, he strode from the study, not bothering to close the tall doors behind him. He moved into the open front reception area and paced impatiently about the room.

Moments later. a large military guard with a goatee rushed in through the front entrance, not bothering to knock. He paused before the colonel's angry presence. "We've found nothing so far, Colonel. His room is undisturbed," Boto reported.

"Your men are certain Kasim didn't return to the compound?"

"Yes, sir. No one saw him come back after marching the second prisoner through the back wall. And no weapons or vehicles are missing."

Tazeki thought hard for a moment. *Wait.* His eyes narrowed at the sergeant. "Repeat that part: a second prisoner?"

"The surveillance tapes—yes, sir. He marched out the first man. Then came back inside. Then...about an hour later...he marched out the second man."

"There was no *second* prisoner!" barked Tazeki. His brain felt like it was folding in on itself. In a stern voice, he shouted: "I must prepare for the ceremony. I want you to study every tape, every camera, every angle. From the moment those two men arrived today."

Sergeant Boto's skin had paled. He saluted and turned to leave.

"You find him, Boto... And he'd better have Pazuzu with him. Or the leopards will enjoy your fat arse as a midnight snack tonight."

Tazeki watched as his underling went rushing back out the front door.

Forced to swallow his rage, back in his study Tazeki picked up his desk phone. "Sergeant Ditt. Issue an immediate search for those two foreigners... Yes, the ones who were at my house." He listened for a moment. "Shoot on sight. They are terrorists." He hung up the phone.

Imbeciles.

***

It was dark now, after nine o'clock, when they crossed into River Cess County. They drove over the bumpy, muddy road, careful of potholes and deep, water-filled ruts. The jeep's twin headlights were lasers piercing the road ahead, catching the occasional flash of yellow eyes through the jungle brush. All this while the persistent drizzle continued. Cale imagined he knew how old Noah from the Bible had felt: Forty days and nights of this crap weather, and he'd be building an Ark of his own.

At the moment, Cale decided, he'd take a quiet and pleasant Wisconsin snowfall, any day.

During the drive, Cale had tried his mobile phone again, but couldn't manage a signal. He couldn't call Maggie to let her know he was even alive. He'd use Jacek's SAT phone when they took their next break. Yet he understood they had to conserve the battery—it was their lifeline. Stretching his legs, struggling for a more comfortable position, Cale felt the canvas sack on the passenger side floor nuzzle against his feet. Souvenirs from Liberia, he chided himself. Maggie will be impressed.

They were in a remote part of the country now, moving south, keeping the vast ocean on their right. At least they were still on an actual road. They had passed a place called Buchanan a while back and were headed to a shingle-and-tar shanty village on the coast called Cesstos. Cale shuddered to think how far they'd have made it on foot. Between the hyenas and packs of wild dogs, the full-on military search, the gun-toting teams of looting juvenile warriors. Well, it didn't take a math genius to calculate their odds of survival. This was the old Wild West times about a hundred.

"You look tired," Jacek said, glancing at his partner. Cale knew his eyes were sunken, his cheekbones edgy. He guessed the shadow of his stubble made him appear drained in the dimness. "Like a nine-year-old boy who's had a long day."

"Every time I close my eyes, you hit a pothole. Not much point in trying to sleep."

"Welcome to Africa. At least it's warm outside."

"You're a glass half-full guy, Jacek. I'll give you that much." Cale was lost in thought for a moment. "Can I ask you something? What happened back there? Between you and that Kasim character?"

Jacek shrugged. "First he had the upper hand—then I did. Survival works a switcheroo sometimes. Last man standing walks away."

It was a condensed summation, but Cale got the gist. Jacek had killed Kasim, perhaps just as easily as he'd sliced through the slab of roast beef in the colonel's kitchen. He felt too weary to engage in a lengthy conversation with his partner. He decided it best to conserve energy, save his strength for when he needed it. A time coming soon, he guessed.

Still, there was one thing that continued to niggle at Cale. "I'm having trouble wrapping my mind around our colonel friend. The *botono* part... Where you suggested he might be a witch doctor? What—he's some kind of sorcerer?"

"Voodoo is the indigenous religion here. The entire continent. It's a part of these people's souls—their afterlife." Jacek's words were sincere. "Just because we might not believe in a botono's power, doesn't mean it doesn't exist."

Cale held off mentioning about Chloe: How Maggie's sister's psychic powers had helped him in solving the Chemist case. How he'd given her props with the press afterwards. Though, truth be told, he was still having problems believing in the mystical. Angels and witches? Demons and spirits? Magic spells and folklore? They all played against Cale's brick-and-mortar version of reality. *Once a skeptic, always one,* his inner voice surmised.

"Seems kinda out there," he said, after a minute.

"If the Colonel is a botono, and he's working with Kinsella," Jacek offered, adding a shrug, "then he must have something to do with this trafficking ring." He was silent for a beat. "A religious mystic, and a military leader besides. He'd have just about all sides under his spell."

"Suppose so." Cale was growing too tired to think straight.

"Forget about it all for now, Mr. Packer." Jacek shifted in his seat. "We concentrate on getting out of this purgatory. Our reward will be getting some sleep in a soft, warm bed."

Cale did not reply. He had already allowed his eyes to close. Despite the bumps and swerves and rain pools in the road, he drifted off to sleep.

***

He must have been dreaming. Lanky slime-creatures with teeth outside their mouths, running upright, chasing him around the grass of Lambeau Field. This mixed with Jacek's reverberating descriptions, like an announcer speaking in a garbled voice over the PA system, rendering the full-house crowd a play-by-play.

This all happening just beyond his range of consciousness.

In lizard-like fashion, Cale blinked open his eyes. He looked around as the jeep's driver's door swung open, and his soggy Czech companion slipped back inside. Closed the door.

"Back from your beauty rest, Mr. Packer?"

"I miss anything?" Cale asked, groggy.

"Got through to Pharaoh on the SAT," Jacek reported. "We're set for pickup." He glanced at his wristwatch. "On schedule. Long as we don't get attacked by some amorous rhino."

Cale felt too disoriented to attempt anything clever. "'Amorous rhino,'" he repeated. "You're not serious, are you?"

"It's mating season. Rhinos have been known to attack trucks and jeeps in an aggressive sexual manner."

"Great," Cale mumbled. "Rhinos wanting to mate with us." He closed his eyes and drifted into a half-sleep. But not before asking himself: *What crazy bullshit comes next?*

CHAPTER 37

Like a caged cat pacing about his study, Tazeki decided this act was getting him nowhere. He sat rigid in his leather chair and glanced at his watch—close to running out of time. He had to get moving on the ceremony. Regardless of Kasim, regardless of the whereabouts of Pazuzu. To hell with them both. He had important things to do. As the old saying went—one he'd learned years ago, while attending college in America—"The show must go on."

He picked up his latest burner phone, noticing he had a text message from Kinsella. It announced in concise words: "Project complete. Crenshaw dead. Escape clean. Chicago. Orders?"

Orders, thought Tazeki. Yes. Thursday night was now upon them. The *Kwensana* was waiting dockside in Monrovia, ready to set sail for the U.K. once the final load was tucked aboard. He would see to it later this evening. One of his business colleagues, Prince Mir Al-Sadar, had invited him to attend his private Fetish Festival this coming Saturday. Tazeki, though, was hesitant at showing his face at the sordid, illicit—read *kinky*—affair. And even more now that the American detective had tied Kinsella, and maybe him as well, to the Emer Saud prince.

Imagining the worst, Tazeki could not prevent himself from picturing his face on law enforcement surveillance cameras. The simple solution? He could send Kinsella in his place to function as a guest judge. Besides, it was smart to move his henchman out of the

States. Kinsella was running hot. An APB might even be out for his apprehension. Sending him to Belgium, Tazeki decided, would kill a pair of birds with one stone.

He glanced at the time again: late afternoon in the Midwest. On his phone he texted "Prince Mir needs you. Dinner at the château. Tomorrow evening."

Flipping the phone into the lined garbage container, Tazeki rose and strode toward the high doors. His booted steps clicked over the polished hardwood floor as he vacated his study, walked down the hallway, and climbed the stairs to his dressing room on the second floor.

The show must go on.

***

Whup-whup-whup-whup...

The throb of the helicopter rotors could be distinguished from a half mile out. Flying low beneath the swollen purple clouds, the private Euro-copter out of the Ivory Coast had no fear of invading Liberian airspace. The war-torn country had no national air force, having dissolved it for good back in 2005.

Jacek had parked the jeep on the quay near the wide mouth of the River Cess, at the point where the jungle bush met the sand crusted shoreline. No one about. The only sound was the ever-present roll of the breakers as they crested and swept their way to shore, crashing with spray against the jutting rocks forming the inlet. No moon was visible. They were surrounded by the black-as-pitch jungle behind them. The ocean spread out like a flat, dark tablecloth, as far as the eye could see.

They had passed around the city of Timbo, then skirted the village of Cesstos. The village consisted of a couple thousand residents, and none of the citizens who spotted the covered U.N. jeep bouncing past on the muddy road paid them the slightest heed. They proceeded toward the seashore, unencumbered.

The timing was perfect, Jacek told Cale, for the vehicle was running low on petrol. On this wretched, drizzling night, there were no military jeeps about, no signs of local law enforcement. Still, they needed to maintain a watchful eye.

Colonel Mabutu was powerful, his resources limitless, and by now, they guessed, he was beyond angry. Not a good combination for their well-being.

Made even more serious, Cale reminded himself, glumly, if the man actually was a witch doctor. And not just some poser; or some two-bit charlatan.

Sheltered inside the covered jeep, they waited, understanding it would not be long. There was no need to phone. The helicopter was GPS-ing their position via the SAT phone. Tired, sweaty, too frazzled to maintain meaningful conversation, they sat in silence with their thoughts. After fifteen minutes, Jacek spotted the lights of the approaching helicopter. They were reflected off the low bank of soot-colored rain clouds.

When it made sense to reveal their position, Cale watched his partner open the door of the jeep and flash his penlight signal upward, into the night sky. The chopper swooped in a low arc, banking in along the beachhead, then lowered its approach and hovered. It created a dervish of blowing water and mushy wet sand below. They had planned ahead for a fluid pickup, and the chopper stayed perched at thirty feet above the beach. When the side door slid open and the weighted nylon ladder was unraveled, both Cale and Jacek understood it was time to vacate the jeep's dry sanctity.

A shout came from somewhere. Cale spun his head around, eyes searching the thicket of jungle opposite the quay. He grabbed his canvas sack and they began moving toward the dangling ladder. A blue light flashed, a whistling sound followed, and Cale felt Jacek tackling him to the ground. A second later their jeep exploded, lifted into the air from a mortar shell. Dirt and metallic debris and wet sand flew shrapnel-like around them, and the ground trembled a second time as the bulk of the jeep's carcass landed on the beach.

Smoke clotted the air, and jeeps could be heard rumbling across the way, gears grinding. Headlights swept the road behind them, cutting through the fog. Jacek pulled Cale to his feet and they began sprinting toward the shadow of the helicopter above. The pilot flicked the search beam on-off for a brief second. Through the darkness, the two men ran toward the lifeline. Jacek ordered Cale to climb first, keeping his Luger drawn and ready.

Grabbing hold of the lower rung of the ladder, Cale began his ascent, canvas sack in one hand, clawing his way upward like a palsied macaque.

Behind them a pair of military jeeps caromed off the road, rocking over the rough stones and onto the beach. Tires spun in the muck. Cale heard Jacek fire three rounds from the Luger. He was at the copter's open door when Jacek leaped onto the swaying ladder below. Cale heard automatic fire, saw flashing muzzles below, heard bullets whisking through the drizzle and humid night air. Jacek swirled his weapon wildly over his head, signaling the pilot.

Cale held the ladder for dear life as the helicopter leaned into a sudden acceleration, banking left, moving out over the black water until they were at last out of bullet range. The chopper hovered again, rocking, and Cale clambered aboard through the opened rear slide-door. Jacek hung puppet-like in the shadows, swaying in the down draft. The dark ocean undulated, a churning cauldron, and raindrops pelted the water's surface below them.

The crack of gunfire fell silent on the beach.

Uncertain if they were still within mortar range, Cale worked as fast as he could to aid Jacek, bring him up on board. If it was a heat-seeking missile their enemies were loading, he knew they were in deep trouble. He held the rope ladder steady, grabbing Jacek's elbow, pulling upward until his partner was safely aboard.

Moments later, they were holding on tight and felt the helicopter climb, then it lurched and banked and sailed off into the night. The introductions were meager. The pilot, Cale later learned, had fought side-by-side with Pharaoh in Somalia, during the 2010 uprising. The man owed Pharaoh a favor and was repaying in kind.

Only after they'd strapped themselves in did Cale allow himself a sigh of relief. He checked his limbs and body parts for injuries. His adrenaline rush had caused his heart to tom-tom against his sternum, but now, the excitement over, he could feel his system crashing.

Buckled at last in his seat, when Cale closed his eyes a minute later, he fell into the deep exhausted sleep of a cherub.

CHAPTER 38

Green Bay, Wisconsin

"Now I know how Ma Barker felt, after being sprung from prison." Maggie shot Slink Dooley a resigned look from the passenger seat. He was driving her back to her Mazda, which remained parked in a church lot a block from the downtown courthouse.

Slink shook his head at her, the way a dad would admonish his teenage daughter. "Hope you learned your lesson."

"Right. Don't get caught with an unregistered, just-fired handgun in your purse. Especially during an assassination."

"For starters." Slink cut his eyes toward her while navigating a turn. "Good thing you weren't charged. It might've messed up your chance for a PI license."

Maggie huffed. "Right now, that's the least of my concerns." She watched as they neared the parking lot. "Thanks for getting me out of there, by the way."

"You can owe me one." Silence hung for a moment. "They gave you your phone back, didn't they? Any message from Cale?" He understood they had demanded her phone and examined it for calls and text messages to Cynthia Hulbreth, the woman who'd been wrestled to the ground with the weapon in her hand.

It was protocol. They had to rule out any chance the women had concocted some strange conspiracy together.

Withdrawing her phone from her purse, Maggie stared at it. "I don't know what they did to it. The battery's out. I'll have to charge it when I get home." She frowned, frustrated. "Besides, Chloe's going to kill me. With all this happening, I stood her up for lunch."

Slink reached inside the pocket of his jacket. "Here. Use mine. Give her a quick call."

"No. I'll take my lumps in a few minutes."

Maggie's dark hair was pulled back, but a few wayward strands had worked themselves free. Lines of concern creased her forehead. Slink pulled the Taurus into the lot, now emptied after the day's earlier excitement. Her Mazda sat by itself, looking forlorn in the empty lot, as they eased to a stop close by.

Earlier at the station, Slink had considered recusing himself from the interview with Maggie, allowing Detective Blum or another detective to talk to her about her presence at the shooting. Why she had a just-fired handgun in her purse. But what kind of friend would he be, he'd asked himself, if he stood by and let the department's wolves descend on his partner's fiancé? Not a very good one.

While they were sitting in an interview room, with a secretary bringing in sandwiches Slink had ordered from the nearby deli, an officer had poked her head into the room. She informed Slink how Maggie's claim of spending time at the private shooting range that morning checked out. The range's owner faxed over written proof, her ID, the exact time she was present, everything indicating her Kahr PM9 had been used for target practice.

It was enough to allow them to release her.

As for the rest of it, Captain McBride had assigned Slink to the case as lead detective. He'd been on site when the shooting occurred. And although there were officially no deceased persons yet (Tobias Crenshaw was on life support, with severe cranial trauma from a gunshot), there was little question an attempted homicide had occurred.

Maggie now leaned across the front seat and gave Slink a thank-you hug. Then she pulled back, giving him a nod, reaching for the door handle,

Slink said, "Hey, can I ask you something?"

Turning back to him, Maggie raised her eyebrows.

"Just want you to know we're here for you. Janet and I, you know?" Slink hesitated, looking her in the eyes. "With everything. No matter what."

"Does Cale know?" She eyed him, her wariness playing across her features. "That I'm—"

"Pregnant? Yeah." Slink's smile was genuine. "We're detectives, remember? Our job to figure shit out."

Maggie opened the door, stopped halfway, as if deciding on saying something further. She chewed her lower lip but said nothing.

"Call me later. After you speak to Cale," Slink insisted. "Or if you need to talk. Okay?" Anything else she wanted to add, he decided, she would say when she was ready.

Gracing him with a cutesy salute, Maggie stepped from the Taurus. Still holding open the passenger door, she asked, "When can I have my gun back?"

"Soon as ballistics clears it. I'll let you know."

Watching her drive off, Slink could feel the relief wash over him. He was on her side, and now she knew it. Not that she had thought otherwise, but with women...well, how did you ever know where things stood? He knew he wasn't good with heartfelt discussions. He always ended up going for the crass one-liner or humorous rejoinder. But here, with Maggie, he had done his best to be the kind of friend she needed at the moment.

Slink decided he could now return to the station with a clear head, start unraveling what had taken place on the courthouse steps that afternoon. Start to get somewhere on a reason, a motive. Like most men he knew, Slink was far more comfortable dealing with murder, than he was discussing pregnancy or relationship stuff with his best friend's fiancée. But with Cale not around, he knew he had to step up to the plate. Do what he could.

That's what friends—and partners—did for one another.

***

The updated, remodeled police audio-visual/computer area is in the basement of the downtown Adams Street station. It's part of the Investigations Unit. They supply photographic equipment for surveillance, cameras, wiretaps, digital recorders. Even drones. Anything that will assist the officers or forensic techs in their investigations. The computer/electronics team consists of four officers and four video techs. They are specialists unto themselves.

Sergeant Peter Rosera (affectionately called "Pete Rose" by the officers) was the unit's leader. He now sat staring at a bank of video monitors, studying the CCTV surveillance tapes from the Brown County courthouse.

"Thorp," he barked to one of his junior technicians. "Get me a still shot of the crowd forty seconds before the first shot was fired."

Three chairs away, Tiara Thorp did as ordered. She enhanced the footage of the front steps of the courthouse, a wide-angle view of the gathered media and onlookers. She froze the shot at forty seconds. The computer scanned the shot, and from the laser printer a few seconds later emerged a detailed photographic blowup of the crowd.

"Rodriguez." Rosera barked at another tech. "Get me the sequence shots of vehicles leaving the parking lot right after the shooting. Let's assign numbers to them all so we can track them."

Two hours later, when Detective Slink Dooley entered the AV unit with a hearty, "What you got for me, Pete Rose? And it better one-up Zapruder," Sergeant Rosera was ready.

***

Slink sighed and blinked his eyes, glancing away from the monitors. He leaned forward and placed both hands on the back of a chair, staring back at the bank of glowing screens again. "A sniper shot? And you are guessing some cameraman in the crowd is our shooter?"

"We broke down the video as requested, Detective," Rosera explained. "Every camera, each possible angle, the entire time-sequentials. Using the gathered forensic data, we concentrated on the frontal kill shot."

"Cut to the chase, Sergeant," Slink said, shooting a glance at his watch. "If you don't mind."

On the large high-def monitor, Rosera pointed at the row of cameramen gathered around the steps of the east side courthouse entrance. He indicated how they all continued to roll their footage, staring through their viewfinders in spite of the sound of gunfire. "All of them except—" The sergeant directed Slink's eyes to the monitor as he zoomed on one particular image.

"Except this guy! Right here." said Slink, picking up the cue. One of the cameramen appeared to be peeking out from around his camera. "The black guy. In the BET jacket."

"Bingo."

Slink glanced at the sergeant. "I'm not seeing anything resembling a weapon."

Rosera went on to explain his idea—theory, at this point—on the potential conversion of a video camera into a sniper weapon. How it was possible, even though they had never laid eyes on a tricked-out model, such as this, in real life. Nor did they have any evidence supporting the idea.

Slink was staring at the monitor. "Rewind it," he said, pointing at the screen. "Back to where our guy is peering out from behind his camera."

Rosera did as requested. The large cameraman wore a baseball cap and was crouched low. The closed-circuit camera angle, twenty feet up the courthouse wall, could not discern his face.

"I'll enhance the video," said Rosera, "see if we can get a better blowup on him."

Slink rose from his leaning position. He turned to depart. "Do everything you can, Pete Rose. Get me the photo. Then let's see if we can get any A.I. facial-rec on this character."

***

Before he left the office that evening, one of the secretaries buzzed Slink at his desk. He was informed a series of photographs was being e-faxed to his computer from the video forensics department. Sergeant Rosera had managed to isolate and enhance the BET cameraman's face. She was sending the images over to Slink's attention as they spoke.

Watching his screen as the file downloaded, Slink felt a grin spread across his face. Studying the trio of enlarged images: *Bingo!* Buzzing the secretary back, he told her he was sending the file to her computer. He gave her a pair of email addresses and informed her where he wanted the images sent.

"And tell Pete Rose he's a genius!" he added, before flicking off his computer. Rising, Slink headed out the door. He now had a potential suspect and solid evidence in the shooting. All he needed was to track down the perpetrator's identity, and they could make an arrest. If their guy was in the wind, well, that's where the FBI's nationwide ID registry would come in handy.

Moving toward his car in the parking lot, Slink couldn't shake the image of the shooting suspect from his mind. Despite the ballcap and BET jacket, he could swear he'd seen the shooter's face before: the anaconda neck, beady eyes, bald or shaved head, were registered somewhere in his mental criminal registry. Along with a thousand other faces. Slink just couldn't put his finger on where. Deciding to not dwell on it, he figured the memory would come to him.

He needed to allowed the image to simmer for a while. Rest in the cellar of his subconscious; allow it to breathe there like a fine wine. It would come to him when it was ready.

Slink didn't want to shake the confidence he felt. With a couple of breaks, in a matter of days Green Bay's first public assassination case might be cracked. And when that occurred, one question would remain: the all-important question of motive. Once they established who had committed the crime, the solitary missing puzzle piece would be *Why?*

Why had Tobias Crenshaw taken a bullet to the brain? Why would anyone want him the infamous Chemist out of the way? So much so, that they'd risk executing him in the public square? The list of those wanting him dead was long: the fentanyl dealing cartels; members of the shadowy, international human trafficking ring; families of the kidnapped victims, whose lives had been ruined.

Just to name a few.

Slink imagined it would all come out in the end. As in most high-profile cases, it usually did. He understood that all he could do from his end was work the case. Let the chips fall where they may.

CHAPTER 39

Liberia, Africa

Drums echoed through the rainy African night. Another ceremony of virgins, the second one this week. This time it was a different location, on the opposite side of the same range of soaring mountain peaks.

Tipa was a small village near the Putalla Mountains, close to the banks of a wide inland river estuary. The parade of participants—dancing, shuffling, bearing torches—wound its way from the village, up a narrow path, moving beneath the overhang of trees whose leaves dripped with rainwater. The climb was steady as they traversed the base of the mountain. To an observer a mile away, the torches could be mistaken for fireflies in the night.

Tonight's ceremony inside the cavern would provide a welcome respite from the soiled gray clouds that quilted the heavens, crying rain on the heads of those gathered for the botono's blessing. Tonight, was a ceremony of protection. The residents of Tipa would pay the price of a dozen young virgins to fulfill the witch doctor's needs.

With the backbeat of talking *tanbu* drums and gourd rattles echoing, the torch-bearing villagers slipped inside the opening in the rocks, one after the next. They spread through the main central chamber of the high cave, gathering around the center pole-tree—*poteau mitan*—where a skull was perched on top like a Christmas angel. The pole was decorated with markings and feathers and an array of colorful gifts drooping from its extended branches.

To one side of the chamber, a huge granite altar had been gifted with a multitude of carved statues, shiny bottles, photographs, colored stones and gourds, handmade knives, biscuits, bowls of cornmeal. These all gifts for the loa. The worshipers—in their colored caftans or striped grand boubous, or canvas pants with bare torsos—ringed the chamber, forming a circle around the central totem. Hands clapping in rhythm, swaying, chanting, shuffling in place, they awaited the arrival of Botono Mabutu.

The drums turned low, continuing a guttural throb.

At the edge of the deep cavern, he appeared in a magnificent black robe, arms spread wide like a soaring hawk. White paint circled his eyes, and tears of paint spotted his dusky cheeks.

The drums ramped up their fervor.

From the crowd, a mambo emerged, a bone necklace, bushy tufts and colored bracelets adorning her arms and legs. She wore a top hat with a large raven feather pierced through the brim. A fat cigar was held between her lips, her face painted like the botono's. The mambo took her place across the chamber, opposite the witch doctor.

An elderly village *houngan*, a healer, stepped from the ranks of swaying participants—many of them shirtless, dark skin gleaming—and emptied a bottle of rum around the center pole: a gift for the loa. He shuffled back into the group.

The botono began a chant in an ancient African tongue; and the drum beat slowed again. The crowd shuffled in place, swaying, a maelstrom gathering in the room's central core. Lighting a fiery brand, he touched it to the fire pit. *Whoosh.* Bright sparks danced and sizzled. When the flames died down, the witch doctor raised his left hand. He was summoning a petro loa, a dark god. The rhythmic gourds rattled, along with the low, guttural thumping of the tanbu. A young female let out a sudden shriek, indicating the arrival of the loa. She jerked and lurched about like a seaman being flogged by sharp leather whips. The others continued to dance, whirling, surrounding her, protecting the loa and its horse.

The village chief stepped forward, leading a goat by a leash-cord. Assisted by strong young males, he maneuvered the animal, so its neck draped over a large wooden basin. The botono stepped toward the creature, long-knife in hand.

From the dark recesses of the cavern came the silent parade of twelve young virgins. All dressed in white, they marched forward, lining themselves near the dark back wall of the cave. Barefoot, frozen, their expressions were blank. Minutes later, the botono and mamba together began administering the "blessed" sacrament. Bread dipped in fresh blood.

The virgins, one by one, were carried from the cavern, safely out of sight.

***

In the same fashion as four nights earlier, the large canvas-covered military truck sat with its cargo loaded: twelve young females to be transported to the port city of Monrovia. The cargo vessel *Kwensana* was floating in the harbor, awaiting the final delivery.

Emerging from an invisible back exit of the cavern, now in military garb, face cleansed, Colonel Tazeki Mabutu strode to the driver-side door of the vehicle. Its engine was running. To the driver, he asked, "You have the correct papers, Shoppa?"

The uniformed soldier replied, "As always, Colonel. All is ready."

Both men in the truck's front seat were armed with TEC-9 automatics. Thirty-two round bloody punches of death. Mountain rebels were always a threat to hijack the shipment. The soldier's eyes gleamed in the darkness. Tree branches swayed around them, and the backdrop of the mountain peaks stretched in earnest against the night's thick velvet curtain.

"Text my mobile phone when you arrive. Tell the captain the ship sets sail when he is ready." The men saluted, and Tazeki watched the truck as it began easing away down the sloping mountainside.

Swollen, grease colored clouds swept across the purple heavens, serving to blot out *Lshne* and her bridesmaid stars. Tazeki thanked the loa for allowing a letup in the rains. It would allow for a smoother helicopter ride back to his compound. A long night awaited him. He understood he would not be able to rest. Not until he discovered what had happened to Kasim.

And even more disturbing: what had happened to his old friend, the wind demon Pazuzu?

CHAPTER 40

Green Bay, Wisconsin

It was Thursday afternoon at the Mood Indigo Beauty Emporium, and Chloe Ravelle sat alone in the break room. She was sipping from her cup of ginger tea—decaf—and in quiet she cussed-out her sister. Maggie had stood her up for lunch. Missed it. No phone call, no message. Nothing. While it was out of character for her sibling, it didn't make it any easier for Chloe to digest.

Sitting at the table in the quaint restaurant they usually dined in, disappointment at last giving way to concern, Chloe had called Maggie's phone. No answer. Left one message, two, then three. Where on earth could she be? Had she forgotten about their lunch date? It was possible, she supposed, with Cale out of town and all the things Maggie had going on in her life at the moment.

Yet it still wasn't like Maggie. So, Chloe was worried.

After consuming a quick salad, Chloe had paid the bill and driven back to work. After leaving yet another message, she decided to wait a few hours before calling again. It would serve Maggie right, allow her to wallow in her guilt.

Earlier that day, Chloe heard the news reports of the shooting at the courthouse. Tobias Crenshaw was gunned down, shot in the head, odds on dead by now, if she had to venture a guess. Had Maggie gotten caught in the traffic? The police cordoning off possible escape routes? Attempting to contain the suspect in the shooting? Or was she—Chloe—watching too many crime shows on television? It was the more plausible explanation. While it might be true Maggie could have been trapped in traffic, it still didn't explain why she hadn't at least phoned, called to tell her she couldn't make lunch.

This was the part that irked Chloe the most. Now it was three p.m. and still no word from her sister. The CD player in the hair salon was spinning a selection most of the younger girls liked, music Chloe didn't seem to get. Some rappy-blues with an operatic backbeat, complete with garbled lyrics. She grabbed her tea mug and wandered down the hallway, headed toward the back area of the shop. Entering the long storage room, Chloe located the cardboard box, which held Leslie Dowd's personal belongings. Items left unclaimed by her parents when the girl had disappeared from the Emporium over a year ago.

Spotting the perfumed, rose-patterned handkerchief, Chloe reached for it. She held it delicately to her cheek, inhaled the perfumed scent...and within mere moments, she became dizzy and dropped to the floor, the vision grabbing hold of her, freezing her body, locking her the way a seizure overcomes an epileptic.

All Chloe could do was lay and watch as:

An opulent dining room with tall French windows, thirty-foot frescoed ceilings, filled with occupants. The table set, fine china, silver buckets of iced Cristal.

Attractive young females dressed in feminine finery, beginning to take their seats. An array of other guests garbed in shades of leather and latex and even rubber. Feathered eye-masks. Uniformed maids bustling about, whispering to one another how you are missing, how you're late for the gathering.

In your bedroom on the second floor, you sit brushing your hair, running late, wearing your undergarments and a terry robe. Everything in the room is antique, and you cannot be sure if it has stood here for a hundred years or was purchased just before your arrival, a year ago. Standing, you turn and face the long mirror; you spin around, examine yourself. Nary a flaw or a blemish. Your body is lean, muscles hardened from the exhausting efforts and countless hours of long practice.

You turn from the mirror, grab your dress from the back of the chair. Slip the slinky garment over your head, smooth the fabric over your hips. Shimmy, turn, making certain no lines or creases exist. Luxurious. Step into the closed-toe pumps—for you dislike open-toed, strappy heels. You free your hair from its pin, sweeping it forward, blond tresses cut at a modest length. You brush it back with the stiff-haired brush, teasing forth the luster.

A knock on the door. "I'm almost ready." You call this to whom you imagine is one of the maids. The doorknob turns, but you do not turn around. Your shoulders tense. You know who stands in the doorway, know by his silence, his aura, the way the air shifts inside the room: the lean, dark suited man in the sharp goatee. His black eyes wash over your every curve, his tight gaze penetrating the back of your neck. You despise this man with all your heart...and this is the reason you do not afford him a glance. Now, as the narcotics invade your brain, buzzing like a swarm of insects, this is your choice, and you understand he will not force you to look at him. At least not this time...

He pauses in the room's center, statue-like. "I want you to behave yourself tonight, my dear."

"I will behave as I choose." Defiant.

"You understand the consequences. Do not challenge me."

"What I understand, is you are a pervert and a liar. Not to mention a cannibal."

He seems amused, and you imagine him stroking his goatee with his fingertips, the way he does when he fears losing control. "You remember our bargain?"

"How can I forget? If I—if we—win the competition tomorrow, you will set me free." You release an unfeminine snort.

His words turn sincere. "I will keep my promise to you, Leslie. As long as you hold up your end."

"We win, and I go free. We lose..." You shrug your bare shoulders.

"Losing, my dear, is not a healthy option for you."

Chloe blinked, the vision fading. She now saw a faint light surrounding her. She inhaled the musty odor of the storage room, which engulfed her where she lay on the floor. She lifted herself to an elbow, then into a sitting position. The migraine was back, and she touched her fingertips to her temples. The vision again.

"Leslie," Chloe heard her own voice murmur out loud, asking, "where on earth are you?"

Pulling herself from the floor, Chloe gathered her bearings. Spotting the rose-patterned kerchief on the floor where she had dropped it, she plucked it up and slipped it into the pocket of her smock. No doubt about it: her visions were back.

Chloe made her way unsteadily out of the storage room, moving like a punch-drunk boxer attempting to locate his dressing room. Still disoriented, she wandered back toward the front of the salon.

***

When Maggie returned home, Hank came trotting to greet her. His feline face bore a look of contrition. She imagined he was apologizing for having growled at her during the earlier ride to the vet. Whatever nasty vibes he had thrown her way, he seemed now to regret them. All was forgiven.

She lifted the plump tabby in her arms, gave him a smooch and listened as he returned a contented purr. "My brave little guy," she said, staring at him with their noses touching. "Did that nasty vet hurt you? Are you all right now?"

Hank stared at her like she might be an angel, his bright green eyes seeming to smile as she nuzzled her face against his round furball head. Then he squirmed, and Maggie let him drop to the floor. He was back to his normal self. When she opened the refrigerator door, he rubbed against her shins, aware she was withdrawing a can of his favorite cuisine. His appetite appeared no worse for the wear.

While Hank ate his dinner, Maggie swept up the steps and changed into shorts and a white Packers T-shirt. She fashioned her hair back in a ponytail and plugged her mobile into the charger. Back downstairs, she phoned Chloe on the dining room phone.

"Hey, I'm back home." Maggie kept her tone light. "Mea culpa regarding lunch. And not calling—they took away my phone. Thanks again for taking care of Hank."

"No, uh...problem," Chloe said, a bit terse, as well as confused. "Care to tell me who *they* are?"

"God, Chlo. You're not going to believe what happened."

Maggie opted to give her sister the abridged version, concluding with how Slink had come to her rescue. When Chloe asked, Maggie admitted it was strange she had yet to hear from Cale. Not a word all day. If she didn't know he could take care of himself, she might begin to worry.

"Glad you're okay," Chloe said, warming, unable to stay mad at her sister. Not when she'd had the vision she'd just experienced. "Listen, Mags, I just had the strangest dream. More like a vision. And you're not going to believe this—it was about Leslie Dowd."

"The missing girl? That Leslie Dowd?" Maggie thought about it. "The one Cale's trying to locate?"

Chloe exhaled. "Yes. She's *alive*, at least. She was dressed all fancy, getting ready to attend a dinner party. In the home of some dark and mysterious man—a man she *despises*."

Maggie shook her head.

"You sure you're not reading those Harlequins again?"

"Ha-ha." Chloe let a beat pass. "If you want, I'll come over tonight and swap stories with you."

Maggie agreed, saying she needed to relax. And company would be nice. Especially with all that had happened on this crazy day. She would even supply the wine—although she couldn't drink much, herself, she allowed.

She promised to fill Chloe in on everything.

CHAPTER 41

Liberia, Africa

"This is bloody insane," whispered Tazeki, sitting in his quiet, late-night study.

On his computer screen he was viewing the security tapes from the CCTV cameras from earlier this afternoon. Watching the bizarre footage as it unfolded before his eyes. Watching for the third time this night. First, he saw Kasim—unmistakable in his Nehru jacket—marching the Czech, Tumaj, toward the concealed exit door at the back wall of the compound. Both men had swarthy skin tone, appearing close to brothers on the colorless monitor. The garrote was tight around the prisoner's neck. Kasim appeared in complete control, his footsteps careful on the wet back lawn.

There was no doubt, Tazeki decided. The image didn't lie. It was real; this *had* transpired. The pair of men disappeared through the outer wall, out of camera range.

Fast forward to the second set of images, showing Kasim returning, alone, back through the outer compound door. The time-stamp read 11:42 a.m. Over *seventeen* minutes—Tazeki pondered the puzzle—why did it take so long to garrote the man? He racked his brain for clues. Was there something different about Kasim on his return? His servant walked with the identical rigid, upright posture, his chin down, head lowered against the annoying drizzle. But something *was* different. He just couldn't put his finger on it.

Tazeki rewound the video, attempting to pinpoint what he was missing. *There!* There it was! It was the trousers. That's what had changed. Though the Nehru jacket covered Kasim's legs down to his upper thighs, his pants were dark in the first sequence. On the second, the return walk, they appeared a degree lighter. Though the difference was almost indiscernible on the black-and-white monitor—factoring in the persistent drizzle, which would dampen the clothing—Tazeki would swear he could spot a difference in the shade.

Was it his imagination? An artifact of the drizzle? Or the dreary lighting? The different time of day, perhaps, causing the fabric to appear a somewhat lighter shade?

Fast forward to the third view of Kasim. And this one caused the hair on the back of Tazeki's neck to rise. First, there was *no need* for a third trip. Nevertheless, in this shot—fifty-five minutes and nineteen seconds after the last—Kasim was marching *a second prisoner* out of the main house. Marching him across the back lawn. Controlling him with the garrote wire.

Only it wasn't Kasim, Tazeki decided. *It can't be.* And the prisoner? No one in the compound was reported missing. It left but one other possibility, remote as it seemed: the prisoner was the American detective, Van Waring! The Czech, Jacek Tumaj, had somehow survived his encounter with Kasim. He'd returned, *disguised in Kasim's jacket*, to rescue his American friend. How the detective had not been devoured by the eels was but another unexplained miracle. Still, in the dimness of the study, in the middle of this rainy and darkest of African nights, the video proof looked incontrovertible.

The surveillance tapes did not lie.

Tazeki leaned back in his desk chair. There was no mistake. He was witnessing the escape with his own eyes. He focused on the pair frozen on his screen, staring at the canvas sack the American was carrying as he was marched toward the outer wall of the compound. It appeared to contain something heavy, something of weight, of substance. Something that swung heavy with each step as he walked.

Was it something stolen? Anger was swelling inside him by the moment. Something that, if he were not mistaken, could well be his missing statue of Pazuzu?

"Son of a bitch!" Tazeki let loose a howl, bathed in the purple glow of the computer screen. Withdrawing the Ruger 9mm from his holster, he fired two quick rounds into the monitor. Then he shot the betraying electronic image—now long gone—three more times for good measure.

In better times, Kasim would have rushed into the study to investigate the sound of gunfire. Now no one came. There was no Kasim. Inhaling the oily smell of the spent weapon, Tazeki swore on the death of his loyal servant: He would find the American detective, wherever on Earth the cur might be hiding. Hunt him down. The man responsible for the unacceptable state of how things now stood. Responsible for harassing Kinsella, responsible for Kasim's death; and worst of all, responsible for the disappearance of Pazuzu.

Even, Tazeki further imagined, responsible for the missing shrunken head.

Yes. The American detective would pay a terrible price. He would pay with his life, as well as with the lives of his loved ones. And their loved ones after that.

Until Pazuzu was recovered, until he—*the botono*—decided the debt was repaid.

First then did Tazeki hear the footsteps of his security guards approaching.

***

Two hours later, alone once again in his study—his guards having carted away the carcass of the old computer, replaced it with the backup Dell they kept at the ready—Colonel Tazeki Mabutu had pieced together what he guessed had transpired. Between the video, his guards' reports and a few phone calls, the storyline had been verified. A missing U.N. jeep had been recovered: blown to bits. A border patrol unit reported firing shots at a lone helicopter near the mouth of the River Cess. A pair of men had escaped aboard the chopper. The patrol guessed they were arms smugglers. Or illegal rhino horn poachers.

Tazeki, however, knew better.

"Were they carrying anything with them?" the colonel demanded.

"Yes, Colonel. One was firing a handgun. The other carried what appeared to be a canvas sack." He paused. "Could have been rhino horns inside, we suppose."

So, there it was. The Czech and the rude American detective had escaped. And no, they hadn't been pilfering stolen horns. Instead, Tazeki guessed, the sack contained the shrunken head and his beloved statue of Pazuzu.

Escaped by helicopter. They wouldn't fly out to sea, would they? Some awaiting American vessel? It was doubtful, he decided. So where would they go?

The colonel made a few more phone calls. He had connections with his military counterparts across the border in the neighboring country, the Ivory Coast. The IC military police head informed Tazeki that they had confirmation, via satellite radar reports: a non-military helicopter had arrived at a U.N. base. Thirty minutes afterwards, a military cargo plane had taken off. The plane had filed a flight plan. She was headed to the U.S. Navy military base in Naples, Italy.

Tazeki wondered about the destination: Naples. Just down the coast from Rome, for one thing. It was also home to a naval base. It would be the nearest thing to a safe-haven for an American on the run. But the colonel was a spider with many long and poisonous fingers. And his web was dripping with deadly venom.

Through his international European slave-trafficking business, Tazeki had connections across Central Europe. Italy, he well knew, had forever been a country flavored by both political and religious intrigue. Two areas the botono was most adept at.

Withdrawing a well-used Rolodex from the lower desk drawer, he began flipping through it until he located the number he sought. It was late in the evening, and Tazeki understood he must move with haste. His agile mind had already formulated a plan of action. He reached for one of his untraceable burner phones and punched in the number.

The voice on the other end answered in Italian and Tazeki advised the man the switch to English.

"A long time, Colonel," the voice said. "What brings such a surprising phone call? And at this late hour, no less?"

Tazeki explain the situation. He conveyed to the man all the details he needed to know. Security presented a challenge at any European airport, but even more at a military landing strip, as was the case at Naples International. "I'll fax you the target's photograph in a few minutes."

"Clean or messy, Botono? Or does it not matter?"

Tazeki thought for a moment. "An accident. But if not, well, you *Italianos* are quite notorious for mob assassinations in public places." He paused. "Above all, I want the American terminated. And I want the contents of the canvas sack returned to me, without a scratch."

"As you wish, Colonel."

After ending the call, disposing of the phone, Tazeki strode across the room to his wet bar and built himself a drink. He flung open the doors and stepped out onto his veranda, which overlooked the undulating seas. The wind had picked up, and he stared through the drizzle at the rain-soiled clouds that painted the coastal night sky. By sunrise, this whole business with the American and his search for Kinsella would be over. In a day or two, he would have his possessions back. Then he and Pazuzu could share a good laugh about the adventure.

With the rain dampening his forehead, Tazeki raised his glass in toast to the rolling waters, the crashing waves, the heartless moody night.

CHAPTER 42

Ivory Coast, Africa

The military cargo plane proved to be as comfortable as riding in an old RV from the '70's, whose insides had been stripped down and gutted of all amenities. Still, Cale couldn't complain. The on-board Navy medic had cleaned and bandaged his wounds and patched him up as best she could.

She'd also administered a cocktail injection of broad-spectrum antibiotics to "Knock out the nasties," as she'd unceremoniously put it.

Fine with Cale. After what he'd been through on the Dark Continent, knowing he'd be free of viruses and parasites and God-knows-what-else, was worth any discomfort involved. Riding strapped-in like a paratrooper on the cargo plane, his muscles throbbing and sore, he'd been too numb to feel the injection, anyway.

The medic did the same to Jacek, though his own battered body had not been through anywhere near what his partner had experienced. Cale concluded that the jeep ride through the rainy African night, hitting every ditch and pothole in six counties, was akin to an hour-long ride inside a cement mixer. It was the only comparison he could think of.

The authorities had confiscated Jacek's Luger at the Ivory Coast air base. Had even inspected Cale's African "artifacts" (confiscating the long-bladed knife), before handing them back the canvas sack. Cale had discarded his phone before they'd boarded the cargo flight. It was useless, the battery fried.

"Mementos from Africa?" the inspecting officer had asked, elevating dusky eyebrows beneath his tight military buzzcut.

"Early Christmas gifts." Cale was too exhausted for small talk.

The man held up the lacquered shrunken head. "I'll be damned. Looks close to real, if you stare at her long enough." Cale shrugged at the man's grin.

"This place will spook you, no doubt," the officer added, his smirk unyielding.

"C'mon, Mr. Packer," prodded Jacek from behind him. "You're holding up the line."

After inspecting Jacek's SAT phone and wristwatch (still functioning), the man had handed them back their passports and pointed across the tarmac, where Navy grunts were finishing their loading of the large cargo plane.

"Y'all enjoy your flight back to Italy," beamed the officer, mimicking every flight attendant in the history of air travel. "Come back and visit the Ivory Coast anytime."

Cale nodded, and he followed Jacek toward the back of the transport.

***

Naples, Italy

Nito "Nine Lives" Passetti felt no hesitation in accepting the phone call from the Liberian colonel, when the private number had shown up on his mobile. Twice before, in fact, Nito had done jobs in Naples for Colonel

Mabutu. And two things could be said about the Liberian: he paid fast, and he paid well. Often three-to-four times the going rate. In the hit man business (especially in Italy, where you couldn't pass a busy street corner without spotting some Tony Montana wannabe), it was high praise, indeed.

The fact was, the colonel could have selected any number of local Napoli operatives to accomplish the job he was requesting. Such being the case, Nito had accepted the contract with little hesitation. Although it was short notice—termination jobs were seldom contracted inside a three-day window—it went without saying that he would accomplish the task with utmost professionalism. It was the simplest way to guarantee return business: do a job neat, do it fast, and keep your mouth shut afterward.

It was the code *"Nove Vivere"* lived by.

Upon receiving the fax from Colonel Mabutu ID-ing the target, and being fed the logistics of the situation, Nito had an immediate decision to make. The target's plane would land at Naples International, and the man would be funneled through the American military terminal—surrounded by armed security personnel and surveillance cameras. The fact he wasn't traveling alone further complicated matters. Working in Nito's favor, however, was that it would be after three a.m. when they arrived.

The dark and lonesome witching hour.

Nito understood he had to come up with a fast, dependable plan. And he had. It was, after all, what he was noted for. That and *palle bronzo* (balls of brass).

So here things now stood, with Nito sitting in the front passenger seat, angling the taxi's rearview mirror to check his false mustache, as they waited in the six-cab queue leading up to the front doors of the terminal. He knew he'd have to pass through a metal detector scan before entering, so the mission was proving more intricate than a simple armed snatch-and-grab. Despite the security guards and military personnel in the area, a blitz attack, Nito decided, was still the best way to go. Yet it would prove tricky, due to the colonel's insistence on the target being taken out with no harm to the canvas sack (or its contents). It meant no rapid-fire weapons, no wall-shattering explosives.

Nito's plan was now in motion. Everything would depend on a couple well-timed maneuvers, and if it all went as hoped, he'd soon be sailing away from the scene of carnage, canvas sack tucked beneath his arm. Colonel Mobutu would gift him with a generous bonus later. Just as he had on three previous occasions.

After a glance at his wristwatch, Nito nodded to his partner in the shadows of the driver's seat. He exited the cab, walking toward the lighted entrance of the airport's military terminal. As he moved, he thought of the words Americans often employed in situations like this:

It's showtime!

***

The landing had been a little bumpy, but no one complained. The flat concrete tarmac of the Naples International Airport seemed to undulate a little, and as he walked, Cale felt as if he'd spent a week aboard an aircraft carrier. His legs were rubbery, the sensation a marathoner gets hitting the twelve-mile plateau. Moving inside the sliding doors, he lagged a step behind

Jacek. Cale imagined they appeared like weary partiers who'd just stepped off the redeye from Las Vegas. To anyone who'd listen, he would explain he felt even worse. No one was listening.

"Mr. Packer," Jacek said, not bothering to smile. "If I didn't feel so rotten myself, I'd say you look like shite warmed over."

"Never without a complement, Jacek. You'll make some lucky woman quite happy one day."

"Woman?" Jacek grunted. "Right now, a barnyard goat wouldn't have me."

"Don't sell yourself short, my friend."

Cale had managed a couple hours of sleep on the flight, though not the restorative sleep his body needed to repair itself. As he'd dozed off, his thoughts kept flitting from being trapped in the eel pit, to the lurking menace of Colonel Tazeki Mabutu and his band of armed henchmen. After that, to the sadistic hulk named Kinsella; and finally, to Maggie, his pregnant bride-to-be. To make matters worse, Cale admitted to himself that his trip had been a failure. He was no closer to locating the mystery man (Kinsella), whom Tobias Crenshaw had fingered as the "true killer."

Nor was he one bit closer to rescuing the two missing girls—Leslie Dowd and Mary Jane Moore.

The single thing he had managed to accomplish was coming close to getting himself killed. More than once. That he remained alive and upright was but through the grace of God.

After presenting the guards with their passports, they were wanded and passed through airport security. Because this was the U.S. military personnel terminal, set apart from the main airport, guards were positioned at all entry points. Even at this godforsaken hour, terrorism did not sleep.

The image of Pharaoh lumbering toward them from across the terminal lobby, however, summoned a grin to Cale's face. The kind he usually reserved for long-lost friends. It was a form of delirium, he decided, reminding himself he'd known the man for just two days. Beside him, Jacek called out: "A guardian angel. We must've been on a plane flight to heaven, Mr. Packer."

Pharaoh's lip curled into a sneer, as much a smile as they were going to get. "Traveling light, I see, Jacek?"

Jacek lifted his chin toward Cale's canvas sack. "My partner here, the souvenir collector." He sighed, weary and spent. "Prized artifacts from Africa. He never told us he was a collector."

"They worth anything?"

"Sentimental value," Cale said, with a tired shrug.

Jacek waved his hand. "Nothing he couldn't have purchased in an airport bookstore."

Pharaoh's dark eyes surveyed the almost deserted terminal, as if memorizing it. Cale followed his gaze. A pair of Navy enlisted man sat on un-cushioned chairs, ditty bags tucked beneath their feet. They appeared to be awaiting a flight. Two rows behind them, a soldier with a mustache and mirrored sunglasses appeared to be asleep. His long legs were extended in front of him, arms crossed, chin tucked. Elevated on one nearby wall were monitors, which indicated flight arrivals and departures.

Beyond the video monitors, a lone female agent worked the counter. Across the opposite side of the room, a security guard was sitting on a chair, talking in Italian with the cleaning girl, who was spraying and wiping the waiting area. Nothing but a skeleton crew this time of night.

Pharaoh explained to Jacek how he parked the van in the nearby visitors' lot. His handgun was inside the glove box, aware it wouldn't pass through the scanners at the entry doors. The country itself was a terrorist tinderbox, ready to explode.

"Cheetah?" Jacek elevated one bushy eyebrow

"Around. Somewhere. Best we don't know." Pharaoh's eyes lifted toward the sliding outside doors, and it didn't take much guesswork for Cale to know Cheetah was hidden somewhere in or out of the building, alert for apparent threats.

"Paranoia" was the word that came to mind. But Cale was reminded himself how these people operated. They lived by different rules than did average citizens. As if at last remembering where he was, he glanced at his wristwatch, then asked if he could borrow Pharaoh's phone. A quick call to Maggie was in order.

"We've got to hit the road," Jacek said. "It's ninety minutes back to Anzio."

"Two minutes. Just a courtesy call."

After Pharaoh handed Cale his mobile, his partners stepped a few paces away. In a low voice Jacek began conveying the story of their African trip. It was a tale, Cale guessed, his friend was certain to embellish with extravagant detail.

Cale punched in the numbers and forced himself to stare across the small terminal at the departure monitors. Either that or his eyes would close by themselves. He was bone tired. It was ten p.m. back in Green Bay, and he felt his spirits lift as Maggie answered on the fourth ring.

CHAPTER 43

Green Bay, Wisconsin

It was just before nine that evening and Chloe was ready to call it a night. She paused in the kitchen, ready to exit the back door.

"Remember to drink your peppermint tea," she called back to Maggie. "You'll thank me in the morning." She stepped outside and eased the door closed behind her. Made sure it locked.

Through the window, Maggie watched her sister move through the glow of the outside security lights and slip inside her Buick. Certain Chloe was safe, she let the curtain close and double-bolted the door. When she turned around, Hank was sitting in the middle of the kitchen floor, his green eyes wide. She patted his head, thinking how pleased she was that her sister hadn't given her too much grief about missing their earlier luncheon. Despite everything that had transpired on this eventful day—the first public assassination in Green Bay history, after all—Chloe letting her have it with both barrels would have been understandable.

Maggie was in the bathroom now, washing her face, when she heard the house telephone ringing. She darted into the bedroom to answer, guessing it had to be Cale. Hoping, anyway.

"My God, Cale!" she stammered. "You've got to come home right away. Please. You're not going to believe what happened."

"I'd believe just about anything right now." His voice sounded thick with fatigue.

"Tobias Crenshaw"—the air gushed from her lungs—"he's been shot! Could be dead by now." Her words were met with deep silence and she glanced at her phone. "Cale? Can you hear me?"

"You can't be serious, right?" His tone rose the barest notch.

"They had a press conference on the courthouse steps. They're thinking Cindy Hulbreth might be the one who shot him."

Maggie took a breath and wiped her eyes, wondering why tears were forming. "Where are you? I've left you a dozen messages?"

"Phone got destroyed. I'm using a loaner. We just landed in Naples. A military base."

"Naples? You mean Italy?" It took a moment to sink in. "How did Liberia go? Did you find out anything?"

"Long flight over. Longer one back." Cale's voice was scratchy, fading. "I'll call you tomorrow. When I can think straight."

Maggie protested, her voice pleading: "Cale! Please come home! I need you back here."

Any reply he might've made, however, was smothered by a sudden clamor of shouting voices. And these sounds were drowned out an instant later by a tremendous explosion...

Followed by the cut to dead silence.

"Cale?" Maggie shouted into the phone. "Cale! Can you hear me?"

Nothing but dead air.

***

Naples, Italy

In the stealthy manner of a shark trolling midnight waters, the attack came from behind. One second Cale was talking to Maggie on the phone, the next all hell was breaking loose around him.

He held Pharaoh's phone to his left ear, the canvas sack in his opposite hand. He was staring out at the bank of Arrival/Departure monitors set behind the terminal counter, his eyes too weary to focus, when the wafting odor of sulfur drew his attention. This was followed by a hissing sound, and when Cale turned his head, he witnessed streams of smoke issuing from near a pillar twenty feet away.

A voice was shouting from somewhere—Jacek's voice?—when an explosion erupted the following second. The blast came from ten feet away, behind the nearby service counter. Cale ducked his head at the sound, hunching his head and pulling his phone arm up to ward against spraying debris.

This reflex movement (he realized later) may well have saved his life.

In nearly the same moment as the explosion, Cale felt one of the assailant's hands gripping his left arm, sending the phone skittering across the floor. Voices were shouting, crying out as the broad, half-empty waiting area descended into chaos.

The attacker's second hand, holding a seven-inch blade, swiped at the back of his neck, just as Cale was ducking from the blast. The blade missed by inches. The impetus of the assailant's errant attempt, however, allowed Cale to spin free of the man's grasp. In doing so, with his opposite hand he swung his canvas sack in an arc, striking the attacker's shoulder, preventing a second charge and keeping the assailant at bay.

Around them red lights were flashing, casting the terminal in a throbbing, disco-like glow. A siren blared. It reminded Cale of an air raid alert. The sulfuric odor and gray smoke seeped through the air. In response to this, the room's safety sprinkler system sent geysers of water spraying from the ceiling spigots.

Ignoring the shower, drenched like a river rat, Cale readied for his attacker's next rush at him. The assailant stood frozen, five yards away, poised, eyes wild, angling his knife.

But before he could attack again, Pharaoh freight-trained into the man, tackling him to the ground. This caused the blade to skitter across polished floor. Pharaoh's momentum, however, carried him beyond the assailant.

The man—Cale now recognized—had been the sunglass-wearing soldier who'd been feigning slumber in the third row of chairs. The man now scrambled up from his knees. His eyes darted to where Cale stood, eyeing the canvas sack, then the exit doors. With Jacek and a pair of security guards bearing down on him, the soldier chose the escape option: he dashed across the waiting area toward the exit.

Cale remained frozen, watching as the man elbowed aside one of the Navy men, who'd himself risen from the chairs. The assailant barreled out the front doors. Once beyond the glass outside the terminal, the next instant a dark SUV came to a screech at the curb. The assailant flung open the rear door and dove inside, just as the SUV accelerated away from the curb.

Jacek was at Cale's side a moment later, asking, "Are you all right? Did he cut you?"

Cale shook his head. The flashing red lights and alarm bells continued. Adrenaline was racing through his veins and he doubted he'd have felt the attacker's blade even if it had struck home.

"He missed. I'm okay."

Pharaoh had risen to join them, his chest heaving. "He was after you first," the large man said, sober, "and also the canvas bag."

A handful of security personnel were now rushing into the area from the main terminal. One of the men grabbed a fire extinguisher and was foaming the room's corner. Someone, unseen, turned off the alarm bell, blessing the room with instant quiet.

Jacek surveyed the chaotic terminal waiting area. He put what had transpired together in an instant, the way a chess master sees twenty moves ahead on a board. "The smoke bomb was a diversion. The explosion was a ruse, as well."

"Plastique," Pharaoh agreed. "It wouldn't trigger the metal detectors. Same with the knife. Ceramic."

"A professional. Cale was his target."

"Why not stab me in the back?" Cale searched them with his eyes. "I never saw him coming."

Jacek's tone was flat. "His plan wasn't to stab you. It was to pith you."

Pith me? Cale frowned. "What the hell does—"

"Like they pith of frog, Mr. Packer." Jacek sliced two fingers behind the back of his neck. "Your cervical vertebrae."

"You'd be on the floor, unable to even twitch," added Pharaoh darkly. "Paralyzed. For life."

A smoke screen diversion...plastic explosives, ceramic knife...a professional assassin. Cale took a few beats to process what they were saying. An attempt to maim him? Permanently? All in effort at stealing back Colonel Mabutu's precious little statue?

He was having difficulty accepting the theory. Why go through the trouble, Cale asked himself, for a pair of items you could purchase at a flea market? Unless the items were worth more than they appeared to be. And unless that person was Tazeki Mabutu—military leader, witch doctor, psychopath. All-around prick.

Cale felt his blood turn cold. The Colonel was no doubt a man with a deep thirst for vengeance.

In the distance, more security personnel were now arriving outside, flashing lights bouncing in the purple-hued dawn. Inside the military terminal, they were now sealing the area where the devices had gone off. They would begin rounding-up everyone in sight, commence a parade of interviews over the next four hours.

"Come on, Mr. Packer," Jacek said, guiding Cale now toward the exit doors. "Time to disappear."

Cale paused. His eyes swept the area under the chairs, the shadows there. "Pharaoh's phone. It skidded—"

"Forget the phone." Hand against his back. "Not traceable."

Outside at the curb, guards were already beginning to erect barriers to cordon off all entrances and exits. A pair of *carabinieri* arrived, likely from the main terminal. They began redirecting traffic away from the area. The cry of sirens could be heard in the distance.

Thirty yards down the street, pointed north, away from the terminal, Cale spied the dark van. Cheetah was inside, the running vehicle waiting for them.

"Hurry," Jacek ordered, his voice low as they escaped the exit doors. They moved onto the congested sidewalk.

Jacek slid left from the entrance, and they followed like scout troopers. A second later, he veered out onto the roadway, fast-walking. He was headed toward the van. Cale followed, surprised his legs could move. Pharaoh, ever the lookout, brought up the rear as they dodged across the four-lane *corso*.

A police whistle sounded behind them. *"Polizia! Fermi, per favore!"* Shouts from an officer back near the exit doors. He tweeted his whistle twice more.

Jacek yanked open the van's rear doors. Cale and Pharaoh piled into the boxy back compartment like schoolboys. Jacek jumped in last, pulling the doors closed behind them.

Cale had landed on a lumpy mattress and felt himself rocked backwards as Cheetah stepped on the gas. They were all pitched sideways a second later, and they searched for some handhold to grip. Cale heard tires squealing as the vehicle wheeled across the wide *corso*, changing lanes, rocking them again as Cheetah careened around a distant corner.

Despite the adrenaline dump of his attack, despite the van accelerating through the predawn streets of sparse traffic, Cale accepted that he could no longer fight off the exhaustion.

He closed his eyes and surrendered, allowing to the thick quilt of blackness to cover him like a shroud.

CHAPTER 44

Green Bay, Wisconsin

Creamy yellow streamers painted stripes across the unmade bed. The Friday morning sunshine rendered the room an artist's golden glow, and although the buttery brightness seemed pleasant, Maggie could not appreciate the caressing warmth.

Instead, she was kneeling on the floor of the upstairs bathroom, one arm draped over the toilet bowl. It felt as if a giant balloon had entered her stomach and was expanding.

She thought, defeatedly: "So much for peppermint tea."

She vomited again.

The morning sickness, retching, the sour taste of bile in her throat. The march of a hundred tiny soldiers inside her head, pounding drums as they paraded around in a circle. Each throb gave off a twitch of pain, not quite as piercing as the Rhine wine hangovers she remembered from college, but close.

Once again, she upchucked, and this time nothing came out. The dry heaves. *Wonderful.* She wiped the sweat from her brow with the sleeve of her robe and flushed the toilet. Rising, she doused her face with cool water at the sink, dried herself with a hand towel. She avoided looking in the mirror.

Maggie brushed her teeth. Twice. At long last. she felt ready to face the day.

While making the bed, she heard a rapping sound from downstairs, heard Chloe call as she entered the back door of the house. Slipping on jeans and a sweatshirt, Maggie discovered her sister downstairs at the dining room table. Hank was on her lap, purring at the pure ecstasy of being brushed. Deciding a cup of regular tea might settle her stomach, Maggie filled the chrome teakettle, set it on the burner. Chloe declined. She was on her way to work, she said, and had just stopped in to check on her.

"How's the nausea?" Chloe asked, sizing her up.

"Same. I'm getting so bored with it."

"It'll be gone soon." Chloe shifted topics. "Any word from Cale? After I left?"

"He called from Naples. Exhausted. I begged him to come home. Then I heard weird sounds, and we got cut off." Maggie frowned. "I did manage to tell him about Crenshaw getting shot."

If only Tobias Crenshaw would do them all a favor and kick the bucket fast, she caught herself hoping. It would sure solve a lot of problems.

"A pervert gets his due. Good riddance." Chloe's tone was unremorseful for the monster who'd kidnapped and raped her sister. "How about Thing Two? The preggers part?"

"Not a good long-distance topic right now." Maggie shifted subjects. "Any more visions of Leslie Dowd? And her mystery man?" Chloe had relayed the entire episode to her last evening.

With a bit of reluctance, Chloe said, "Just this: *He is coming.*"

"Who's coming?"

"That's just it. I have no idea." Chloe plucked a stray piece of cat hair from her pantsuit. Four arm bracelets clacked. "No dream or images this time. I just kept hearing a repeating voice: '*He is coming.*'"

Maggie gave her a searching look. "What aren't you telling me?"

"That's it. Over and over."

The kettle whistled on the stove, causing them both to start.

Maggie busied herself pouring tea. Chloe rose from the table and tongued her fingertips, brushed the lap of her slacks for more cat hairs. "It might not be good, Mags. Whoever *He* is, it might not be good."

Watching her sister depart from the house with a wave, Maggie thought: just as well. She didn't want to hear any more of Chloe's bizarre dreams or premonitions. She had her own nightmares to contend with, her own demons to wrestle.

She sat at the table and sipped her tea, her thoughts five-thousand miles away to wherever Cale might be right now. He'd said he had no phone. She had no way to even get in touch with him. All she could do was hope he was safe and pray that he'd be home soon.

A moment later, Maggie felt herself brighten. It was as if her prayers were being answered. Could it be *that's* what Chloe's dream was about? The mystery was suddenly clear to her. And weren't the simplest solutions most often the best?

He is coming.

It was about Cale, no doubt. It had to be: "He was coming home."

***

Driving to work in the morning, Chloe chewed on her lower lip. She was lost in thought, so much that she almost missed the turn into the salon's parking lot. *My God*, she thought, kicking herself: *I should have told Maggie the whole truth*. On the other hand, how could she? How do you tell someone you love that the evil coming their way is a vicious demon?

The fact was, Chloe couldn't. She had stared into her sister's eyes and given her the exact warning that she, herself, had received:

He is coming.

But was it enough?

No, Chloe decided, it wasn't.

Still, was burdening Maggie's life even further the decent thing to do? Informing her that the entity on the way, planning to pay her a visit, was some stench-breathing, soulless monster from hell? How would Maggie react to news like that? The two-word answer: Not Well. Not when her sister had so many other problems to deal with.

Nevertheless, Chloe concluded that she had to do *something*.

Sitting in the salon's parking lot, she fished into her oversized handbag and withdrew her phone. She dialed directory assistance and was connected to the number she sought. When the receptionist answered, Chloe said in a firm voice, "I'd like to speak to Father Larchezi, please."

"Can I ask what this is concerning?"

Chloe felt her forehead furrow. "I need to know if he's qualified to perform a...a certain ritual."

"Can you be more specific?"

"An exorcism," Chloe said, the final word hanging in the air like a curse.

***

Monrovia, Liberia

It had rained throughout the night. When the dawn broke, gray and mist-filled, the downpour continued to pelt the calm waters of the seaport. As the smoky haze lifted, like a ghost ship rising from the mist, the cargo freighter *Kwensana* slowly began easing away from the wooden docks. The anchor had been raised, and the large ship belched out a single bleat, as she powered out to sea.

Below decks, the guards were armed with machine-pistols. They kept a sharp eye on the twenty-four young girls who were crowded inside a compartment deep down in the hold. Fifteen minutes later, when the freighter had cleared port and begun her customary northwest heading, the guards took their departure, securing the compartment behind them.

On the bridge, the captain turned the ship's controls over to the first mate. He withdrew his mobile phone from his jacket pocket, hit the speed dial, and proceeded to inform the land guards they had an all-clear.

After hanging up, neither the captain nor his first mate spoke. They were content to gaze out through the drizzle that glistened the lower decks, staring at the iron gray ocean, which stretched as far as their eyes could see.

Chateau du Carthairs, Belgium

Prince Mir Al-Sadar's workers had been busy with all the little details it took to make his festival a world class event. One of the highlights was a broad canvas banner, which had been erected by workers late that afternoon. It stretched wide across the front of the chateau, above the huge double-doors of the main entrance. It read:

WELCOME BELGIAN FETISH FESTIVAL

The banner spanned beneath the high, second-story windows and looked down on the curl of circular front drive. The far side of the roadway swept past a trio of stone nymphs, who romped playfully inside the massive gurgling fountain.

Just behind the fountain—where the hill began its gentle slope down towards the track fields below—were a dozen mature oak and willow trees, which stood at attention, beaming like the stiff officials of a welcoming committee.

The dark of evening was upon them now, and though the crickets chirped, and the quarter-moon was arcing its way through the sky, Leslie lay prone in her bed. She was wrapped inside the blankets, feeling the warm sensation of the drugs as they coursed through her veins. Too anxious to do anything else, yet too wound up to sleep, she stayed curled beneath the quilted layers while she considered the next few days. The festival—meaning the race—was a mere forty-eight hours away. And then it would all be over. She would be a winner (of course), and courtesy of Prince Mir, she would be granted her freedom.

Leslie knew it was true. He had promised, after all. Hadn't he?

Yet of the hundred or so idiosyncrasies she, by this time, understood about His Highness, two of them stood out, as far as Leslie was concerned: *First, he was wealthy beyond measure; and second, he was a goddamned liar.*

But why would he lie to her? she asked herself now. His favorite pet? Especially if she brought him a victory in the race he seemed to cherish so much? That was it, Leslie decided: He would *not* lie. How could he? She was his team captain; and she was his prize.

In fact, how many times had he told her as much? No, the prince would keep his promise, Leslie decided. He would grant her the wish they had bargained for. By this time next Monday, she would be on a swift passenger jet headed back to her homeland. Back to America.

At long last, Leslie would once again be free.

CHAPTER 45

Anzio, Italy

On a lumpy mattress on the floor of the office room, Cale roused from his half-sleep to the *whup-whup-whup* sound of rotating chopper blades. He was being jostled, and he moaned, his mouth drier than the sub-Saharan terrain. He squinted open his eyes, and as daylight slapped him, the dreams faded away. No helicopter, but the pain still registered as real. When he shifted, every muscle and joint of his body shrieked a chorus of protest.

Cale eased himself to a sitting position. The events of the previous day rushed back: he recalled the cramped six-hour flight to Liberia, the dropping down into the creature-infested death pit, then the long bumpy jeep ride. This was followed by a bullet-dodging helicopter escape straight out of some jailbreak movie.

To top it all off, he had escaped the blade of a trained assassin by the narrowest of margins. A man intent on "pithing" him, the way a scientist would some slimy amphibian.

Christ! No wonder he felt like hell. What surprised him most was the fact that he'd woken up at all.

Brushing the blankets aside, Cale wondered how he'd gotten back to wherever he was. He remembered little after the airport assault in Naples. Flashes of memory of African countries came and went, some sort of military cargo plane heading back to Italy. After they'd landed, still in a fog, he had borrowed a phone and called

Maggie: just to tell her he was alive. Cale was hard-pressed to remember anything else about the conversation.

After that had come the explosions and attack, then they'd made their escape in the fleeing van. His clothes had been removed, and he'd slept for God knows how many hours. What time it was now, what day it was, he could not say with certainty. He wasn't even sure what country he was in at present.

"I was wondering when you'd wake from your beauty rest," came the accented female voice from across the room.

Cale covered himself with the sheet. Rubbing his bristled chin, he looked up to find Cheetah standing in the doorway. She was holding a plastic water bottle, staring at him with her arms crossed. She indicated a fresh bottle sitting on the room's business desk, and Cale leaned over and grabbed for it. He swigged half the bottle down.

"You tucked me in?" he asked, taking a moment to survey his surroundings, rolling his neck to determine if it worked the way it was designed. "I'm guessing we're back in Anzio?"

She took a sip from her own water bottle. "We escaped Naples without a trace. Courtesy of Agent Fronteer, if I had to take a guess. Otherwise, our photos would be plastered all over the telly. They must have ID'd us from airport surveillance tapes."

Cale nodded. His muddled brain was still piecing the time-sequentials together.

"You slept all the way back here. Good thing they treated you for dehydration and pumped you full of antibiotics on the plane flight. You've got a couple nasty gashes on your ribs and shins. I checked the field dressing. You're intact."

"A regular Florence Nightingale?"

"Multitasking. It's a prerequisite on this job." She lifted her sharp chin, indicating the business desk again. "You've got a new mobile, and I set out some towels. Jacek's provided fresh clothes. I took the liberty of burning yours. Didn't think you'd mind."

Cale glanced around the room. No windows. "What time is it? I'm afraid to even ask what day."

"Friday afternoon. Nearly two," Cheetah said. "You missed breakfast and lunch, but I saved you a sandwich. Pharaoh claimed dibs on it in case you stopped breathing."

"All heart, ain't he?"

She put forth a wan smile. "Shower's down the hallway, in case you forgot. Your Homeland friends have been active since yesterday. They're switching to 'Attack mode.' We'll fill you in when you're up and about."

Continuing to survey the room, Cale wondered if he might be trapped in some dream. "The canvas sack I was carrying?"

"I've got it out front," Cheetah reported. "No worries. Your prizes from Africa are safe and sound. Not a scratch on them."

Cale nodded his thanks and she stepped free of the doorway. "Better get a move on, Detective. Or you'll miss the bus." She slipped away, silent as a shadow. He listened for her departure, heard nothing.

Attack mode? The way his body was protesting even the slightest movement, he wasn't sure he could handle an attack on an eighth-grade playground, yet alone what Agent Fronteer might have planned for them.

Yesterday, Cale remembered, bleary-eyed, he had reminded himself how fortunate he was to have survived. Further, Maggie had begged him to end his trip. And that was before the assassin's attack. So, she was no doubt correct. His excursion had been a dismal failure, an exercise in futility. It was time to return home.

Upright and breathing. It's all I ever promised you, Mags.

Maggie. It didn't take much to realize how much he missed her, how much he loved her. He was thirty-seven-years old now. It had taken him this long to make a commitment to a girl. A true commitment, one that involved getting married, spending the rest of their lives together. Now here he was, five-thousand miles away. And Maggie was sitting back at home, alone and pregnant. Through no fault of her own, Cale reminded himself. He wasn't sure he was the child's father, or not. But what he was certain of, it was something they needed to talk about.

Am I the true father? Or is the father the sick psycho who raped you?

Lying half-naked on the lumpy mattress, battered, disheartened, Cale wrestled with his bleak inner thoughts. If he had an ounce of common sense left, he'd pull the plug on this ill-fated mission. In less than an hour he could be in Rome. An hour after that, he could be on a plane headed back to Wisconsin.

Cale threw off the blankets and rubbed his grizzled face. It was time to get moving.

***

Tobias Crenshaw was shot in the head. Maybe even dead by now.

Cale stood in the shower and allowed the hot spray to pelt his face. Shot by Cynthia Hulbreth? Was that even possible? Did Maggie tell him that? Or did he dream it?

With everything that had happened over the past thirty hours, much of it blurry and running together in his mind, his grasp on reality felt tenuous, at best.

Emerging from the shower, wrapped in a towel, he examined the scrapes and cuts his body had received since they had landed in Liberia. From the neck down, he looked like he'd been in an alley fight with a fistful of Hell's Angels. Neck up, he had a few superficial scalp lacerations. A couple of bruises. Nothing too serious.

It could have been worse, he supposed.

When Cale had entered the shower ten minutes ago, his mind had been made up: He'd be returning home. Pronto. It was what Maggie wanted. And it was what made the most logical sense.

Now, as he stood staring at himself in the steamy mirror, his heart told him otherwise. He had made promises to people who were counting on him, and there remained inside him a deep sense of obligation. Cale understood a few solid facts about himself, and near the top of the list stood one trait: he was not a quitter. When he had decided to fly off on his mission—to locate and bring back Kinsella, to rescue the missing girls—he had promised himself (along with the victims' families), that he'd see the task through. No matter the personal cost.

It was the fabric he was made of.

A few more days away from Maggie wouldn't kill him, would it? No. He could see this mission through. And when he arrived back home in Green Bay, after he'd settled in from his journey, then they could have their heartfelt talk about him, and her, and her *condition*.

After applying fresh bandages to his ribs, antiseptic ointment to his shins, donning the booyah military garb Jacek had left out for him to wear—boots included—Cale emerged out into the central area of the warehouse. The same area Agent Fronteer had employed two days earlier as a "war room."

A voice called out from the workplace, where Jacek sat typing at a computer terminal. "Ah, Detective Lazarus. How nice of you to join us."

Cale gave Jacek a simple nod as he approached. He did the same to Pharaoh, who was sitting beside his boss. Cale said, "You know my motto, Jacek: Upright and breathing." He issued Cheetah a wink, as he moved up to join them.

"So, where do we begin?"

EPILOGUE

Liberia, Africa

The blackest of starless nights. A snarling wind smashes the waves against the rock-crusted shore, the roar as loud as a rocket launch.

Inside the main house of the walled and guarded compound, high on the third-floor—in a rectangular, enclosed space he calls the "Blood Room"—the witch doctor kneels in the center. Six lighted candles surround him. Their flickering shadows cavort on the walls and highlight the painted symbols, vulture feathers, and the dripping chicken blood, which seeps down the surface like leaking entrails.

Tazeki Mabutu is naked, perched like a falcon before the carved wooden bowl. Streaks of colored paint are splayed across his torso, and his face is covered by a lumpy, undulating, purple-scored mask of human bone. From a chalice, he pours warm human blood over the shimmering diamond in the bowl's center. As the gem twinkles in the firelight, the witch doctor whispers in a low voice:

"This is far from over, my American friend. The bones of your loved ones will be crushed like charred firewood; and their hearts yanked free, squeezed and dripping from their putrid chambers."

He pours more fresh blood into the bowl, causing the flames around him to sputter and leap. And when he turns his head around and stares straight up at you, dear reader—from behind the gnarled and scarred mask of human bone—his eyes are crimson pinpricks.

"The dark loa *will be appeased!*" he promises, teeth gnashing. And his lips form a sinister curl inside the mask, his grin more malevolent than the cackling laugh of a lunatic.

ACKNOWLEDGMENTS

A novel is always a collaborative effort. In light of this, I'd like to thank Dawn Mancheski, who continues to render encouragement. Kevin "The Coach" Harbick, whose passion would not allow Tobias Crenshaw (aka the Chemist) to die; to Detective Lieutenant Paul Splawski (retired) of the Green Bay Police Department, who provided insight into criminal transport and how police suspensions and review boards function.

To Scott Browne and Tera Thorp-Harbick, who allowed me to tap their brains regarding the inner workings of African Vodun and witchcraft.

Bart Drage offered insight into the Italian coastline city of Anzio, Italy. D.P. Lyle, M.D., whose text *Murder and Mayhem*, helped me with zombie creation; and Steven Falk, M.D., anesthesiologist extraordinaire, who aided with his particular brand of expertise. Chase DeCleene, college wrestling champion, assisted with tips on hand-to-hand combat and knife fighting.

I'd be remiss if I failed to thank Grant Cousineau and John Helfers of the Green Bay Readers Group, who also provided welcomed suggestions and insights. And best-selling author, Ashley Emma, continues to bestow expert guidance and support; thus, I tip my hat to Fearless Publishing.

And last but not least, to Randy Rose, Tom Ebli, Gary "Chopper" Lambert (RIP), and Dale Berg, as well as all other members of The Corporation—Think Tank, who keep me grounded with their shuck and jive. Mucho thanks to you all.

ABOUT THE AUTHOR

Janson Mancheski is an award-winning author of five novels. The Chemist Series (*The Chemist (2010), Trail of Evil (2011) Mask of Bone (2011*) featuring Detective Cale Van Waring, are all set in Green Bay, Wisconsin. *The Chemist* captured first place for fiction in the Sharp Writ Book Awards in 2010. Voyage Media Productions has accepted Janson's screenplay version of his book, and casting and production offers are currently being reviewed.

Janson has authored a number of short stories and received awards for multiple screenplays. The movie script version of Janson's fourth novel *Shoot For the Stars (2016)* (an historic Green Bay Packers "What If" novel), was a finalist for the 2012 Writers Digest creative fiction awards. His latest novel *The Scrub* (a memoir featuring the ghost of Curly Lambeau) was published in December 2017.

A University of Wisconsin–Green Bay graduate and practicing optometrist (Illinois College of Optometry–Chicago, IL) from 1985 – 2005, Janson worked as the team eye doctor for the UW–Green Bay men and women's basketball teams. He also functioned as team eye doctor for the Green Bay Packers from 1990–2002.

Janson is an ardent Green Bay Packers, UW-Green Bay Fighting Phoenix, and Wisconsin Badgers fan.

His newest novel *Bully Me This!* will be released in summer, 2019. Along with the fourth installment of *The Chemist Series.*

For further information on Janson's books and activity:

SEE **www.Jansonmancheski.com** (Featuring *The Chemist* movie trailer, starring Steve Golla.)

Facebook @ **Janson Mancheski author**

WANT MORE OF THE CHEMIST SERIES?

SNEAK PEEK OF BOOK 3: *MASK OF BONE*

CHAPTER 1

Green Bay, Wisconsin

The serial kidnapper stood at the top of the concrete steps outside the Brown County courthouse. Gone were the orange jailhouse jumpsuit and lace-less canvas shoes he'd been wearing hours earlier. They'd been replaced by gray khaki slacks, a light button-down shirt, and a sports jacket. He was shaved, his hair a little longer than his arrest photos from four weeks ago, and he was leaning on what the cops were calling a "sympathy" cane.

The man was positioned, strategically, a pace behind his attorney, who was addressing the crowd. A brown-shirted county deputy stood on each side, and the eyes of the lawmen scanned the angry, restless crowd that had gathered across the concrete walkway and clipped courthouse lawns.

From this agitated group of citizens, occasional shouts rang out: "Murderer!" "Scumbag!" "You're gonna fry, Crenshaw!"

The members of the media, their recording devices and cameras and cell phones angled to capture every nuanced word, had formed a semi-circle at the bottom of the courthouse steps. This designated "safety arc" was enforced by another pair of uniformed city patrolmen, ensuring that the man speaking—an attorney with glasses and a grandfather's wreath of seasoned gray hair—was allowed his personal space near the top of the steps.

The weather report had verified the conditions: one of those hazy May days, the sky trying to decide what it might like to do. Cement-colored clouds could be seen approaching from the west, casting traces of shadow, bringing with them the metallic hint of coming rain. So far, the drizzle had held off, but for how long was anyone's guess.

The attorney requested quiet, putting an end to the crowd's insolent jeers. When the voices abated, he proceeded to speak in a solemn tone about evidence, due process, and the importance of examining the relevant facts, so nothing could exist beyond a reasonable doubt. He sounded as if he were delivering a lecture on legal ethics.

"Screw you, Crenshaw! You murderer!" someone shouted.

"Hope you burn in hell—you bastard!"

Positioned behind the attorney, Tobias Crenshaw kept his expression blank. He'd been schooled at keeping it that way for this event, and he stood frozen, feigning disinterest, as the small crimson dot appeared just below the hairline on his forehead. His demeanor remained unfazed as the back of his head exploded. At this same instant, he dropped to the ground like a life-sized puppet whose strings had been snipped.

Those who had been listening close might have distinguished a faint coughing sound in the same millisecond the crimson dot had appeared on the target's forehead. But this mild idiosyncrasy was forgotten by most everyone who'd chanced to hear it; and it was no surprise, for an instant later, pandemonium broke loose.

The shooting on the courthouse steps had taken place yesterday.

After a day of tech analysts consolidating the data, putting together a timeline from a variety of digital sources, reviewing every angle and shadow and movement, the detectives were at last viewing the finished production.

Inside the Green Bay Police Department's Electronic Forensics/Tech Analysis lab, Detective James "Slink" Dooley watched the replay of the grisly event unfold. Five other tech officers inhabited the room, walking him through the various sequences. They were focused on the first monitor on the left of a bank of eight. Slink watched Tobias Crenshaw—the man charged with being the infamous serial offender dubbed "The Chemist"—take the bullet to his head and disappear from view.

If you enjoyed this sample, please view Trail of Evil on Amazon here: https://www.amazon.com/Mask-Bone-Chemist-Book-3-ebook/dp/B00DU1GLN6

Printed in Great Britain
by Amazon